THE POISON
WITHIN

RACHEL MARIE PEARCY

ISBN: 9781724180421

383 pages

To Cece

If this book is my baby than you're definitely it's cool, fun

aunt.

The Kingdoms
of
Kelda

Nestian Ocean

Northern
Tribe Lands

Sunken Peaks

Ivory Cape

Ashen
Forest

Vail Lake

Trava

Castil
Sea

Imani
Plains

Halton Sea

Bardo Mountains

Cira

Obsidian
Isles

Deserts of
Asta

Kael
Reef

Emeraldi Ocean

PROLOGUE

The carriage shuddered as it rolled over another fallen log. The old man inched forward on the driver's bench, gripping the reins tighter in his hands while he ignored the sweat rolling down the back of his neck. It had been three days since the storm had swept in without warning, covering the kingdom in a blanket of dark clouds, and pelting the land with hard rain. In its wake the dirt roads were left soft while bushes blown free of their roots littered the open space, making the already delayed journey even more grueling.

Another dip rocked the coach side to side, and he winced. His back was arched in a permanent curve thanks to the years of driving, but it was the woman inside the coach, rather than his terrible posture, that caused him anguish. He could hear her grunts of displeasure as they rambled along, and after another sharp jolt her voice called out from behind the curtained window.

"Stop the carriage."

Even at a high volume her tone was calm and even, but he had been in her service long enough to know better. His hands trembled as he obeyed the order, guiding the horses to a stop near the edge of the road. He dropped his eyes and focused an intense stare on the holes in his shoes. He could hear the swish of her dress as she exited the carriage, followed by the sound of soldiers riding up on all sides as they surrounded them. He didn't have to look up to know how they felt; the tension radiated off them as they dismounted and stood waiting for their orders.

"Where's the driver?" She asked a nearby guard. "What's his name—Ronald? Bring him to me."

Without warning a strong hand reached up and grabbed the old man by the pant leg, yanking him off his perch and down to the ground below. The impact knocked the air from his lungs, and he choked for a breath as he stood up.

"Ah yes, there he is," she sang as she walked towards him. Determined to keep his head down, the old man tucked one arm behind his back and the other across his stomach, dipping into the lowest bow his crippled body could manage. He remained hunched over, shaking with the effort, until a thin finger slid under his chin, pushing his head up and forcing him to meet her eyes. An expression of worry that didn't quite ring true played across her face as she spoke.

"Tell me Ronald, how long have you worked for the royal palace?"

"Your Majesty, I've served the Isles' royalty for over forty years."

"After so many years of service, would you say you're an expert driver by now?"

He stammered, "Your Grace—"

"Since you have so much experience," she interrupted, "I'm going to assume the reason I'm being tossed around my cabin is because of something other than your ability to steer these horses."

"My apologies My Queen." His heart beat hard against his ribs. "The rain has turned the dirt to mud, and avoiding the fallen branches has been difficult, Your Majesty."

"I appreciate your attempt at returning me home," she sighed. "But it won't do me any good to arrive battered and bruised. Seeing as you have no control over the condition of our roadways I'll have to find my own way to remedy the situation."

Ronald swallowed the lump in his throat as she turned away from him, his muscles tight.

"Bring me the prisoner," the queen called out.

Two guards approached, each holding an arm of the man they dragged between them. His thinning hair was pushed up on one side, and his left eye stuck out from his face in nasty shades of blue and black. A trail of dried blood trickled from the corner of his mouth down onto the front of his torn shirt. His gait was hindered by a limp, either caused by some recent abuse from the soldiers, or the shackles connecting his ankles and wrists together. As they reached the queen the guards tossed him down, leaving him on all fours at her feet.

"Your majesty?" The man sneered as he pushed himself to his knees.

The young queen stood over him, a sly smile playing on her crimson lips. "You understand you're being taken to the work fields to pay for your crimes, but as I am a kind and generous ruler I've decided to offer you a different option. I'll be sending you ahead of my carriage to clear the roadway of any object that might make my ride uncomfortable. If you do an adequate job, and we reach the outer wall without issue, then I'll release you. You could be heading home by nightfall."

The man frowned, his swollen eye squinting at her. "You think I'd trust you, after everything you've done? You invaded my home, taking from me anything you wished. The bit of theft I'm accused of could have been paid off with a few bits of gold, and yet you've sentenced me to years of manual labor. You're wicked and a liar, and I refuse to do anything you ask of me."

The last of his words spat from his mouth, and a bit of saliva flew past her cheek, missing her face by an inch. Still, the queen never flinched.

"That's a shame," she frowned. It was the only warning before a shower of embers shot from the tips of her fingers, and Ronald cringed as one landed on the sleeve of his coat. He swatted at the singeing fabric as she continued. "I was going to undo your chains while you worked but given your sudden outburst I'm afraid you'll have to complete the task as you are."

"I already told you," the man snorted, "I won't do it."

"Refuse me again," she sighed, her face relaxed and bored, "and I'll have your wrists tied to the rear of my carriage, and I'll drag your helpless body all the way back to my castle. Watching your broken bones bounce off each branch and rock we ride over will have to serve as distraction enough for the bumpiness of the ride."

The man's good eye burned with a mixture of hate and defeat as the soldiers picked him up off the ground and pushed him into the road. Ronald watched as he shuffled out in front of the horses, kicking aside rocks, and struggling to lift larger branches with his bound hands.

Around him the guards had relaxed. They seemed to assume the worst was over, and they began to mount their horses and line up against the road once more. Ronald turned to walk back towards his seat atop the carriage when a soft hand on his shoulder stopped him.

"We'll give him a little bit of time to get ahead of us," the queen smirked. She was next to the old man, watching the prisoner work in the mud. "Once I give the word and we start moving again, keep the same pace as before. I'd like to spend the night in my own bed."

"Your Majesty," he said, eyes widening. "If I do that, the horses will trample him within minutes."

She stood silent, looking at him with her hard, cold eyes.

"What I mean Your Grace, is that without his work the ride will be as rough as before."

"I'm willing to risk it," she shrugged. "As I said, make sure you keep the pace."

ONE

The dry leaves crunched under the young woman's feet with each stride she took up the steep hill. The tree line was growing closer, and she could start to make out the etchings burned in the bark; the crude rendering of a shield with a wide slash through the middle. She pushed her legs harder, trying to fight against the weight of her boots which grew heavier with every second that passed. The bottom of her once elegant gown was now tattered and torn, and a thick strip of mud caked the edging. The young autumn sun washed over her bare shoulders, but it did nothing to chase away the chill cutting to her core.

"You think a few scratches on a tree will stop me?" The man laughed somewhere behind her, but she refused to turn. Her body screamed with exhaustion, and the throbbing in her shattered wrist had spread into her arm.

She held it tight against her chest, trying to shield it from the jarring motion of the chase.

The slope began to even out, and as the sun dimmed behind the canopy of yellowing leaves, Rya's heart soared. She spun around, expecting to find the man's expression hard with anger, but instead he was sauntering towards her with a wide grin.

The running had knocked back the hood of his cloak, revealing the gaunt young man underneath. Dark bags hung under his black eyes, sinking them further into his face. She could see the thick white scars running down his brown skin, starting behind each ear and disappearing under his collar. She recognized them immediately and knowing who he belonged to only increased her heartrate.

"You can't touch me here," she said, backing away from him. "I've reached the border."

He moved around her like a cat stalking its prey, each step deliberate and calculated, closing the space between them.

"I didn't kill him," she continued. The palm of her left-hand tingled as the emotions swelled within her, and the burn grew around the broken bones in her right.

"That should matter to me?" He asked in a playful tone.

"Of course," she replied, still stepping backwards. "It's why you're here, isn't it? You're one of the Kael."

2

The man's laugh was sharp and loud. "That I am. I've been hired to cut your still beating heart from your chest, and return it to your kingdom. To be honest, I'm only interested in the reward, not the reason."

She grew dizzy as she watched him move from side to side, pushing her further into the cover of the trees. "Your name's Nix, isn't it?" She asked. "I heard Father Kasen call you that. Nix, I can offer you more gold, or even land. Whatever he's paying you, I promise I can give you more."

His smile faded. She could see the fire burning in his pupils, the yearning to hurt her, and she regretted calling him by name.

"I don't want your money," he sneered. "I want your blood."

"But I'm innocent."

"You may not have killed King Gerrod, but to the people who sent me, you've done enough to deserve the pain you've got coming to you."

"They're all fools," she shouted in response. Her one good hand balled into a fist, the fire from her fingertips burning into the flesh on her palm. It was the type of hurt she'd experienced a hundred times before, but the feeling in her broken arm was new and unpleasant. The pain churned with her anger, scorching her from the inside out.

3

The mixture of rage and agony had distracted her, and she hadn't noticed how close he'd gotten. He pulled the two long daggers from the sheaths on his thighs; the bone white handles flashed in the streaks of sun as he spun them in his palms with ease.

Turning on her heels, Rya took off into the woods, darting between the trees. The trunks gave her brief cover, but she knew it wouldn't last. Her body was too worn, and this was what he'd spent his life training for. In desperation, she zipped from right to left, and back again, hoping the obstacles would allow her to gain some ground. When she could no longer hear his footsteps, she felt a brief glimmer of hope, but the burst was short lived as the ground disappeared from under her with a sudden jolt.

The ditch caught her off guard, and before she could brace herself, Rya fell face first to the forest floor below. She landed with a thud on her already mangled wrist and let out a shrill howl as the searing pain burst in all directions. The blow stunned her body, and she laid on her stomach, frozen and unable to move. Something warm and wet ran down her forehead and she tasted the metallic sting of blood in her mouth. After recovering from the shock, her panic took control and she flipped onto her back. She scrambled to push herself up the soft side of the ditch, but the loose dirt crumbled under her feet and she slipped back to the bottom.

4

"Your power as queen has ended," Nix said, now standing over the trench looking down at her. "And now, so will your life."

Rya braced herself for the blow. She bit down on her lower lip, not wanting to cry out, refusing to give him the satisfaction of her fear and pain. He lifted his foot, ready to move in, when his body rocked backwards with a grunt. A single arrow shaft protruded from his shoulder, the pointed end erupting from the back side. The black of his cloak masked the blood she knew was spreading across the fabric, but when he reached up to snap the wood in two, his hands came away stained bright red. He threw the feathered end to the ground, and took a slow, deep breath. His eyes locked with hers, and without flinching he pushed the end of the broken shaft further into his flesh, his index finger sinking into the open wound. The wet sound sickened Rya as the wood slid out the other side and fell from his body. The metal tip bounced off the leaves on the ground below, and he smiled.

"You take one more step towards her," a girl's stern voice said, "and I'll put the next one through your eye."

The shuffle of footsteps came from somewhere behind Rya, but from the bottom of the ditch she could only see Nix, and the new hint of worry playing across his face.

"I wouldn't risk it," a young man added, making the assassin's lip twitch. "Don't think the first one was an accident; it was a warning."

"This woman is a criminal," Nix responded, his words sounding reasonable and measured now. "I'm in charge of taking her home to face her judgment. Give me two minutes and we'll be on our way."

"This woman," the girl answered, "is in the Ashen Forest, and is now under our protection. Those trees you ran past mark the boundary. Even the Kael knows the laws we keep, though most are smart enough to stay away."

Rya's heart skipped a beat as Nix begrudgingly returned his blades to their homes and held up his open hands to her mystery saviors.

"You may have her now," he said with a sick smile, "but I'll get her in the end. Even the Ashen know the Kael don't leave a job unfinished, though most are smart enough to stay out of our way."

Rya watched with relief as he backed away a few feet, and then turned and disappeared the way they'd come. She fell back against the cool dirt of the ditch and shivered. The danger had passed, and the thudding in her chest had slowed, allowing the exhaustion to take over. Her head swam and the trees started to sway in her vision. The pain once throbbing in her arm now pulsated in every inch of her, keeping with the beat of her heart. She could hear the

6

small group of people moving around her, but as the dark corners of her sight started closing in, she couldn't make out their faces. The world began to fade away, and for a moment she could have sworn her body was floating.

TWO

Cam's hand was wrapped tight around her bow as she watched Thane double check the ropes. He had placed the queen's broken body on the long, brown and red stained slab of wood. The sled usually transported large game from the hunt back to the castle, but today it would be serving another purpose. Cam sighed, thankful the unconscious monarch couldn't smell the blood that had saturated the grain over the years.

Thane stood up to examine his work. "She doesn't look so regal right now, does she?"

Cam knelt down next to the sled and reached out a hand, brushing the dark brown hair from the queen's face. Without looking up at him she asked, "Do you think the rest of them know it's her?"

He glanced around at the half dozen others, each scanning the surrounding woods, keeping guard in case the assassin chose to return. Only one of them wasn't watching the trees, instead eyeing the newcomer with caution.

"If they don't know now, they will eventually. There's no way to hide something like this."

Thane finished securing the sled, while the squat man continued to glare in their direction. Finally, he spoke, nodding towards the queen's body with a scowl, "Are we really taking her with us?"

"Why wouldn't we Ruben?" Cam replied, standing up. The rest of the hunting party all shifted, trying to keep one eye on the woods while they watched the confrontation, but the man had begun shrinking away, already regretting his choice.

His brow pinched together as he chose his next words with caution. "Your Highness, she's the Black Queen. That name comes with a whole lot of trouble. I'm not sure us bringing her to the castle is the best choice for the kingdom."

"Alright, since you seem to know more than I do, what would you do with her? What do you think is best for the kingdom?"

"The law dictates we protect her. The Kael man has left and the danger is gone. I say we leave her here. We've done our duty, and she's alive. No one would think less of us for the decision."

Cam felt the blood rush to her face. "You believe we should abandon her here, unconscious and alone in the forest? Is that really your idea of protection Ruben? Because if it is, I may have to reconsider having you in my company."

"No, of course not Your Highness." His face glowed red. "I only thought maybe there's another option besides taking her straight to the castle."

"She's royalty, and she's injured. We will take her with us," she replied. "I'm not going to throw away the entire history of our people because you're scared of one woman."

"I'm not scared," he grimaced. "I was merely trying to be cautious. But you're right; we will of course follow your orders Your Highness."

The hunting party all mounted their horses and began the slow walk west towards home. As they all fell into line, two by two, Thane rode next to Cam in the middle, his own mare pulling the queen's sled. They had both noticed Ruben had lagged behind, taking a spot in the far back of the group as he continued to pout.

"He can lie all he wants, but I know he's scared," Thane said, glancing over at her. "He won't be the only one either."

"I know," she nodded. "But the law is absolute. We've taken in numbers of other criminals, I don't see why this one should be any different."

"Because she is different. She's the Black Queen, remember?"

"That name," Cam scoffed. "She's the queen of the Obsidian Isles. You'd think people could be a bit more creative in coming up with a nickname for her."

"I believe the name comes from the blackness of her heart and not the land she rules, especially since she's a foreigner to them."

Cam glanced down at the sleeping body bouncing behind them, her eyes passing over the bare skin of her shoulders. The salt-filled air rolling off the sea, and the constant cloud cover, gave the people of the Obsidian Isles dull skin that was rough and weathered. The queen however was smooth with an even, olive tone. Her complexion, paired with her dark mahogany hair, made her a stand out among the people she reigned over. It was no wonder why King Gerrod had chosen her.

"You've heard the rumors, haven't you?" Thane asked, bringing her gaze back forward.

"Some of them," she answered, "but it's hard to tell the facts from the exaggerations."

"I heard she can summon fire from under the earth, and that she can rip a man's heart from his chest with her bare hands. Although, those do seem unlikely."

"I'm not sure," she smirked, "but when she wakes you're free to ask her about it. I only hope she doesn't decide to use you as an example of those powers." Thane shot her an annoyed look from the corner of his eye and Cam chuckled to herself.

As the sun began to drop in the sky, the horses came over the top of the hill, exposing the valley below them. At the heart of it, the dark stone wall cut through the white birch trees, creating the barrier shielding her home. The gray capped turrets clashed against the pink and purple swirled sky. To the south the water glimmered in the distance; the Halton Sea wasn't far, and in the afternoon light the glare almost blinded her. A road emerged from the port village of Wynlis and carved its way across the land like a river, guiding travelers to the castle. It was a smooth path compared to what they were on now, which forced them to trudge over the low plants and rocks of the hillside. She weaved her mare through the trees, and with each step her home grew closer, and a small weight began to drop in Cam's stomach.

"I'm doing the right thing," she said out loud, reassuring herself.

12

"I know," Thane nodded. "In all the years we've known each other, I've never doubted your judgment."

"I can only hope my father agrees."

He reached his arm out over the distance between them and placed a comforting hand on her shoulder. "You need to trust your choices as much as the rest of us do. You know what's right, and you're going to make a great queen someday. Stop second guessing yourself."

"I know," she nodded. "You're right."

"Aren't I always?" He laughed.

Cam shook her head at him, and with another click of the tongue, her horse began to trot down the hill, headed towards the Ashen Castle; headed towards home.

THREE

A warmth spread along Rya's side, while a gentle weight on her chest kept her pinned in place. Her eyelids were heavy, struggling against her as she willed them open, desperate for one more moment of peace. The dim light of the room burned, and she sat still for a moment, blinking away the white spots in her vision.

What is this place? She'd had flashes of memories— the forest border, the assassin behind her, the voices from the woods. The thoughts swirled together in her mind, mixing into a jumbled mess and making her head ache. She couldn't recall any details about the people who rescued her, but based on her current surroundings, she guessed they weren't lowly woodsmen.

Lush fabrics and over-sized furniture decorated the humble room, each combating the coldness of the thick stone walls. The door to her left sat ajar, open just enough to show the darkness waiting on the other side. Next to it, the fireplace burned with the embers of the night's fire, providing the heat she'd felt before. Along the same wall hung a copper framed mirror, the clear glass reflecting the twinkling stars in the window opposite it. The sight of the night sky made her question how long she'd been asleep in the room. *A few hours? A day?*

Her body was stiff and her muscles all hummed the same dull ache. She moved to sit up, pushing herself with her hands only to flinch when the pain in her wrist was quick to remind her, she couldn't. She removed her arm from under the covers laying over her, examining the white wrapping running from her fingers to her elbow. Throwing back the blankets with her other hand she looked down at the rest of her body. Someone had stripped away her old clothes and placed her in a fresh, thin nightshirt. The various scrapes and scratches along her now bare legs had been tended to as well, and her entire body had been scrubbed clean. With a weak hand, she reached up and ran her fingers over her forehead, feeling the few rough stitches on her left temple.

"Great," she grunted. "That'll scar."

She swung her legs over the side of the bed, placing the soles of her bare feet on the cool floor, and a shiver ran through her body. She leaned forward to test the strength, uncertain if her weak legs could handle the rest of her weight. The door was only a few steps away, and her desire to have answers outweighed her pain. If she could make it to the hallway, maybe she could find out where they'd taken her. *The sooner I know where I am*, she thought, *the better*. She took a deep breath and pushed herself up.

Once standing, her legs began to wobble under her. She managed a single step, pausing before the next. Her muscles ached and her head was throbbing, but she shuffled another foot forward, ignoring her body's pleas. Another step and she was able to reach the handle. She pulled open the door in one swift motion, collapsing against the frame to keep herself upright while her legs trembled in protest.

The hallway outside the door was dark and narrow. Small glass sconces had been lit sometime during the night, but their flickering did little to shed real light into the space. Rya squinted, following the muted color of the carpet running to the end of the hall where it made a sharp turn, when two figures appeared in the darkness.

"What are you doing?" A young man's voice asked, his shadow jogging towards her. The other figure, smaller than the first, followed close behind. Rya turned, trying to dart back inside the room, but her muscles failed her. She crashed to the hard ground inside the doorway with a groan. The stone was cold on her face as she lay waiting, begging her legs to push her forward, and cursing them when they refused.

"You weren't even awake a few hours ago." The man fell to his knees at her side, hovering over her. His straw-colored hair hung down around his face, long enough to brush the top of his shoulders. He frowned down at her. "You can't go running around like that."

Behind him a young woman stood with a smirk. The familiarity in her face caught Rya by surprise, and a short yelp escaped the queen's mouth.

The boy scooped her up into his arms, the ends of his hair tickling her face as he held her to his chest. He carried her the few feet to the bed, laying her gently against the headboard. "You need to take it slow. You don't need to hurt yourself any more than you already have."

"Where am I?" Rya demanded. She was afraid to meet the girl's eyes as she covered the queen's legs with blankets. "And who are you?"

"You're in the Ashen Forest," the boy answered. "Can you remember anything from before?"

"I remember passing the border, but after that it all gets a little hazy. Where exactly have you taken me?"

The girl leaned back against the wall, her arms crossed over her chest. "You're in King Mikkel's castle, as a guest. All things considered you should count yourself lucky. Not everyone wanted to bring you here."

Rya sighed. "I see my reputation has proceeded me. I'm surprised you even picked me up off the ground. I

17

would have expected you to leave me there rolling around in pain."

"I would never leave a lady in distress," the young man replied. He smiled at her while he rubbed the stubble along his jawline. "Neither would Princess Camreigh. She was in the woods when we found you and she insisted you stay here with us."

"You two were in the forest?"

"I was," he answered before gesturing to the girl next to him. "Norell doesn't hunt with us, but she's been taking care of you since we brought you back."

"I'd hate to know what you did to be punished with such an assignment."

Norell frowned, pushing herself off the wall. "I volunteered." Without another word, she stomped from the room, leaving Rya alone with the young man.

"I apologize for her. She can be a little protective at times." He paused, his gaze locked on the empty doorway before shaking his head. "You really should get some more sleep. I'm sure tomorrow will be a busy day now that you're awake. People are bound to have questions."

"About that," she asked, "how long was I unconscious?"

"Three days. Well, I guess four since it's practically morning now. In addition to your injuries, and the exhaustion, you ended up fighting a pretty nasty fever for a while. You've been through a lot Your Majesty."

"Please, call me Rya. After saving my life, I think you and I can do without the formalities."

"Thank you Your—Rya. I'm Thane, and it's a pleasure to meet you. Like I said, though, you need more rest."

"You might be right," she yawned. The pain spread all over her body, banging against her insides like a drum, draining her energy with each strike.

Thane gave a small bow as he excused himself, closing the door behind him.

Rya slumped down, resting her head on the pillow. Four days were gone and lost forever. At least she'd ended up in the royal palace. It was the safest place in the Ashen Forest, which meant Nix couldn't touch her. As long as she could stay, she would be out of his reach and able to plot her next steps. The sleep started to weigh down her eyelids, and as she drifted off once more, she promised herself one thing—she was going to do whatever it took to keep herself safe.

FOUR

Cam paced outside her father's throne room, peaking through the gap in the doors with each pass. It was right off the entry hall, and between the thick oak separating her, and the chatter of the servants as they worked, she could only hear bits and pieces of the conversation. It had been almost an hour since Guthry had slid by her with a glare and hobbled down the aisle to her father. His shaky legs and hanging skin showed his years, but his eyes were as sharp as they'd ever been. She didn't care if he had been adviser to two kings before Mikkel, she hated him. The fact he was allowed inside while she stood waiting only made the feeling stronger.

"We need to remove her immediately," his shrill voice called out. It had been the third time he'd yelled those words. Cam knew his intentions, and the anger grew in her chest. Unable to hold back any longer, she pushed open the doors, storming down the length of the room towards the men.

The throne had been carved from the largest tree in the forest hundreds of years before, but under her father it looked like a child's seat. His thick limbs and wide shoulders made him twice the size of any man and, combined with his mass of red beard, he terrified anyone who didn't know him informally. Cam took in the gentle look on his face and she knew this outburst wouldn't be enough to upset him. It was the old man waiting at the end of the aisle that would be the problem.

"What are you doing?" Guthry sneered as she stopped next to him. He raised his ancient hand, waving a finger in her face as he addressed the king. "She's the one who caused all this. She brought that witch into your home."

"I wasn't going to leave her," Cam answered, swatting his hand away. "She was in trouble, and I helped her. It's what the Ashen do; we're the protectors."

He scoffed. "She doesn't need protecting. She's evil, with magic greater than any we've seen before. She will inflict horrible curses onto the people of this forest, and when she does it will be your fault."

"She's been unconscious since we found her, what exactly do you expect her to do?"

"I expect many things now that she's awake."

Cam's mouth dropped open. "She's awake? Why didn't anyone tell me?"

"I heard she came-to just before daybreak. To me, that's plenty of time to plot something sinister."

"Right," Cam replied, rolling her eyes. "I'm sure the first thing she did after being knocked out for a few days was jot down a villainous plan."

"Don't make light of this," Guthry warned. "She will destroy our home."

"If the Ashen Forest is truly your home," she retorted, "then you'll remember how we behave here. Or has it been too long since you were a criminal on the run yourself?"

"She's right," Mikkel nodded, finally adding to the argument. His voice boomed in the open space. "You came here as a young man fleeing his home, begging for someone to help you. The Ashen took you in and gave you safety. My grandfather liked you so much he made you a royal adviser. None of that would have happened if we were to turn away those in need."

"Your Majesty, I was running from a lord for sleeping with his wife, I wasn't chased from my own kingdom for murdering a king. She's killed a member of royalty before, what's to stop her from doing it again? You are an imposing force, and the princess can take care of herself,

22

but what about your son? What's to prevent him from being the target of her powers?"

Cam snapped, "you leave Eirik out of this."

"I'm only pointing out," he continued, ignoring her anger, "the Black Queen has magic stronger than any of our weapons. We can't fight it, and she uses it against people as a form of amusement. The stories I've heard would turn the strongest man's stomach."

"Rumors and stories," Cam groaned, throwing her hands in the air. "Can you provide any real proof of these stories? Or are you relying only on the drunken tales you hear second hand in the taverns?"

"Her reputation is proof enough," he spat back. "Mark my words, you allow her to stay and with a snap of her fingers this whole castle will be in flames."

"Oh, that won't be happening," a soft voice laughed. Cam turned around to see the queen standing in the open doorway, wearing a dark green dress and a teasing smirk. Two guards flanked her sides, but with a nod from Mikkel they relaxed their shoulders and turned to step out. Rya walked forward. Her hands had been hanging at her sides, but as she sauntered down the aisle they swayed with the rhythm of her hips. Cam couldn't take her eyes off her, fixated on her gliding towards them until she came to a stop between the princess and Guthry.

"It's a pleasure to see you on your feet," Mikkel smiled, bowing his head towards her.

Rya returned the gesture. "Sir, if you allow me to put your worries to rest, it's because of your hospitality and your daughter's bravery that I am here today. Seeing as I owe you both my life, I can say with absolute certainty I won't be setting anyone on fire."

Cam covered her mouth, choking back a laugh. As Guthry shouted his disapproval, the queen gave her a quick wink.

"This is outrageous," the old man barked. "She's making a mockery of you and your court."

"Enough," Mikkel warned, glaring at him. With Guthry's mouth shut the king turned his attention to Rya. "My apologies, but we've had some concerns about your arrival. While your situation is more sensitive than some, I can't give you special treatment. Each person seeking safety in our land stands here before me. I will interview you, and if I feel you're worthy of staying, you'll be under our full protection. Just know that if I allow you to remain in the forest you will be held to our laws, and the punishments can be harsh. If you're willing to agree to all those rules, I can continue with a few questions."

"Of course," Rya nodded. "I'll answer whatever I can."

"The accusations against you are quite serious. They're saying you murdered your husband, King Gerrod, in order to take the crown for yourself. Is there any truth to this claim?"

"He was barely my husband, but no, I had nothing to do with his death. Gerrod has had a bad heart since his youth and failed to adhere to the mender's advice. As far as I'm aware he passed without any outside assistance. If a plot to end his life existed, I had no hand in it."

"These rumors have led to your own people chasing you from your kingdom and sending you on the run. How do you explain that?"

"They are being misled by the leader of the Isles' temple, Father Kasen. If he truly believed I was to blame for the king's death, why would he wait three years to bring the charges against me?"

The king looked perplexed. "What would this man have to gain by falsely accusing you?"

"He's been trying to control me since I was named queen, and I've never allowed him to gain hold. After years of failing it seems he's decided replacing me is easier. I believe he plans on having me executed and allowing Prince Gavin to take my place on the throne."

"Lies," Guthry interrupted. "Everyone knows the prince of the Isles was kidnapped and then murdered years ago. This only proves her deceitfulness."

"No," Rya replied. "Since his disappearance people have spread rumors of the prince surviving, and I believe Kasen has located him. It's why he chose now to strike. Even if Gavin was to return, the only way he could take the crown is if I give it to him, or in the case of my death. Kasen believes these false charges will be enough to send me the gallows."

Cam watched her father's face, trying to decipher the stern look he was giving. Her stomach twisted as she glanced again at the queen.

"I'm not sure what you're expecting from us," Mikkel added. "As a rule, we offer refuge to anyone who seeks it, but we will not go to battle in your name. I won't risk my people's lives over the squabbles of another kingdom."

"I'm not asking for anything which hasn't already been offered. I need a safe place to stay while I heal, and once I've recovered I will leave here, on my own, to reclaim my crown."

"And what about your magic?" Guthry added. "What's to stop you from putting us all under some spell? How are we to trust you won't use your powers against us?"

The queen rolled her eyes. "Since it's clear you have no idea how magic works, I'll enlighten you. Magic flows through the entire body, it's part of you as much as the blood in your veins, but it can only be channeled through your hands. As you can see," she said holding up her bandaged arm, "I'm a little broken at the moment. The hands are the doorway for the power to escape, and until my bones mend, the doorway is blocked. The magic is halted within me, and I am incapable of doing all those things you're so worried about."

"Well, that settles it," Mikkel said, standing up. "I feel safe saying you pose no danger to the Ashen people, and you're welcome to stay in our kingdom as long as you wish. But be warned, if you commit any crimes while you're here, or I find out you're plotting against us in any way, you'll be returned to the assassin hunting you. That is, if I don't deal with you myself."

"I'll be on my best behavior. I promise."

"That's it?" Guthry hissed. "You're just going to take her word? How can you ignore the concerns of your people?"

"I've made my decision," Mikkel warned, his voice echoing off the walls. "It would be wise of you to respect it."

The old man shrank away, bowing to the king. "Yes, of course Your Majesty. I'll be on my way."

Cam watched him slither from the room, satisfied at the grimace he had as he left. When she turned back to her father she saw the worn look on his face. The last few days had taken a toll on him as he sat through dozens of meetings with various people, each worried about the new arrival. He had stood by her decision to bring the queen to the castle, but it was clear he was dealing with the fallout when it should have been her burden to bare.

"If you'll excuse me, ladies," he sighed. "I have some other matters to attend to and need to visit my library. Cam, why don't you give our guest a tour of the grounds."

"It'd be my pleasure," she replied.

Mikkel tipped his head once more to the queen before walking towards the doorway. As he disappeared, Rya relaxed, taking a seat on the step leading to the throne. She rubbed her calf as she frowned down the aisle.

"I can't believe that fowl old man is allowed to speak in that tone."

"He's always like that," Cam shrugged. "But he's been royal adviser for decades, and he feels he's earned the right to say what's on his mind. Personally, I think my father should have fired him a long time ago."

"It doesn't seem enough. If he was in my service I'd have his tongue removed so I'd never hear his voice again."

"I wouldn't worry about it. Papa rarely takes any of the stuff Guthry says to heart."

Rya chuckled. "That's a relief."

Cam had checked in on the queen often since she'd brought her home, always worrying about how pale she'd grown. When the fever took hold her color turned, glowing red as her body fought against the sickness. Watching her now, Cam was pleased to see the only hint left behind was a pink tint on her cheeks.

"About that tour," Rya smiled.

"Right." Cam reached out and took both of the queen's hands, pulling her to her feet. The brief touch sent her heart pounding in her chest, and the air caught in her lungs. Heat rushed to her cheeks as she held on a second longer than normal. Cam spun towards the door, attempting to hide her blushing from the queen. "We wouldn't want you getting lost."

FIVE

When Rya thought of a tour of the grounds, she
expected to see the grand hall's high ceilings, or the
treasury, or perhaps the glorious gardens that flanked the
front steps; she certainly didn't expect what Cam had
planned.

"Where are you taking me?" She cringed. The
corridor was long and dim, with no doors along the length
of it. Skinny flat windows popped out along the top,
allowing the sun's light to spill inside, but the shadows still
swallowed the end of the tunnel, lost in the darkness ahead.

"I figured starting in the inner ward was the best
plan. This leads from the castle to the kitchens there. We
used to play down here as kids; racing each other from one
end to the other. It drove the servers mad having to dodge
us as they carried trays of food up for meal time."

Rya smiled. "You must have been pretty quick."

"I wish," Cam replied. "My friend Thane usually won. He's always had longer legs than me, giving him an advantage."

"You mean he didn't let his little princess win?"

She laughed. "No way. Where's the lesson in that? If anything, I had to fight harder because I was the princess. There was a line of kids wanting to say they beat the future queen. I grew up knowing if I wanted to win, I needed to actually be the best."

Finally, they appeared to have reached their destination. Cam pushed open the single swinging door and led Rya into the kitchens. A dozen people dashed between large iron pots bubbling with various broths and soups. Others peaked in on the ovens, checking the meats and seasoning vegetables. The air was heavy and sweltering, filled with the scent of spices and garlic. Rya could already feel the sweat beading on her neck as Cam stopped to pluck two rolls off a stack nearby, waving to one of the women who responded with a kind smile and a shake of her head. The princess handed Rya one of the balls of bread and pushed open the front door.

Outside, the cool autumn air washed over her, brushing away the stuffiness of the kitchen. The girls walked through the inner ward, tearing off pieces of their rolls as they talked. While Cam chatted about the various buildings, Rya watched the people going about their days.

31

Young couples were lounging on benches, teasing each other with coy looks. Children played in the streets, bouncing balls off the sides of the homes, or squealing as they chased one another through the alleys. Around another corner, a group of women cackled while exchanging gossip and beating the dust from their rugs.

"Most of the people who work within the main walls live here in the inner ward," Cam explained. "It's a tight community, but it's only a small percentage of our population."

"A number of your subjects live in the woods themselves, don't they?"

"Yes, the woodsmen make up a great portion of the Ashen, but there's also Wynlis Port. It's grown quite a bit in the last few decades, nearly tripling in size."

They continued their walk and a light breeze swept across Rya's bare shoulders. The queen raised her hand, running it through her cropped hair and sighing. Cam's words became distant and muffled, driven away by the memory flooding her mind.

She'd been running for days, struggling to keep moving, but as her body fought against her she decided to take rest in a small inn. The last of her gold clanked together in the leather pouch as she handed it to the keeper, her face hidden behind a thin shawl she'd managed to keep with her during the trek. Once upstairs, she found the accommodations to be nothing more than a bare mattress on the floor, a chamber-pot, and a kettle resting over a pile of ash. In the corner sat a small plate, flies buzzing around the remnants of the last tenant's festering meal. In a fit of rage, she kicked at the brass chamber-pot, sending it clanking across the wood floor and bouncing off the wall. Without thinking she balled her hands into fists, the pain from her freshly shattered bones shot through her fingers and she cursed as her thumb went numb.

Rya fell onto the mattress, exhausted and infuriated, and found an agreeable spot to sit between the lumps and various stains. She leaned over and peeled off what remained of the thin leather shoes she'd been wearing, rubbing the sore spots left from the worn away areas. When she looked up she caught her reflection staring back at her in the metal of the chamber-pot and she winced. It was wide and distorted, stretching her face into an odd shape. Despite the warped face mimicking her scowl, there was no mistaking who she was; she'd always be the Black Queen.

She couldn't remember making the decision, but she could still feel the weight of the knife as she plucked it from atop the discarded plate. Her teeth grinded together as she forced her injured hand to wrap around her hair, biting back the scream wanting to escape her lips. With the other she began sawing away, watching the dark brown curls

33

litter the ground at her feet. As the last clump of hair fell free, she sank back onto the mattress and wept.

The sound of water brought her back to the present, and she looked up to see Cam's worried face staring at her.

"Are you alright?" She asked. "You look—I mean, do you need to rest? You just woke up, maybe this has been too much."

"No," Rya answered. "I'm just a little light headed for a moment, no need to worry, Princess." She could feel the edge of her hair brushing the base of her neck, suddenly aware it was no longer uneven and jagged. That too had been cared for while she slept.

"If you're sure," she nodded, leading her into the courtyard. "And you can call me Cam—just Cam."

The queen smiled. "This is a beautiful place, Cam."

The grand fountain sat in the middle of the courtyard, surrounded by paving stones. It was made of white marble, and water spouted from the top of a six-pointed crown which capped the third tier. It then flowed over the lower two ledges before splashing into the basin below. A light mist hung in the air around it, catching the sunlight and turning it into faded streaks of color suspended above.

"This is one of my favorite places," Cam smiled, taking a seat on the fountain's wall. "Something about the rushing water makes me feel peaceful. I come here whenever I need to get away from everything else."

"I can see why," Rya replied, taking a seat next to her. From the corner of her eye she could see the princess staring at her.

"I'm sorry." Cam looked away, her cheeks turning pink. "You look so different than what I remember. We met once, while I was in the Isles, but it was nearly three years ago. I know a lot can happen in that time, it can change a person."

"Yes, it can." Rya smirked. "For example, you're not the spindly girl you were back then."

"I'm surprised you remember me at all. You were so busy, I can't imagine making much of an impression."

"I remember everything from the week Gerrod died," she sighed. "The advisers told me it was my duty to sit on the throne and entertain anyone wishing to mourn the king's passing. I was forced to sit in that chair for days while people, one after another, came in with their tear-stained faces howling over his death. As if any of them knew him at all." Her words trailed off, and she frowned at the anger boiling inside her. She took a deep breath, calming herself before continuing. "I remember you and your father coming to offer condolences."

Cam nodded. "We had been moving through Trava and Papa said we needed to pay our respects."

"I'm sure you know your father is one to stand out among a crowd," Rya joked. "I remember laughing at the look on my soldiers' faces as he walked in, towering over them all. And there you were right next to him, walking with as much grace and confidence, as if you were the same size. It made the advisers nervous; they weren't accustomed to a girl being so bold."

"They obviously hadn't spent much time with you," Cam laughed. "I'm sure they wouldn't even notice now."

The image of the young princess was as clear in Rya's mind as if it were yesterday. She had been all limbs and thin as a rail, not like now. She could tell, even with the loose tunic she wore, Cam had grown into the curves of a young woman. Her round, childish face had thinned out, sharpening her nose and chin. Her shoulder length hair had grown longer, and the strands of blond were twisted into a braid that reached the middle of her back. The only feature remaining the same were her eyes; the color of a storm over the sea and as piercing as a dagger.

"How old were you when you came to see me?" Rya asked.

Cam thought for a moment. "It would have been just past my fourteenth birthday."

"Only two years younger than myself. Funny how such a short amount of time can mean so much. One of us was still an innocent child, and the other a new queen."

36

"Time might make a difference when you're younger, but the effect fades as you age. There's not much that separates us now."

Rya looked over at the girl and a flutter in her stomach caught her by surprise. For a moment, she thought the light breakfast she'd consumed was going to reappear, but seconds later the feeling had passed, and Rya was left confused.

A stampede of small feet broke the moment and she looked up to find a thin boy charging at the pair of them. His pale-yellow hair bounced with each step and a smile stretched from ear to ear, revealing the gap where his front tooth should be. As he got closer he slowed down, skidding to a halt just before crashing into their knees.

"Are you the witch?" He asked, still beaming.

"Eirik," Cam gasped. She grabbed the boy by the arm, yanking him to her side. "I'm so sorry, it seems my brother has forgotten his manners. I might have to beat them back into him."

"I haven't forgotten anything," he replied. He squirmed, trying to free himself from her grip, but kept his eyes on Rya. "I've never seen anyone with magic before. I had to get a look at her."

The queen placed a gentle hand on Cam's arm and she released him. The boy took a small step back and looked Rya up and down before shrugging.

"It doesn't matter, she's not a witch. She's too pretty."

"He's rather charming," Rya laughed.

"It's true," he added. "Everyone knows people with magic are old and ugly. It's in all the stories, that's how you know to stay away from them."

Cam smacked her forehead with her hand, hanging her head in embarrassment.

"I'll let you in on a secret," Rya whispered, luring him closer. "Anyone, at any age, can have magic within them. It's born inside you as you take your first breath, and it's there until your last. It's up to the person themselves to harness the energy and make it work for them."

"So—" the boy said in a hushed voice, "I could have magic?"

Rya giggled. "I'm afraid if you did, you'd already be showing signs at your age. But then again, it's always possible."

"It's true then, you have powers?" He asked. "Can you show me?"

The queen nodded, then cupped her hand and dipped it into the fountain. The boy watched with wide eyes as the water she'd scooped out began to float and twist in the space above her palm, shaping itself. When it had finished, a blast of cold air shot upwards and the water turned solid, falling into her fingers. With a triumphant grin, she handed

38

him a perfect rose made of solid ice, her joy made even greater by the look of wonder on his face.

"This is for me?" He gasped, hardly able to speak.

"Not all magic is bad," she replied. "Remember that when you hear people talking."

"I will."

Rya patted him on the head. "For now, let's keep this little gift a secret alright? If lots of people knew I could make you a rose, they might want one themselves, and that would make it less special."

The young prince nodded in agreement, then took off with a grin, cradling the ball of ice in his small hands as he ran up the castle's steps. Rya couldn't contain the smile on her face, even as Cam's glare burned into her.

"If you have something to say," the queen sighed, "you might as well just say it."

"You said you couldn't do magic. You lied. You said the break in your wrist wouldn't allow you to use your powers, but that's obviously false."

"What I said," Rya clarified, "was I'm unable to do the things the old man was babbling about. I've been training my powers since I was a child, and a little trick like I just did takes almost no effort at all. Now, putting an entire castle under a spell, or setting a forest on fire, is a different story entirely. If it makes you feel any better, freezing that water did leave my arm aching."

39

Cam crossed her arms over her chest, staring down at her feet. Another feeling struck Rya, one which was as equally foreign as the first. She swallowed, hoping the sick feeling would pass as quickly as the other, but it didn't.

"Look," Rya huffed, "I promised to be on my best behavior and I meant it. I really do owe you my life for what you did in the forest. I don't know anyone else who would have saved me."

"That's not true," Cam replied, relaxing her arms a bit. "I'm sure most people would want to help a damsel in distress."

"Not when they find out they'd be helping the Black Queen. I know what people think of me, and I know if it weren't for you I'd be dead right now so—thank you."

Cam put her hands back at her sides, her fingers grazing Rya's. The brush of her soft touch sent a shock through the queen's hand, and her mind scrambled to find something to say, anything to distract her from the princess' skin on hers.

"I didn't realize Mikkel had any other children," she said. "I thought the queen passed away years ago."

"Seven, to be exact," Cam answered. "My mother died giving birth to Eirik."

"I'm so sorry."

"I'm blessed with wonderful memories of her, but when I think about it, I get sad for my brother. He won't have any of that. He'll have to grow up never knowing his mother."

Rya frowned. "Some would consider it a blessing."

The princess opened her mouth to speak when she was stopped short by Thane waving from the other end of the courtyard. Rya had been so distracted earlier that morning she'd missed how tall and lean he was. As he jogged towards them, she watched his muscles move fluidly, reminding her of the large desert cats she'd seen in her homeland.

"Good afternoon ladies," he smiled. His front teeth overlapped just a bit, only adding to his charm. "I see you're looking better today Rya."

"Thanks to you I'm sure," she replied. "I have to stop falling to the ground all the time, in case you're not around to pick me up."

Cam's brow furrowed as she watched the two of them banter. "Is there something you needed?" She asked in a clipped tone.

"I apologize for the intrusion but I was sent to fetch you. My father wants to see us both in the armory."

Cam turned to Rya. "Will you be alright on your own?"

"I think I can find my way back inside," she answered with a grin. "If, however, I'm missing from dinner, please send a search party."

41

"Of course," Cam laughed. "I'll always make sure you're safe."

SIX

The dining hall was bustling with movement as the servants prepared the night's meal. Some were dashing from table to table, setting plates and flatware, others were arranging the centerpieces, while another small group mopped the floor from one side of the room to the other. It was a dizzying dance of a dozen bodies lost in their work, making it easy for Rya to cross the space without notice. She slid through the double doors along the wall and disappeared inside.

The rotunda was dim, but she had no trouble seeing it was beautiful. The high-pitched dome was painted gold, and bright white columns traced the arc of the wall, but it was the six stained glass windows which drew her gaze. They stretched from floor to ceiling, and each was a glorious tapestry of color depicting a different scene.

"Wonderful, aren't they?" Mikkel's voice echoed in the empty ballroom, making her jump. He chuckled, "I'm sorry, I didn't mean to startle you."

"No, it's my fault. I didn't realize I'd been followed," she answered, looking back at the windows. "They're amazing."

"The castle was built by the first kings, but this room was added almost a hundred years later. Each window shows a different piece of life here in the Ashen Forest. The first one is a woodsman hut tucked in the trees, and that one is a group of hunters taking down a deer."

"I've never seen anything like it. It's not surprising, your whole castle is unlike any other."

"What do you mean?"

"I've traveled to a handful of kingdoms, both within Kelda and beyond the seas, but they all seem the same. The entry halls are showrooms for their treasures, littered with jeweled vases and gold trinkets. The only vases I've seen around here are made of painted clay. Other rulers have over-sized portraits made of themselves, each exaggerating the battles they barely fought, or portraying them as better looking than they really are. Your walls are home to small family paintings and the mounted heads of past hunts. Even your throne is an oddity. It's not on a tall platform but sits just high enough to make sure you're seen without your presence looming over your subjects. And it's not even made of gold or silver, but instead it's been carved from wood."

Mikkel smiled, pleased with her assessment. "The Ashen have always had a special connection to the nature around us. It's what sustains us. We are a great kingdom because of our lumber trade. We are well fed from the animals in our forest and the surrounding sea. We respect that which gives us life, and we like to honor it in the way we decorate."

"Yes, I understand, but how do you display your authority? How do you keep your people under control? Those other kings and queens, they flaunt their wealth for all to see because it's a way to show their titles. Their thrones are a physical display of their power."

Mikkel stroked his beard. "I found balancing a firm hand, integrity, and respect are the key to being a good ruler. Though, I am aware it's not everyone's chosen method." He paused, taking a breath before asking, "And what about you? What's on your castle's walls? What does your throne say?"

"Nothing." Her words were as stony as her face. "The throne of the Isles was forged from black metal long before I existed, and it will remain long after I'm gone. The walls of the castle are bare; I had the portraits removed when I took the crown. I have no connection to those past kings, and I didn't care for their eyes following me through the halls. I've found more creative ways of displaying my power."

The king sighed. "So, I've heard. You know, the things they say—they give people a good reason to be afraid of you. I'm sure you realize how hard it is for some that you're here."

Rye kept her eyes on the windows, but they were far away from the current moment. "I was talking to Cam before, about the day you came to the Isles after Gerrod died. I saw hundreds of people during that time, but you will always stand out to me. Do you know why?"

"No," he said shaking his head. "Why?"

"You offered condolences to the kingdom, and you wished me luck and prosperity as the new queen. You never spoke of any sadness. You never called Gerrod's death a loss. You knew what kind of man he was, and you weren't going to praise him just because he was dead. You stood in front of me and blessed me with your honesty. It was a gift no one else had ever given me before, and no one has given it to me since, and I will forever be grateful for that."

"I couldn't pretend he was a great man," Mikkel answered. "I can never understand how he stood by and allowed his own son to be murdered. Even if it isn't true, he believed it was and that makes the difference. Who refuses to pay ransom for their only child? If it were me, I'd give my land, my castle, even my life for my children. Anyone with such disregard for their own blood couldn't have been much nicer to anyone else."

"That's an understatement."

The king crossed his massive arms. "Do you honestly think Prince Gavin is still alive?"

She nodded. "I know the advisers weren't happy with Gerrod near the end, and when I took the throne they thought they would use me as a figurehead while they ruled the Isles. They were disappointed to learn I wasn't so easy to control. If I know anything about Father Kasen, he'd have a backup plan. When it became clear I wouldn't stand by while he ran the kingdom, he threatened to find someone who would bend to his will. Gavin, in this case."

"You knew he was after the crown this whole time? Why didn't you try to stop him?"

"Gerrod's advisers made it clear what they expected. Unfortunately for them, I had other plans. I stripped their titles and status and banished them from the castle. The only one I couldn't dismiss was Father Kasen."

Mikkel nodded with understanding. "Because his title comes from the temple and not the king."

"Exactly. I knew even attempting it would rile up the people of the Isles. Burning offerings to the volcano god is not a custom I take part in, but most of the old families take it pretty seriously. So, Kasen remained in his position, and

47

through the years we've been in a silent battle. Each of us waiting, placing pieces here and there to push the other one out. He made a move before me, and here we are. I showed those other men how wrong it was to underestimate me, and soon enough Kasen will learn that lesson as well."

"Rya," he said, his docile voice not matching his mammoth size. "Just tell me one thing—are the stories about you true?"

She looked up at his kind face. "Since you were honest with me all those years ago, I'll do the same for you. I never broke any of our laws. I am the ruler of the Obsidian Isles, and everything that happened was within my rights as queen. Not all my decisions were popular, but it's part of running a kingdom. I'm sure you understand, especially after allowing me to stay. I may not know the specifics of the stories you've heard, but I will say that they all contain bits of the truth."

"You see the window in the middle?" Mikkel asked, gesturing in front of him. "The one with the king holding a massive shield. It represents what we are as a people. From the first king until our last we are the protectors. I will never turn away someone who hasn't wronged me. I kept you here because even if the rumors are true, you've done no harm to my people and I have no proof of any evil from your past."

"You're a good person Mikkel, which is why I knew I could come to you."

"I know you have good inside you as well. You just lost sight of it somewhere along the way."

"No," Rya replied, "I have rage, and hate. I have the determination to take back my throne, and I have the power to destroy anyone standing in my way. Those emotions are worth so much more than the good I once held inside. Those are the qualities that will put me back on top."

The queen turned on her heels and walked towards the doorway, leaving Mikkel standing in the darkened ballroom, shaking his head.

SEVEN

Night had fallen, and as her first day with the Ashen drew to a close Rya stood before the large mirror in her room, focused on the contours of her face. Her fingertips brushed her cheekbones, noticing the way they stuck out a little more than when she'd first fled. There had always been a crease between her brows, but it had only appeared when she was especially angry or stressed. Now it never left. Her hand moved to the stitches on her temple. She had already started to heal, and soon it would be nothing more than a thick scar left on her skin, but that was too much.

A woman's stern face appeared behind Rya, staring at her over her shoulder. The queen spun around towards her, her chest pounding with fear. She expected to see the woman's thin mouth pulled tight together, and her eyes burning with rage, but there was no one. She was alone. The image of her mother was only a memory; a disgusting trick her mind played on her when her defenses were down, and right now she was tired and unprotected.

Turning back to the mirror, she ran her finger across the large cut, pressing slightly to test the pain. *A lady doesn't play in the dirt*, she thought to herself, *a lady doesn't have scars*.

It had been years since she was allowed to run free and without care. The garden behind her house had been a sanctuary for her as a child, and she could still remember the time she spent outside. A small portion was off limits, separated with a fence that encased the plot of dirt and few short bushes, but the rest of the yard was all hers. She could recall the way the air smelled fresh and fragrant, changing depending on which plants the wind passed through on its journey. She would run with her hands stretched out, touching the bright colors of the flowers as she moved. One spot in particular was extra special. She would lay down with her back against the cool earth between two large bushes, watching the clouds pass overhead, or laughing as the bugs buzzed back and forth. It was her escape from the stuffy restrictions she had to follow indoors.

Her father had inherited their home from his family, but her mother was the one who kept the rules. There was never to be a single piece out of place. She was not allowed to run down the halls or jump and play in the sitting room. She was to walk without scuffing the floors, and she should never have a reason to raise her voice above a civil volume. She had always done as she was told, but out in the garden, she was her own master. It was the only place she was free, until it was stolen from her.

She was nine years old when everything changed. The day was warm and dry, and after a few hours spent in the garden she had gone back inside to get some water. She hadn't expected her mother to be waiting for her. The woman stood with her mouth pinched together, and her cheeks bright red. Rya looked down at her dust covered dress that was once yellow, and she understood the rage on her mother's face. She grabbed the young girl by the arm, yanking her through the rooms and up to the bath. Without a word she ripped the clothing over Rya's head and pointed to the tub. Once the basin was filled with hot water, she scrubbed Rya down with a brush until every inch of her skin was pink and swollen. The silence was more painful than anything. Rya knew when her mother had passed the point of scolding she was in for real trouble.

Finally deciding Rya was clean enough, she handed her a fresh dress. Rya pulled it down over her head, wincing as it passed over her still-raw skin. Her mother left the room, returning a moment later with a stool and a mirror.

"Sit," she said to the girl. Rya immediately climbed on the stool, her hands folded in her little lap. Her mother placed the mirror in front of her and handed the girl a brush. "No less than two hundred strokes to start. You will do this every day, brushing out your hair to whatever number I deem acceptable. From now on, you are not allowed in the garden. Young ladies to not play in the dirt, and I won't have you living like some filthy dog. You will keep yourself clean and pretty. You will make sure you are groomed each day, and your clothes will always be pressed and neat. You'll never become a queen if you're not perfect, and I won't have you being anything less."

Looking into the Ashen mirror, Rya considered the wound once more. Her anger pressed inside her temples, her head pounding from the memories that hurt her.

"A queen can't have scars," she said out loud, mimicking her mother's tone. "A queen has to be perfect."

"Is that really what you think?" Cam stood in the doorway wearing a sheepish look. She realized the queen hadn't expected an answer, and her arrival had startled her. "I'm sorry to intrude," she added. "I wanted to make sure you had everything you needed before I headed to bed."

"Can you really intrude if you own the castle?" Rya answered with a weak smile. "Come in."

Cam stood behind her, the princess' face hovering over her shoulder where moments earlier her mother's scowl had been. She studied Rya in the reflection, then reached up and pulled back the neck of her own shirt. A long, thin mark, pale and ghostly rippled across her smooth skin. It stretched from the crook of her neck down over her collarbone.

"That one's from my first time with a real sword. I'd like to say I got it fighting, but truth is the blade was too heavy and I dropped it on myself. With my luck it landed on the one spot my armor didn't cover." She pulled up the sleeve of her left arm to reveal the crisscrossed scars just below her elbow. "I got these jumping between the rafters of the guards' quarters. I managed to keep myself from falling to the ground but scraped myself against the rough wood in the process. There are others," she grinned, "but they require removing more clothing than what's appropriate."

She tugged on Rya's shoulder, turning the queen to face her.

"Do you think I'm unfit to be a queen?"

"No," Rya huffed. "Of course not. But our situations are different. I have a reputation. I was chosen by Gerrod because of my face and my body. I'm only a queen because of my beauty."

"Your beauty might be what got you to the Isles, but it's your spirit that kept you there. You didn't hold onto your title because of your face. Your body didn't keep the advisers from snatching your power away from you. This—" she said, brushing the skin just below Rya's cut "—this

54

isn't going to make you less of a queen. It's going to show the world you aren't afraid to fight for what you want. It's going to reinforce who you are. If anything, this mark makes you more."

Rya's stomach fluttered under the soft touch of Cam's fingers, and a heat started to form in her chest. For a moment she forgot where she was, and what had led her there. All she knew is that she wanted to stay frozen in this moment.

"You're the Queen of the Obsidian Isles," Cam added. "You can do anything."

The words crashed through the bubble surrounding her, and suddenly she had snapped free of the feelings attempting to grab hold.

"I know who I am," Rya replied, standing up. She pushed down the warmth growing inside her, burying it someplace dark. "I don't need to be reminded of that. My power is legendary, and no one will see a scar on my face when they are staring in awe at my magic."

Cam nodded, shrinking back towards the door. "As long as you know who you really are."

With that she was gone, and Rya was again alone. She sat on the edge of the bed, resting her face in her hands as she calmed her breathing. Her insides twisted and tumbled over each other and she could feel her stomach bubbling with sickness. Despite her mind telling her the outburst was necessary, her body seemed to disagree, fighting back against her with force. Guilt had felt different as a child. It was always fueled by fear and shame, occurring when she knew her mother would disapprove of something she was doing. Even when the emotion sprung forth in her chest while fleeing the Isles it was bound to her by rage and a promise. As she sat in the flickering light of the fire, she had trouble grasping the sadness that clung to her guilt. It burrowed inside her like a small animal waiting for winter to pass, heavy and cold in her gut.

What's happening to me? She thought as she threw herself backwards onto the mattress. Her eyes closed and she began to drift to sleep with the image of Cam's face behind her lids.

THE MARKET

The boy held his breath as the stack of crates wobbled beneath him, his feet clinging to the shaking mound.

"Get down from there," his father shouted. "I swear Byron, if you're not going to help me, I won't bring you next time."

It had been a long journey, riding from their home on the edge of the kingdom to the center market, but his father had promised it'd be worth it. This village was the largest in the Obsidian Isles, and the closest to the castle's grounds, making it a prime spot for vendors.

There was a lot of work to be done setting up the stall, but the trip had left him with a load of energy and a need to climb. From his seat on top of the wooden boxes he could see the entire square stretched out ahead of him, including the elegant carriage stopping along the outer road.

"There's a lady coming pop," he said. "A fancy one at that."

"A fancy lady huh?" His father repeated in a bored voice.

"She just got out of a nice coach. Got some men with her too."

"Wait," his father said, suddenly looking excited. "She's got men with her?"

The boy nodded, "Men in shiny armor. And they got swords."

"Byron, get down here and straighten yourself up." His father's eager tone had him equally excited, and he clambered down the stack. The man reached out, trying to slick down the tufts of hair on the boy's head.

"Who is she, pop?" He asked, squirming away. "Who's the lady?"

"She's no lady," his father answered. "She's the new queen of the Isles. Now look sharp, I heard she can be particular about things, and it's safer not to test it."

The boy brushed the dirt off his knees and stood tall, scanning the passing people for any sign of the woman. It wasn't long before he heard the guards shouting orders to part the crowd. The queen walked between her men, eying the stalls around her as she passed. His face lit up, and he craned his neck, standing on his toes, trying to get a better look at her. His straining must have caught her attention, because a moment later she pointed his way and headed straight for him.

"Good day, Your Majesty," his father said with a bow. "Such a blessing to find you out and about today."

Byron followed his example, bending at the waist. He stayed still as a statue until the queen came forward and stopped in front of the crates.

"What do we have here?" She asked, peering inside one of the stacks. "Apples? From what I understand, that's unusual for this kingdom, isn't it?"

"Yes, Your Majesty." The man answered. "I own a small plot of land along the southern border, and I found the soil is just right for growing apples. I haven't had much luck with the other crops I've tried, but these here--these are the best apples you'll taste in all of Kelda."

"Is that so?" She said, picking one up. "With such a bold claim, I'd better try it for myself."

Byron held his breath. She put the fruit to her lips and sank her teeth into the bright green skin. A sparkle of juice hung on the corner of her mouth as she slowly chewed the bite. Each second felt like forever, and as they ticked by a growing sense of fear rose in his stomach. It was impossible to judge her face.

"What's your name?" The queen asked, finally swallowing the chunk of fruit.

Byron's father was sweating now. "Morgan Parson, Your Grace."

"And who is this young man?"

"This is my son, Byron."

"Well," she smiled. "I'm happy to say Mr. Parson this is in fact the greatest apple I've ever tasted. You should be quite proud of yourself."

His father beamed. "Thank you, Your Majesty."

"In fact, your product is so superb I've decided I'm going to buy your entire stock. I'll even give you double the price."

"That's nearly 200 gold for the lot," Morgan stammered. "That's too much, Your Majesty. I don't believe they're worth that amount."

"There seems to be some misunderstanding," the queen replied. "I meant, I'm going to buy your entire stock from this moment on. I will be the only person in all of Kelda you sell to from this day forward. Your apples will be found exclusively in my castle, and my castle alone."

"I see." He nodded. "Yes of course Your Majesty, anything for the Queen of the Isles."

"Good. I'll have my men help you reload your cart and you can deliver this batch today. After that, you can set up a schedule with our bookkeeper."

"Thank you, Your Majesty. It's such an honor."

Byron tugged on his father's shirt, and as the man leaned down towards him the boy mumbled in his ear. "What about the man from before?"

"What's that?" The queen asked.

"Oh, it's nothing Your Majesty," Morgan replied. "A man stopped by shortly before you arrived. He only bought a small basket full. Nothing more than a dozen I'm sure."

"That does pose a problem," the queen replied. "I believe I was quite clear that I'll be the only person to have these."

"You did, Your Majesty. I'm sure he couldn't have gone far. I bet he'd be happy to gift them to his queen."

The young woman turned to the two men standing behind her and with a wave of her hand said, "find him."

The soldiers darted off into the crowd, and Byron felt the sense of dread from earlier rising up inside him again. He stood to the side, the queen next to him, nervously tapping his foot as the rest of the men helped his father load the crates onto his wagon. They had just picked up the last of the boxes when the two soldiers reappeared. The one in front had a sick smile on his face. He held a lumpy brown sack in one hand, and a bloodied sword in the other.

The queen glanced down at the items and back at the man. Movement around them had stopped. It seemed the entire village was frozen, each person waiting and watching with baited breath.

"I trust you got them all?" She asked after a moment.

"It took some coaxing," the man laughed, "but in the end, he handed them over without much of a fight."

"Good," she nodded. She turned back towards Morgan, "I trust you can find your way to the castle's gates."

"Yes, Your Majesty," he answered, his voice barely above a whisper.

With a final nod, she turned and walked away. This time the queen stepped in front, leading her party back towards the carriage, and unlike before, there was no need for the soldiers to shout. The crowd parted way without word, bowing their heads and keeping their distance as she strolled past them.

EIGHT

The past ten days had all started the same, and that morning was no exception. A sour-faced Norell pushed open the queen's door and stormed past the bed in a flash of dark hair and frustration. With both hands, she grabbed the heavy fabric covering and thrust it open, allowing the morning light to flood the room in a yellow glow. Grumbling, Rya rolled over and buried her face in the pillow.

"It's time to get up," the girl said, stripping the blanket away. "If you had it your way you'd sleep until sundown."

"There has to be a more pleasant way to wake me," Rya growled, glaring at her from under her tussled brown mop. "You could at least say hello before blinding me."

"Where's the fun in that," she replied without humor.

Rya swung her legs over the side and stood up, stretching her arms overhead with a groan. Norell wasted no time, sliding between her and bed to smooth the covers and fluff the pillows. The queen eyed the small stack of clothing sitting on a nearby table and looked to the girl.

"What's that?" She asked mid yawn.

"Your outfit for the day."

Rya walked over and picked up the top piece, unfolding it to find a pair of dark gray riding trousers. "You're kidding, right?"

"The princess has asked me to bring you to the stables this morning," Norell explained. "I've been told she's taking you riding. I thought this outfit would be better suited for the activity than the low-cut dresses you seem so fond of."

The girl's words dripped with bitterness, and Rya couldn't help but toy with her. She smiled as she pulled the pants on under her nightshirt. "I'm sure I can find a way to show some skin in any outfit. It's all about being creative."

Norell rolled her eyes but refused to take the bait.

"You don't like Cam spending time with me, do you?" Rya asked.

"My opinion doesn't matter," she replied, handing over a white shirt to the queen.

"Let's say it did matter, how would you answer the question?"

"If I'm being honest, I believe there are better things she could be spending her time on."

"Better things?" Rya prodded. "Or better people? People like you maybe?" Norell snorted in disgust as she picked up the queen's discarded clothing off the floor, but the reaction only fueled Rya's amusement. "I still don't understand why you volunteered for this. You hate waiting on me, so what's in it for you?"

"My reasons are none of your concern, Your Majesty." The title always sounded wrong coming from Norell's lips, as if the words were drenched in a foul taste. "I suggest you move quickly, you don't want to keep her waiting."

"Is it to raise your status?" She wondered. "Or maybe you just want to get closer to the princess? I've seen you watching us this past week. Does it bother you when we're together? If so, then this ride she's taking me on must really upset you."

The girl continued her work, dumping the water jug onto the last few embers of the previous night's fire. Rya could see the anger burning beneath her cheeks.

"I'm just curious why you'd keep this position. It's clear that it is torture for you."

Norell glared and turned towards the door, stopping only for a moment. "And it's clear you enjoy other people's torture. I'll be waiting in the hall when you're ready."

As they walked, Norell placed herself directly in front of Rya, pretending to lead the way when they both knew it wasn't needed. The queen wasn't used to being a long-term guest of a kingdom, which had left her with a great deal of free time. In the beginning, she spent the day wandering the gardens and sticking to the interior of the castle, but that grew tiresome quickly. Soon after, she ventured to the inner ward. She had braced herself for the whispers and stares, resolving to keep her head held high in defiance of whatever the people thought about her, but as she walked down the narrow streets she found it unnecessary. Children smiled at her as they passed, and some of the adults had even waved and greeted her good morning. No one eyed her with disdain. No one altered their path to move away from her. If any of them were fearful or angry about her presence they kept it well hidden, treating her as if she were just another normal face in the crowd.

It was by the fourth day she'd found herself in the outer ward. The training circle was situated in the corner and offered a bit of excitement during the day. Guards would practice their swordplay, challenging each other with childish taunts and personal jokes. Rya had been surprised to see a fair number of women dressed in the heavy leather armor, waiting their turn to exchange blows. In the Isles, the army was made up of the men only and included those far too old to be marching into battle. Back home in Asta, women were allowed to fight but only if there were no men of age left in the family. Despite it being legal, many women chose to forgo the opportunity, believing they would never be able to make a decent marriage if they were viewed as rough and callous.

The ring was where she found Cam most days. Thane would be next to her, exchanging tips for swordplay or setting up for their next archery training. As the time passed, Rya found herself drawn to the outer ward to watch them. It wasn't long before Cam started to wait for Rya at the doors to the castle, offering to walk to the circle together. The sight of Norell leading her now was a disappointment compared to the princess' company.

The archway to the outer ward passed above and they were suddenly walking side by side. In the brief moment Rya couldn't help but steal a glance at the girl. She was trying to study her dark eyes and round face, desperate to take in her features without notice.

"Is something wrong?" Norell huffed.

"No," Rya replied, looking forward again. "Why do you ask?"

"It seems I'm not the only one who's been watching people this week. I've caught you staring at me a handful of times now, like you're waiting for something to happen. There must be a reason I'm so interesting to you."

Rya frowned. "If you must know, you look a lot like someone I used to know."

"Someone important?" Norell questioned, coming to a stop. "Someone like Sora maybe?"

"What?" Rya snapped. She froze to the spot. The color had drained from her face and her heart dropped into her stomach. She hadn't expected to hear his name, not now, and certainly not from this girl. The shock of it left her void of words.

"You were calling for him while you had the fever. I expect he's quite special to you for that to happen." Her face twisted into a smile. "You've reached the stables, Your Majesty. I hope you enjoy your ride."

The girl was gone, disappearing back into the inner ward, but Rya's emotions were still surging. Sora's face flashed in her mind, and all she could see was the pained look he had the last time they spoke. It was like being punched in the chest. Each breath was deep and focused, each an effort to keep her stomach from emptying itself. The blood kept pounding in her veins, and the ringing in her ears grew so loud she'd almost missed Thane calling to her from the stables' entrance.

"Over here," he shouted. He was leaning against the wood siding, with one leg propped up against the wall. A small horde of children gathered around him, but with a wave of his hand they scattered, returning to whatever duties they'd been neglecting. "I would never have guessed Cam would be the one running late," he laughed. "Maybe you'd care to keep me company until she arrives?"

"Certainly," Rya said with a forced smile. She clasped her shaking hands together behind her back, and as she'd done a hundred times before, she put on her mask for the world to see. Pushing the last bit of anxiety away, she followed him into the barn, ready to distract herself with the new surroundings.

The walkway led down the middle of the long building, opening to the stalls which lined each side. The roof was pitched in the middle and Rya could see the stacks of hay stored above in the rafters. The smell of the fodder was mixed with the scent of packed earth and animal; all familiar, and all painfully tied to the memory she didn't want to have.

The children she'd seen before now scurried from one end of the stable to the other. Some carried pails of fresh water from the outdoor well, others were dropping armfuls of feed into the troughs. They passed an open stall door where inside a small girl stood on an old wooden stool, brushing out the coat of a large beige stallion.

They'd walked about halfway down the length of the building when Thane stopped, slid open one of the doors and stepped inside. Rya stayed in the aisle way, leaning over the side wall, watching him pat a mare on the neck.

"This is Rainy," he smiled, picking up the bristled brush closest to him. "Isn't she beautiful?"

Rya couldn't agree more. Rainy's rich cream coat seemed to shine against the blackness of her mane and tail. Both front legs had matching black stockings, but the back two were dipped in white. "She's gorgeous," she nodded. "But aren't you the head of Cam's personal guard? Why are you out here grooming your own horse?"

"My job is to protect the princess, but she makes it hard to do. You've followed her around this week; you've seen her with a sword, and how amazing she is with a bow. I'm sure you'll agree she's not the type of girl who needs protecting."

"That much is true," she nodded. "I just wouldn't imagine you would want to spend your free time in the filth of the stables."

Thane laughed, stroking the mare's nose. "Rainy's my soul mate. I would never leave her out here alone."

Rya returned the laugh. "She isn't exactly what I pictured your type to be, but you did pick a pretty one."

"Rainy was a gift from my father when I was ten. Cam had just named me her Kinsman, which is the official title I've been given. It's an old tradition the royal family has, and it's the highest honor our people can receive. By agreeing to be her Kinsman, I swore in that moment I would always protect her, even at the risk of my own life.

Even above my own blood. It's not a position one takes lightly."

"It seems like an important job for someone so young."

"It is, which is why my father awarded me with my own horse. I already knew how to ride, but he taught me how to ride Rainy specifically. He showed me how to read her movements, and how to know her thoughts. He wouldn't allow the children working here to groom her because he said it was my job, and mine alone. I've been out here every single day since then, brushing her down, making sure she's fed, filling her water. In the end, I'm a better Kinsman for it."

"How so?" Rya asked, shaking her head in confusion. "How does brushing the horse make you a better guard to the princess?"

"I've spent each day for the last nine years with Rainy, building the bond between us, and it has taught me everything I need to know about her. I know her personality, her quirks, her habits, and I know what spooks her. Spending all that time together has allowed her to know me in return. She moves where I want before I ask, and she can tell what kind of mood I'm in. When we ride now, we ride as one mind. We are always together, and always in sync—"

"And that's how you are with Cam as well," Rya finished for him.

"Exactly. I only spent an hour or two each day with Rainy, but I spent ten times that with Cam, so you can imagine how well I know her."

His eyes flashed, hinting his statement was hiding a secret he wasn't going to share with her. Rya shifted her weight back and forth, feeling uncomfortable and suddenly exposed. She was about to find an excuse to leave when the footsteps broke the tension. From the far end of the stable, Cam was jogging towards them.

"I'm sorry," she puffed, stopping at Rya's side. "I hope you weren't too bored."

"Not at all," Rya answered. She shot another quick glance at Thane who had returned to his normal cool and calm composure.

"Well," Cam smiled. "If you're ready, follow me this way."

As Rya walked after the princess Thane breathed one last comment.

"Be careful out there," he said with a hint of warning. "We don't want anyone getting hurt."

NINE

Rya shifted her seat on the all-black gelding, listening to the main gate clicking closed behind them. Her body was humming with nerves, and her hands were sweating under the soft leather gloves she'd been given. Seeing Cam relaxed on top of a dark brown mare she'd called Zara, looking cool and collected, only made her feel worse. The lump in her throat grew larger, and she tightened her grip on the reins. The feelings she'd pushed down for years were rising up inside her, twisting her stomach into a knot, and there was nothing she could do to keep it at bay.

"Are you alright?" Cam asked, noticing the green twinge to her face.

"Yes," she nodded. "It's just been awhile since I've been on a horse; I usually ride in my coach. I'm hoping it comes back to me quickly."

"I'm sure you'll be fine. Eclipse is one of the sweetest horses we have. He'll take good care of you."

Cam clicked her tongue and the horses began walking west into the open forest. The trees were spread out enough to allow the animals to pass without issue, but the terrain was rough and uneven, and Eclipse bounced Rya around in the saddle as he trotted up the hillside. She was just starting to find his rhythm when Cam looked at her with a wicked grin. In the blink of an eye she was off, galloping into the distance. Without thinking, Rya gave a gentle nudge and took off after her.

The trees blurred around them as they raced through the forest, swirling in a tornado of greens, yellows, and browns. The sound of the birds chirping disappeared under the thunder of the hooves on the ground, and Rya could smell the fresh dirt being kicked up in their wake. The wind whipped around her face, throwing her hair behind her, and stinging her cheeks. The rush of freedom was just as she remembered it, and it tore at her as it mixed with the pain in her heart.

After a few minutes Cam slowed down and allowed Eclipse to catch up.

"You could have killed me," Rya said half pouting, half joyful.

"I knew you could handle it. Besides, from what I hear you're not afraid of anything. A little ride should be no issue for you."

Once more, Cam galloped into the woods and, with an arrogant smirk, Rya followed.

They'd been riding for a few hours, alternating between a brisk walk and a full run. Each time the horses took off, Rya's heart jumped and then sank. The constant flux of emotion was as exhausting as if she was doing the running herself. She felt a sense of relief as Cam slowed Zara to a stop on one of the hilltops. Rya came up next to her, looking out over the sprawling kingdom.

"You can see all the way to the ocean from here." Cam said, gesturing to the water glistening in the distance.

"And those?" Rya asked, pointing to a dozen pillars of smoke scattered across the treetops.

"They come from the chimneys of the woodsmen. They prefer living among the trees rather than within the village or castle. It makes their work easier."

"Aren't they harder to control when they're spread out like that? I would imagine it's easier to tame them if they were given less freedom."

"If you were to put a pack of wild dogs in a small cage does it make them any less wild? If my subjects are angry, having them all in one area isn't going to change how they feel. It won't solve the cause of the problem. They don't follow my father because he's hovering over them, they follow him because he's a fair and just ruler."

"Not everyone responds well to that kind of leadership," Rya replied.

"And not everyone can be that type of leader," Cam retorted.

Rya eyed her with sympathy. "His shoes will be hard to fill, but I have no doubt it can be done. The ideas and beliefs of the Ashen have held up for centuries, they're not going to come crashing down so easily."

"As the time moves forward and our kingdom grows, the people change. They want to protect their way of life as much as anyone else, which makes them afraid of anyone from the outside coming in. But that's who we are. If we close off the Ashen Forest to those in need, how can we still call ourselves the Ashen? How can we still consider ourselves the protectors if we refuse to offer our hand?" Cam sighed at some unspoken thought before giving Rya a weak smile. "Come now, I know of a small clearing nearby, we can give the horses a chance to rest."

Rya followed in silence, watching the smoke disappear behind the canopy, thinking of her own subjects. She couldn't imagine the rough and ragged people of the Isles following her without the fear in their eyes. They had hated her from the moment she arrived, and she was smart to use it to her advantage. Part of her was jealous of Cam;

she would inherit a kingdom that loves and adores her father, only now was it obvious his legacy would be a hard one to uphold. Cam's future would never be smooth and without turmoil, and Rya's arrival was just the first sign of that.

The ground evened out, and the sun broke through the leaves, shining down on the circle of green. Coming to the edge, Rya dismounted and secured the reins to the saddle while Eclipse lowered his head, nipping at the soft grass. Cam found a fallen log near the other side, and plopped herself down, smiling at Rya across the open space.

"I know it's nothing fancy, but it beats sitting on the ground." She patted the open spot next to her. "I don't bite," she joked. "I promise."

Rya shook her head as she joined her. "Yeah, but I might." She looked down at the bow Cam had propped up next to her feet. "Do you always arm yourself when you go for a ride?"

"The forest is full of animals, and not all of them are friendly. It's easier to fend off a hungry bear from a distance with a single arrow than up close with a sword."

"Magic's always easier," Rya teased.

"I'm sure," she laughed. "I bet you'd just wave your hands and turn him into an angry squirrel instead."

Rya couldn't help but laugh at the mental image. Cam waved her hand with a flourish, and Rya caught the small bit of black ink peeking from under her sleeve.

"What's that?" She asked, motioning to Cam's forearm.

"The royal mark?" Cam pulled up her sleeve to expose the small tattoo. It was made of thick black lines, and matched the etchings on the trees which had saved Rya's life. Without thinking, Rya reached out and ran her fingers over the outline.

"I didn't know the Ashen still practiced that tradition." Rya's cheeks burned red when she realized she was still touching Cam's soft skin. She pulled her hand back.

"Each immediate member of the royal family gets one when they come of age. It used to be to identify the king if he died in battle, but these days it stands for so much more. It's a symbol of who I am, and where I came from. I'm proud to have it on my skin forever."

Cam's face turned pink as she spoke, followed by a wave of red when she saw Rya grinning at her passion. She took a breath, smoothed her braid, and asked, "Are you having fun?"

"Yeah, I had forgotten how great it can be."

"I don't understand, as a queen you should have your pick of horses, why wouldn't you take one out now and then?"

"I just don't." Rya replied. The memories twisted her insides, and her jaw jumped as she clenched her teeth together, fighting back the emotions. The corners of her eyes burned as she blinked away the tears threatening to spill out.

"It just seems like a waste."

"Well, it's not," Rya snapped in return. Cam bit her bottom lip and leaned away, and Rya immediately regretted the anger that slipped out. "I'm sorry. I didn't mean to shout at you. There's just a lot you don't know—a lot that's happened, and it's hard to deal with sometimes."

"No, I'm sorry," Cam sighed. "I can be a little overzealous and nosy. You don't ever have to explain yourself to me, okay?"

"But I want to," Rya replied, surprising herself with the words. She had never thought to share the story with anyone, not even Sora, but as she stared at Cam's caring face she found the words spilling out of her mouth.

"The year I turned seven, my parents took me on my first trip to the Isles, traveling up and over the Bardo Mountains instead of heading all the way west to go around. I had listened to stories about snow as a child, but growing up in the Deserts of Asta made it impossible to believe in. It wasn't until that trip that I'd actually seen it. As we crossed the mountain range a blanket settled over the rocks without a sound. It fell from the sky in little tufts of white, soft and cold, kissing everything it touched. It was the most beautiful sight and the most peace I'd ever experienced. I didn't know anything could make me feel that way.

"After our time in the Isles was over, when we were about to leave, my parents gave me a gift: a three-year-old mare they'd bought from the castle's stable. Every part of her was stark white, and the second I sat on her I felt the same sense of peace I'd had in the mountain pass. I named her Snowfall, as she was equally as wonderful and magical as the stuff I'd watched dropping from the sky. I cherished her."

"Did you have to leave her back in the Isles when you fled?" Cam asked.

"No," Rya frowned. "I'm afraid Snow was gone long before this mess I'm in now." The sadness filled her chest, and she winced as the pain grew.

"Hey," Cam whispered, placing a gentle hand on Rya's arm. "It's alright. You don't have to tell me—"

"He killed her," Rya confessed.

"Who did?"

"Gerrod. Years later, once I was brought to his kingdom. He killed Snowfall. He stabbed her right in the heart, and he did it in front of me. He told me it was a punishment for an offense I hadn't committed yet. He'd feared that I would try and run from him, run away from the Isles, and he wasn't wrong. It had crossed my mind. As a way to stop me, he took the only thing that was mine. He wanted me to know he was in complete control. He wanted to prove he was the king and while I was in his land, I was nobody. I knew in that moment he owned me, I was just another trophy for him to display, and I would never be free. I haven't ridden a horse since then...until now."

"I'm so sorry," Cam said, covering her mouth in shock. The absence of her touch left Rya feeling empty. "I had no idea, if I had I wouldn't have pushed you to come riding today. I feel horrible."

"No, I'm glad you did." The queen replied. "I needed this. I needed to remember what it felt like to be happy."

Cam's hands moved to her sides and the soft skin of her fingers once again brushed against Rya's hand. The slight touch brought goosebumps to her skin. She looked at the princess, taking in the details she'd somehow missed before. Like the small spatter of freckles on the bridge of her nose, or how the wind blew the one strand of hair she could never get to stay put, no matter how many times she tried to braid it. Another brush of the hands and Rya's stomach flipped over itself. It was a wonderful feeling, one she'd long forgotten, but also one she had never wanted again. As it registered in her mind she jumped to her feet, brushing the dirt off her pants and taking a few steps away, trying to distance herself from the girl.

"I think my arm's feeling sore," she lied. She looked away towards Eclipse, not wanting to meet Cam's eyes. "We should start heading back."

"Of course," Cam replied. She hadn't questioned the queen's reason, but Rya could hear the confusion and disappointment in her voice. She kept her gaze away from the princess, keeping her face down and taking several long, deep breaths. *I won't let this happen*, she thought to herself. *Not again. Not ever.*

TEN

A light breeze rustled the leaves above, separating a few and sending them to the floor below to meet their fallen brothers. Birds chirped and whistled from the surrounding bushes, and Rya spotted a gray squirrel scurry from one tree to another. The natural music of the woods was calming, until the sound of foreign footsteps interrupted it all.

The young man stepped out of the forest, hovering near the edge of the tree line, keeping his face masked in the shadows. The dark copper stain covering his shoulder stood out as a reminder of their last meeting.

"I thought you were smarter than this, leaving the safety of the castle," Nix said with a sick smile. "It's a shame you won't be returning."

Rya could feel her insides buzz as the power began to surge in her blood. Her bones shook with the force of her magic, and the pain in her wrist grew with each second ticking passed. Cam's hand slid across the small of her back as she passed her, putting herself between the queen and the assassin before Rya had a chance to protest.

"As the princess of the Ashen Forest, I demand you leave this land at once."

"I know who you are," he laughed. "You're the one who stuck an arrow through me. Only this time, you're without your little gang, and without your weapon."

Cam looked down at her empty hands, her face pale. The bow she usually carried lay propped against the log a few feet behind them, forgotten in the chaos of his arrival.

The assassin took a few steps, closing the distance between them. "Lucky for you, I'm here for the Black Queen and nothing more. Allow me to take her, and I'll leave you and your kingdom untouched."

"Once again," Cam growled, "I'll remind you she's under our protection. She's not going anywhere."

"Tell me, has she explained the things she's done? Has she told you about the man she killed over a basket of apples? Or the woman she had burned to death in a bath of boiling water?" He paused, waiting for a response, but found only silence. "Ah—I thought not. There're another hundred stories just like those. You might not be so willing to put yourself in danger's path if you knew the truth behind that woman."

"I don't care," Cam replied, her words shaking. "I won't let you take her."

"Then I'll just have to kill you as well."

Nix pulled one of the ivory daggers from its sheath, and the anger boiled over inside Rya. She lifted her good hand and pointed her open palm towards the assassin. A smile spread across his face as he took another step forward, but when her fingers curled into a fist he froze.

"What are you doing?" he barked. "Release me!"

The vibration in Rya's chest grew, and heat spread down each of her arms, but she kept her focus steady. The sweat started to bead on Nix's forehead, and his arm trembled under her forceful grasp. The dagger shook along with his hand, unable to move forward and unable to break free of her power. The burn inside her broken arm grew to an inferno, devouring her bones, but she refused to yield. The corners of her crimson lips curled into a smile as she dug her fingers in deeper.

"What's happening?" Cam gasped. She was still at Rya's side, her face frozen in horror as she watched the assassin fight against the unseen force.

Nix's knuckles had gone white, clenched around the hilt of the knife. The tip twisted towards him as his hand pointed the blade at his own face. Another grunt from him and it stopped moving. Rya was pushing her magic further, but he was fighting back with all he had. Cam gasped as the blood began to roll down the assassin's sleeve; five small spots carved out in his flesh, put there by the invisible nails he struggled against. She was weak and had concentrated all her power on his one arm, ignoring the other as it moved to his thigh.

Rya watched in slow motion as the second knife slid from its holster and left his hand. It flipped through the air, rotating end over end towards Cam's chest. In that moment Rya knew she'd lost. She shifted her focus, aiming her hand towards the flying dagger and halting it in midair, the tip stopping an inch from Cam's body. The weapon hung suspended for a moment before falling to the ground, and the queen followed, collapsing into the soft grass.

"Rya," Cam shouted. She dropped to her side and took the queen's hand in her own. "Rya, are you alright?"

"Your bow," she coughed.

Cam scurried over and grabbed her weapon in one hand while the other reached up for an arrow. She pivoted on her heel, arrow nocked and ready to release, but the clearing was empty. She whipped around once more, searching the trees for the assassin, but he was gone. "Where is he?" She shouted, spinning in circles.

"Ran," Rya whispered. "He'll be back." The queen's insides burned in agony, the energy drained from her entire body. It had been ages since she'd used that much magic, and the pain from her shattered wrist only made it worse. "We need to return to the castle."

"There's no way you can ride back now. You can barely sit up."

"I'll be fine," she lied, rolling onto her side. She tried to push herself up only to fail and fall once more. "We can't stay here, it's too dangerous."

"I know of a small cave a few yards down this pathway. We can hold up inside until you're rested. Do you think you can make it?"

She couldn't find the strength to respond, but it didn't matter. Cam slipped her arm under Rya's and pulled her to her feet, shouldering her weight as they shuffled down the worn dirt path. The cave wasn't far, but with each step growing more difficult for Rya, the walk seemed never ending. With the rocky alcove in sight, Cam's face burned red and sweat dripped down her neck as she carried the queen the rest of the way.

"I'll be back," she huffed as she propped Rya against the back wall. "I need to secure the horses. Here—" Cam had plucked the assassin's abandoned dagger from the clearing and was placing it in her limp hand. "If anyone comes for you, use it."

The queen watched through spotted vision as Cam ducked outside the cave and disappeared into the woods. Her hand wrapped around the hilt of the knife, but her flesh couldn't feel it. The hum of her magic dissolving was the only sensation she had anymore. It drowned out the rest of the world as it dissipated. Her heartbeat started to slow, and her limbs grew heavy as if they were tethered to the earth, slowly sinking down into the dark rock under her. Her eyes were equally tired, and without the power to stop them, it all went black.

Cam watched as the blue afternoon sky became streaked with the dull orange of dusk. Hours spent against the solid rock wall had left her back aching and her legs numb. A dozen thoughts had passed through her head as she waited for the queen to wake. Would Nix find them a second time? Would Thane come looking for them? Would she need to use the arrow she held pressed against the bowstring? But one thought popped up more than any other—was she wrong to have trusted Rya?

"It's nearly dark," the queen groaned. Her eyes blinked open, and she moved to stretch her tired body.

"I know."

"Why didn't you wake me sooner?"

"You needed to sleep. Whatever you did before—it wrecked you." Cam pushed herself to her feet, shaking the feeling back into her calves. Rya tried to do the same, steadying herself against the wall with her one good arm while she rose to her feet. The movement was too much for her, and she swayed on weak legs. Cam jumped towards her, throwing her arms around her and pulling her into a tight hug, keeping her upright.

"Thanks," Rya whispered.

Cam shivered as the queen's word tickled her neck. Her bare skin was a breath away, and the heat from her flesh warmed the princess' lips. Cam broke free from the embrace, stepping away and allowing her hands to fall to her sides. "We need to get moving if we want to make it back before nightfall."

"Right," Rya nodded. "Lead the way."

The horses were tied just outside the cave opening. Rya slid her foot into the stirrup but with her arm still aching she was unable to pull her body up. Cam was at her side once more, helping push her towards the saddle so Rya could swing her other leg over. Cam's hand lingered a moment on Rya's thigh before she turned abruptly and checked the straps on Zara.

Once settled in their saddles, she gave a click of the tongue and began the long walk towards the castle. The narrow pathway made it so they had to ride single file, and Cam was grateful. She needed to keep the space between them, at least until she had the answers to the questions that filled her mind. She also knew as soon as Rya looked at her with those big brown eyes, she would be in trouble. The queen's gaze had a way of making her heart jump, and she couldn't help but soften like butter. Cam was successful until the halfway mark, but as they came over the top of one of the hills, Eclipse rode up on her left.

"Are you alright?" Rya asked. "You aren't hurt, are you?"

"No, I'm not hurt."

"If you are, I could help."

"I'm not hurt, I just—what were you doing? I've never seen anything like it. It looked like you were trying to kill him."

"I was," Rya shrugged. "It's a shame I couldn't do more."

"That's the second time you've lied to me. You told me you didn't have the strength to do powerful magic and yet I just watched you try to stab a man without touching him. How am I supposed to trust you when you keep showing me I shouldn't?"

"I didn't lie. I've never been in this situation. I don't know what my body can and can't do right now. I took a chance and trust me, if I was fully healed, he wouldn't still be alive."

"How can you be so calm? You almost killed someone and you're acting like it doesn't faze you—like you don't even care."

"I don't," she replied. The answer was void of any emotion, but as she continued to speak Rya's eyes shimmered with worry. "He was going to hurt you, or me, or both. He deserves to die."

Cam's heart was pounding against her ribs as the next question came out of her mouth. "What about the others he mentioned, did they deserve to die too?"

Rya paused before shaking her head. "The man he talked about was an unfortunate casualty of my pride and my youth. He shouldn't have lost his life, but there was nothing I could do to fix it. There was no way to bring him back."

"Tell me about it; tell me what happened."

"You don't want to hear that story."

"You're right," Cam nodded. "I don't want to, I *need* to."

Rya sighed as she gave in. "It was near the beginning of my reign, and I had been in one of the outlying villages walking through their marketplace when I came across a man and his son selling apples. He promised they were the best in all of Kelda. Imagine my surprise when he was correct; it was the most amazing apple I'd ever tasted. I decided right then I was going to be the only one in all the kingdoms who had access to these apples. We made a deal that he would only sell to me and no one else, and in exchange I'd pay handsomely for it. Unfortunately, he told me how another villager had bought from him shortly before I'd arrived."

"And you had the vendor killed for it?"

"No," Rya sighed. "The farmer and his son went home untouched. I did, however, order my guards to find the man who had made the purchase. I told them to bring me what he had, no matter what."

"Oh," Cam whispered.

"I had been crowned only two weeks before, and I didn't know my soldiers well, so I didn't know the kind of men I had sent to complete the task. They could have just demanded what he'd bought, but these few men were vicious and decided killing him would be quicker. When they returned to the village square with a blood smeared sack, I knew what had happened. I was angry for a moment, because I caused an innocent man to lose his life, and I almost berated my men right in front of the whole town."

"Why didn't you?"

"The villagers were all standing around, everyone's eyes on me. As I looked at each of their faces I saw the fear that filled them. They were scared, but they were compliant. They already knew of my magic, I never tried to keep it secret, but now they'd seen firsthand what kind of person I could be if crossed. I knew no one in the village would ever step out of line, because if they believed I was willing to kill over a bit of fruit, who knows what else I'd do. Soon the word started to spread throughout my kingdom, and the more the people feared me, the more they respected my crown."

Cam shook her head, unable to form a response.

"Look, it's not something I'm proud of," Rya explained. "If I had known they would be so loose with my orders, I would have been more specific, but I couldn't go back on my decision. How would it look if I stood in the middle of the village begging the people for their forgiveness? I needed them to see I wasn't weak."

"So, you paid that price with a man's life?"

"I paid that price in many ways," she shot back.

Rya tried to keep her face emotionless, but the sadness she'd buried deep inside was showing itself in little ways, from the look in her eyes to the way her lips tightened. After hearing the story of Gerrod's punishment, Cam suspected she had many dark secrets from her life that Rya kept locked away.

The thought softened Cam's heart, but she couldn't help but ask, "And the woman he mentioned, what about her?"

"That's a story for a different day," Rya answered as they approached the castle's gate.

ELEVEN

With night settling over the castle it was no surprise to see Thane pacing outside the stables. His hands were clasped together behind his head, and a cloud of dust rose around his feet as he walked back and forth. When the sound of hooves on the packed dirt hit his ears, he stopped and snapped his head around. Cam locked eyes with him and his body unraveled as the relief washed over his shoulders.

"Sorry we're late." Cam apologized. She jumped down and handed off the reins to the boy standing by. She watched him with caution as he walked away, waiting until he was fully inside the stable to begin speaking. "We were cornered by the assassin from before; he hasn't left the forest."

Thane's mouth hung open as another boy ran out to fetch Eclipse. Rya was still seated on the horse, holding her arm to her chest as she tried to figure out how to dismount without falling. Cam wanted to run to her aid, but Thane was already there, holding her until her feet were steady on the ground.

"Are you hurt?" Thane asked, scanning the two of them for signs of blood or torn clothing. "What's wrong with your arm?"

"It's broken, remember?" Rya joked. "I'll be fine, I promise. Cam was the lucky one, she walked away without a scratch on her."

"What happened?"

"First, we need to find my father," Cam huffed. Without explanation, she started towards the inner ward at a brisk pace. She knew the other two would be close behind her, and she also knew exactly where to find the king at this hour. No one spoke as the three of them navigated their way to the castle's entry and then the door of the royal library. Cam pushed it open without knocking and, thankful to find him alone, ushered Thane and Rya inside, closing it behind them.

"You've returned," Mikkel smiled from behind his desk. "You missed dinner, but I'm sure the kitchen can throw a plate together for you." As the glow of the fire lit Cam's sullen face, he knew this wasn't a casual visit. He stood up abruptly, knocking back his chair. "What's wrong?"

95

"The assassin, Nix," Cam began, "he is still in the woods. He found us out on our ride and confronted us. We were able to fight him off, but I have no doubt he'll be back again."

"Are you alright?" He rushed towards her, grabbing her arms and checking for any sign of trauma. "I don't see blood, that's a good sign."

"I'm perfectly fine," she nodded.

"I don't understand," Mikkel said, shaking his head. "How could he know you'd left the castle?"

"He must be keeping watch somewhere near the gates," Thane suggested. "Maybe he's waiting in the trees, biding his time until the right moment? He could have seen them leave, then followed them until they were far enough out that it was safe to attack."

"No, that can't be," he replied. "I know the Kael are not easily deterred, so I figured he might try to get close. I've ordered guards to do double rounds on the top of the wall, watching for any movement. I even have them doing a sweep of the woods surrounding us at the start of each hour. They haven't found a thing; no broken branches, no footprints, no campfire. We haven't seen a single sign of anyone coming close to the castle."

"What are you saying?" Cam asked.

"If he knew you had left it's because someone inside the grounds tipped him off." Mikkel frowned. "Which means we have a traitor within our walls."

"Guthry," Cam spat, slamming her hand on the desk. "I know it was him. He's been angry ever since you allowed Rya to stay."

"That's a serious accusation," Mikkel cut in. "He's the royal adviser and has loyalty to the king. Not to mention he's not the only one to voice his concern. I don't want to upset you Rya, but many people have been cautious about you staying here, and some were downright angry."

"I'm used to it," she replied.

"Is there anyone you are wary of?" He asked the queen. "Anyone you avoid or stay away from since you came here? Anyone make any threats to you?"

Cam held her breath. She knew Rya had suffered through the dirty looks and pouted stares from Norell for the past week. If Rya was going to point the finger at anyone, Cam was certain it'd be her. It was no secret she wasn't the queen's biggest fan, but she couldn't imagine her being capable of such a betrayal.

"No," Rya answered, shaking her head. "I can't say anyone stands out."

The king nodded. "Let's keep this between us for now. If someone is passing information outside the castle, I don't want them to know we're onto them."

They all nodded in agreement.

"Despite the horror of what's happened," Mikkel continued. "I am impressed you fought off a member of the Kael. They are trained since childhood to know nothing but pain and death. How did you manage it without being injured yourself?"

"It was Rya," Cam answered, glancing at the queen. "He wasn't expecting her to fight back, and the element of surprise is a powerful tool. He fled when he figured out he'd have to take us both on. Next time, I don't think he'll take her for granted."

With a long sigh, Mikkel pulled the princess into hug, smashing her face against his chest. She inhaled the familiar scent of him, thankful to be home.

"I'm happy everyone is safe," he said, "but from here on out I want both of you kept inside the grounds."

"What?" Cam tried to argue, but her words were muffled by his shirt. "You can't be serious."

"If Nix is still hiding in the forest, we can't risk sending Rya outside the walls, not until she's healed. He won't stop until he's successful. Not to mention you've defended her twice now, and I can't help but think you've painted a large target on yourself for it."

Cam pushed herself away. "Nix isn't the only one who has been training since childhood. I can wield a sword

98

better than half the men and women here, and I'm an expert archer. I shouldn't be locked away when I can fight."

"You are the princess of the Ashen Forest and the heir to my throne; you need to learn some fights you walk away from, and some you allow others to fight for you. It's why we have an army. I don't rush off to lock swords with every single person who threatens me, because if I did I wouldn't be here now. Do me this favor, and stay within the safety of the castle, at least until I can figure out our next move. Please?"

"Yes Papa," Cam mumbled.

"Now, like I said before, you're probably starving. Head to your rooms and I'll have someone bring up a plate. You'll need food and rest after the day you've had. And remember, tell no one about any of this."

"Yes Papa," Cam repeated a second time.

The trio turned back and exited the library. The door between themselves and Mikkel had barely clicked shut when Thane caught Cam by the arm.

"Something else happened," he whispered. "I know you Cam, and you were holding something back in there. It's not like you to lie to your father."

"It's my fault," Rya said, eying the hold he had on her.

"It's okay," she replied, removing her arm from Thane's loose grip. She checked the queen's face, looking for any similarities from earlier, fearing she might try and crush his hands in response to the touch. "I trust Thane with my life, he'd never do anything to hurt me. And he would never betray me."

"What's going on?" He asked, looking back and forth between them.

Cam sighed. "I didn't tell my father the details of how Rya fought off Nix, because I was worried about his reaction. People are already afraid of her, and knowing she used her magic won't make it any easier, even if it was to save my life."

"You got a Kael assassin to run away from you using just your magic?" He was staring at Rya now, but instead of the anger or worry Cam expected, he looked impressed. "From what I know about them, they train their people with torture, inflicting pain on them until they can tolerate any pain without flinching. The final test to become a full member is to be cut from earlobe to shoulder while standing silent and still. You make a move and you die. You must be more powerful than I thought."

"Not quite," Rya answered. "It took a lot out of me."

"She was wonderful," Cam smiled. Thane looked back at her, raising his eyebrows, and she stammered. "I just mean—she could have sacrificed me and killed him once and for all, but she didn't."

"Sure, that's what you meant," Thane teased with a smirk. "I'm sorry I questioned you, and you can be sure your secret is safe with me. It's been a weird night, and I think your father was right, we could all use some sleep."

"I won't argue with that," Cam replied. She could feel the weight of the day pushing down on her shoulders. Her head was pounding, and she ached for the softness of her bed. The sight of the staircase gave her the smallest boost of energy until she spotted the girl waiting on the second-floor landing.

Norell stood with her arms crossed over her chest, her dark hair cascading over her shoulders. People who didn't know her would think she was always angry. Her mouth naturally turned down at the corners, giving her a permanent scowl, and her eyes were always burning with intensity. Only those who really knew her could decipher her actual emotions, and looking up at her now, Cam knew she was in serious trouble.

"I can't do this tonight," the princess whined.

Thane looked up the steps just in time to see Norell turn around and storm off into the darkness. "Unfortunately, I don't think you have a choice."

Cam trudged up the steps to the third floor, where she knew Norell would be waiting. Her feet were like rocks as she shuffled from the landing towards her bedroom, the sight of her fluffed up bed cover teasing her from behind the body standing in the doorway.

"What were you thinking," Norell snapped. "Running off into the woods with her, without anyone to watch you."

Cam pushed past her and threw herself on the mattress, rubbing her temple with her fingertip. "We made it back safe and sound, didn't we?"

"That's not the point. You should have taken Thane with you, or one of the other guards."

"I've never needed a chaperon on a ride before."

"You've never been alone with someone so dangerous."

"I can take care of myself," Cam groaned. The throbbing in her head was growing worse, and she knew Norell was far from finished. "I'm not a child."

"Then stop acting like one," Norell scoffed. "You're forgetting she's the Black Queen. In Rya's world people die, and she's the one to make it happen. You're acting like it doesn't matter to you."

"Because it doesn't," she shouted in return. She threw herself back onto the bed and covered her face with her arm. She knew the reasons anyone might be afraid of Rya, she'd seen it first-hand, but there was some part of her that didn't want Norell attacking the queen. "If you have so much against her, why did you volunteer to care for her?

It's not your job, you didn't have to do it, and yet you insisted it be you."

"I did it for *you*, I thought it would be obvious. You were consumed with her when you came back that day. You were at her door hour after hour, checking on her. You were so concerned about who was taking care of her, but I was concerned for you. I needed to keep an eye on things. I could see what was happening from the very beginning and the longer she's here the more right I become."

"What are you talking about?" Cam asked, sitting back up.

Norell's hands were balled at the sides of her dress, her foot tapping in anger. "You know exactly what I'm talking about. This is going to be just like last time. I don't want to see you get hurt again. I can't handle it."

"This is nothing like that," she growled, "and Rya is nothing like Hannah."

"No? How can you be so sure? You barely know her."

"I just know. Besides, you're worrying about nothing. There isn't anything going on between us."

"For your sake I hope not. She's already got someone special, remember? Whoever Sora is, he means something to her. You can't pretend he doesn't exist."

"Stop it," Cam exclaimed. "Just stop. Whatever you think is going to happen, won't. And if it did, it's not for you to control. It's not your job to take care of me."

"Yes, it is," Norell sighed, her tears swelling. "It's always been my job, and I'm not going to stop now. It doesn't matter that you'll be queen one day, I'm still going worry. A crown doesn't make you invincible. You of all people should know that."

TWELVE

Rya's arm ached as the mender squeezed it between his thumb and finger. The pain shot into her hand, and she flinched, pulling against his grip. The gesture peaked his interest, and the old man raised his eyebrows, squeezing again. This time she kept still.

He'd been to see the queen several times before, helping Norell in caring for her wounds and tending to the break in her wrist. He was the most experienced mender in the Ashen Forest, but even he had never dealt with such magic before, leaving him curious about Rya's progress.

"I don't understand," he sighed, laying her arm back on her lap. "You were healing faster than anyone I've seen before. Usually it takes weeks for a break like this to fix itself, but you were looking at half the time. I assumed the magic you have flowing inside your body was helping speed the process along, but now your muscle is swollen and tender. It's like you've regressed somehow."

Rya glanced to the princess standing in the open doorway. Cam's face was still and calm, but she knew the fear she was hiding inside. If anyone found out what happened in the woods, it would put Rya's life in even more danger than it already was.

"I hurt it again," the queen lied. "While riding yesterday, I was careless and smacked in on the horse."

"You shouldn't be engaging in such activities until you're fully healed," he scolded.

Rya rolled her eyes. "I know that now."

The man packed away his tools and excess bandages. "Make sure you take it easy, Your Majesty, even if you're feeling better. You're too special to risk more injury."

"Thank you," she nodded, watching him bow as he passed by Cam and exited the room. She looked at the princess and frowned. "I'm special alright. He only wants to study me and my magic. He doesn't care about my well-being, he just wants to use me like everyone else does."

"Not everyone in your life is trying to use you," Cam scoffed, sitting on the edge of the bed. She was flicking the tail of her braid between her fingers. "You had friends and family growing up, did they all try and use you?"

"Yes," Rya answered in a matter-of-fact tone.

Cam dropped her hair. "Okay, what about me? Do you believe I'm trying to use you for a secret purpose?"

"No," Rya replied, shaking her head. "You're the first person in a very long time that I don't suspect, but that doesn't mean I won't find out later I was wrong. It's happened before."

"Always waiting to be hurt is a horrible way to live your life."

"It's the only way I know."

The queen hadn't noticed the heat in her palm until a sound broke her focus, and she shook her hand in the air, trying to relieve it. The whimper had come from the doorway where a frail girl stood trembling. She had the signature blond hair of the Ashen, with beady eyes and oversized front teeth. She was small in stature and if she had to guess, Rya would put her at about nine or ten years old.

"And who are you?" Rya asked, standing from the bed and smoothing her dress.

"Your Majesty," the girl stammered. "I'm Elin, I've been sent to tend to your needs."

"I already have someone for that," the queen answered. "Though I haven't seen that girl at all today. I had to dress myself this morning."

"I'm so very sorry." Elin's voice trembled as much as her hands. "Lady Norell sent me in her place—she didn't tell

107

me until just now. I came as fast as I could Your Majesty—I didn't know."

Cam stood to comfort the girl but Rya was already taking Elin's hand in hers and leading her into the room.

"It's alright," Rya soothed. "You can't be blamed for something which wasn't in your control. Tell me, have you been a chambermaid for long?"

"A year now," the girl sniffled. "My sister taught me."

"I have no doubt you're wonderful at it. Like I said, I've taken care of myself for today, but I look forward to seeing you again tomorrow."

"There's still more to do," Elin answered, perking up. "I have to make your bed and prepare the fireplace for the evening's log. You go about your day Your Majesty, and when you return it will all be in place."

"See, you're better than Norell already," Rya winked. The girl giggled and began to dash around the room. The queen took Cam by the elbow and dragged her into the hall, leaving Elin to complete her work.

"*Lady* Norell?" Rya gasped. "You didn't tell me she was a member of high society. How could I not know?"

"I'm sorry," Cam said as they stepped down the staircase. "I didn't think it mattered."

"It certainly paints a different picture of her behavior. Why would a lady be slumming around as a chambermaid? Am I right to assume it was as a favor to you?"

"Something like that," Cam said sheepishly.

Rya scoffed. "Of course. Her disappearance this morning is connected to you as well, isn't it?"

"I'm afraid it might be my fault. We had a bit of a fight last night. It seems like too much of a coincidence for her to quit the next day."

"She definitely looked mad the last time I saw her, but then again she always does. What were you fighting about?" Rya asked. Cam blushed, looking down at her feet as they exited the castle's doors, and the queen understood. "Right—about me. It's fine, I'm used to being the target of people's anger. You have to have a thick skin if you're going to rule a kingdom. So, what was it this time? My reputation? My magic abilities? My fashion sense?"

"No, nothing like that."

"There has to be some reason behind her anger."

"I'm sure you're right it's just—I don't know what's gotten into her," Cam replied. "She's always been stubborn and protective, but this time it seems magnified. It's like she can't control herself. Every time she sees us together, she has a fit."

Rya shrugged. "It's because she's in love with you."

"What?" Cam laughed.

"It's why she's acting the way she is, there's no other reason for it. She's in love with you, and whatever uh— friendship you and I have growing is threatening to her."

"No, she's not in love with me."

"How can you be so sure?"

"Because," Cam smiled, "she's my cousin. Her father and my mother were siblings. We grew up together, and we're as close as sisters ourselves."

"Oh," Rya replied. She could feel the heat in her cheeks as she blushed, but another feeling had taken hold as well. It was a different kind of warmth filling her body. "That does change my assumptions a bit."

"Like I said, she's always been protective. I'm hoping whatever has her riled up this time fades quickly. I'm tired of the lectures."

Rya looked up as the sounds of the inner ward filled her ears. The chatter and movement always made the area feel alive, as though it was breathing on its own beat. The life they walked into provided a moment of relief, and Rya continued the conversation with curiosity.

"I didn't realize you were related," she added. "You don't look much alike, especially since she's from the northern tribes."

"How do you know that?" Cam asked, surprised by the statement.

"All the stories tell of the first Ashen being fair of hair and skin. Their traits are passed on for generations, and Norell doesn't exactly fit that mold. Her dark features give her away."

"But how could you know about her heritage? That's a pretty specific guess."

"I knew someone else from the northern tribes. They have the same round face and flat nose. It wasn't hard to make the connection."

"Not that it matters, but Norell was born here in the forest," Cam nodded. "Her mother was from the north but her father, my Uncle Harris, was one of the Ashen's ambassadors and would travel all over Kelda and beyond. During one of his trade missions beyond the mountains he met Yukie and fell in love instantly. Thankfully for him, she felt the same and they were married weeks later in her village. After Uncle Harris was done with his duties, him and Yukie both returned to the Ashen Forest."

"And your aunt being different was never an issue? Norell has never faced any backlash for looking like a northerner?"

"Not at all. We take in people from all the kingdoms of Kelda and have for hundreds of years. While a good majority of us look like the ancient Ashen who settled here, we've had enough outsiders come in to mix things up. If you met more of the woodsmen, or the people living in the sea port, you'd see the Ashen aren't as plain as you imagined."

"Plain is not a word I'd ever use to describe you," Rya smiled.

111

She thought about how Yukie married a man from a strange land, and moved away from her home for him, not unlike her own story. The difference was Norell's mother was in love, which must have made the change easier to bare. She couldn't help but envy the woman. During her first days in the Obsidian Isles the people treated Rya like a caged animal, like she only existed for their amusement, and for them to stare at. She spent years living in the castle, some before she was crowned queen, and not once did it feel like home. She was always reminded she was an outsider, and she would never truly belong. Little did they know that keeping themselves separate from her, would make it easier to punish them when she finally ruled.

It wasn't long before the girls had made their way to the outer ward. They stopped along the fenced off ring near the stables, hanging their arms over the wood.

"There he is," Cam said, waving to Thane who stood inside the ring. Rya had been to the circle a dozen times to watch people practice, but today a smaller challenger stood inside. Eirik was wearing leather pads on his chest and legs, a matching helmet wobbled on his small head. With both hands he swung his long wooden sword from side to side, grazing the belly of the large boy standing in front of him. Each strike was dodged, and even with Thane offering tips from the side, he couldn't land his blows. The prince charged his target at full speed before being knocked to the

112

dirt by the other boy's sword. Eirik stood up, tipped his helmet back and smiled, charging him again. Once more the boy swatted him on the back and knocked him to the ground. This continued three more times, and each time Eirik would get up again, smiling and ready for the next one.

"He's got a lot of spirit," Rya laughed.

Eirik brushed himself off, and with a loud yell charged the boy again. The boy once more swung his sword, but Eirik was ready for it, dropping to his knees as the wooden blade passed over his head. The prince thrust his sword out and jabbed his opponent in the ribs with the dull tip. The older boy screamed out, and Eirik jumped up, cheering his victory.

"That's one thing about my brother—he never gives up," Cam smiled. "He's always been stubborn."

"He's smart," Rya added. "You could see him learning and thinking as he fought. He knows he's small, and he knows the enemy will doubt his abilities because of it. The key is to lure them into a false confidence, then when they are no longer alert, you strike." She smiled. "He reminds me of myself."

She could feel Cam staring at her from the corner of her vision. She'd done it before, glaring at her with confusion or doubt, but this time it was different. Her gaze was warm and soft, and it made Rya's heart beat faster in her chest.

For a moment she thought the princess might step towards her. She imagined Cam's hand on her waist, her breath closing in on her own, but the thought was pushed aside as the young prince came bounding up to them.

"Did you see me?" Eirik asked, out of breath and wheezing.

"Yes, I did," Cam smiled.

"What about you Rya? Did you see me hit him?"

"I did, how many was that today?"

"Four," the boy puffed with pride, "and Winston only hit me eight times."

"A new record," Cam cheered. "Look, I have to talk to Thane, do you think you could be a gentleman and keep Rya company for a bit?"

"Of course," he replied, bowing towards the two girls. "It would be an honor."

Cam placed a gentle hand on Rya's shoulder, then hopped over the fence into the ring. As she waited for Eirik to remove his armor she passed the time by staring at the princess in the distance.

The boy trotted over to a small bench nearby, taking a seat on the edge and allowing space for Rya to join him. He was drenched in sweat, and his pale hair clung to his face. With each breath he wheezed a little, but his smile never faded.

"You did a great job today."

"I'm getting better each time," he replied.

"Do you always get winded when you fight? Maybe I should tell someone you don't feel well"

"I'm fine," he puffed. "I'm used to it. I've have breathing problems ever since I was a baby. They say I won't be a great fighter like Cam. I don't have the stamina, whatever that is."

"It means you can't fight for a long time, but only in short bursts."

Eirik nodded, accepting the explanation as if he already knew.

"Fighting is overrated," Rya continued. "You're not bad at it, but that's not where your strength lies. You have charisma."

"What's charisma?"

"It's a great power. It means you read people, you know how to speak to them, and how to reach them. You're good with words; they are both your sword and you're your shield. You may use them to cut someone deep, even ruin a person if you wanted, but you can also do great things with your charm. Your kindness can heal old wounds. Your spirit can lift someone up and give them strength and courage. I've seen people like you rally an

115

army of farmers to their aid with a well-spoken speech alone."

"Whoa," the boy whispered.

Rya smiled. "I've found words hold more magic than I could ever create with my hands. It's a skill I have yet to master."

He smiled up at her, flashing the gap in his teeth. "Don't worry," he beamed, "there's still time."

THIRTEEN

Over the next few days Elin proved to a blessing to Rya. Her mornings started with a pleasant smile instead of Norell's sour pout. She was gently coaxed from her sleep instead of the blinding light that had normally burned through the backs of her eyelids. The girl even insisted on brushing out the queen's hair, which Rya was pleased to see had grown out enough to graze the top of her shoulders, and the ends were starting to curl like they had before.

She shook her head, watching the brown locks sweep across her bare skin. The choice to cut it off had been a practical one, hoping if she looked less like the Black Queen the assassin might not be able to track her. It was a moment of desperation, and it had been the first time since she'd fled the castle grounds that she'd grown lost and hopeless. Unfortunately for her, Nix wasn't as easy to trick as the villagers she'd passed along the way, and he found her again a few days later.

"Your Majesty," Elin said in a soft voice, "what kind of chambermaid did you have in your castle?"

"Oh—I didn't really. A number of girls came and went, but none seemed to get it right. I couldn't find one to keep around too long."

She could sense the unease coming from the girl as she continued pinning the queen's hair to the back of her head.

"Of course," Rya continued, "I didn't have you with me. If I had, I wouldn't have had to look for anyone else."

Elin grinned and stepped back, tilting her head to admire her work. Rya checked the mirror and a smile stretched across her face. Elin had taken a small strand of pearls and wove them through Rya's hair before twisting the whole mass and pinning it up. The result was beautiful. Rya smiled at the reflection, finally able to see herself and not some stranger in the face staring back at her.

With her confidence renewed, Rya glided through the castle, watching heads turn ever so slightly as she passed, no doubt taking in the beauty she was known for.

"Simply stunning," Thane remarked, watching her descend the front steps. He was laid out across one of the stone benches which lined the courtyard, his hair flowing over one end and his legs draped over the other.

"You look comfortable," she smiled, pushing his legs off the side so she could sit next to him. "I take it Cam doesn't have much need of you today?"

"She's busy doing royal stuff with King Mikkel." He sat up straight, collecting his hair in a low ponytail. "I didn't realize when he said Cam couldn't leave the castle grounds, it would make my life boring also."

"You're free to leave without her, aren't you?"

"Yeah, but I wouldn't do that to Cam. I couldn't bare the guilt if I had fun hunting or riding while she couldn't."

Rya glanced around the courtyard, searching for prying eyes. Satisfied they were alone, she whispered, "Have you heard any word about who might be working with Nix?"

He shook his head. "With my father in charge of the Ashen army I've taken to milling around the outer ward. Seeing me in the gatehouse or the armory isn't unusual and I thought I could use it to my advantage, maybe pick up on some whispers or gossip, but I've heard nothing."

"Cam said she was doing the same in the kitchens and while walking the inner ward; she's trying to overhear anyone talking, but she's come up empty-handed as well."

"It's not surprising," Thane added. "If I was going to sell you out to an assassin I wouldn't go spreading it around either. Especially knowing both Cam and King Mikkel are happy to have you here."

119

"Excuse me for not believing it makes a difference. You can't tell me there isn't a single person in the Ashen Forest who would go against the king?"

"I mean—there's obviously *one*." Thane replied. "Otherwise we wouldn't be looking for a spy, but the people love him."

The two paused their conversation as Norell walked into the courtyard. She stopped when she saw them sitting together. Her cheeks flashed red, and her jaw clenched. Without saying a word, she balled her hands into fists and walked away.

"Mikkel might have a loyal following," Rya sighed, "but we both know there's no shortage of people who hate me."

"I've never heard a truer statement," a cruel voice said from next to her. She'd been so focused on watching Norell storm off she'd missed Guthry sneaking up behind her. "Anyone would be a fool to trust you."

"I'm sorry," Rya said, feigning shock, "did you just call the royal family fools? Because the last time I checked, I had Mikkel's blessing, Cam's friendship, and Eirik's admiration. I think the only fool around here is you."

"Your day will come," he spat back. Thane jumped to his feet. In front of the hunched old man he looked twice as tall, and could easily take him down without much effort. Guthry didn't budge but instead peered at him with a scowl. "I won't let this witch be the downfall of our kingdom."

Thane's nostrils flared as he tried keeping his tongue civil. "You'll do exactly what the king asks of you. But, if you insist on carrying on this conversation, we can do it in front of King Mikkel himself. I'd like to know his thoughts on your disobedience."

"You can stand down soldier," Guthry sneered. "I would never ignore the orders of my king, no matter how mislead they may be." He looked once more at the queen and gave a twisted smile which made her sick. "You better watch yourself. I hear the gold on your head is rising each day. Soon that number is going to match someone's price, and you'll be out of luck."

Thane stood like stone in front of Rya as they both watched Guthry slither away towards the inner ward. With the old man gone from their sight he could finally relax, and returned to his seat. Rya's eyes, however, stayed fixed on the archway the adviser had disappeared through.

"He has to be involved," Rya frowned.

"He's not wrong," Thane sighed. "The longer you stay here, the more danger you might be in."

"What are you saying, that I should leave?"

"No," he shook his head. "I would never want you to go before you're healed. I have total faith in your abilities, but sending you home without your full power is too

121

dangerous...That's still your plan, isn't it? To stay until you're able to fight again?"

"Yes," she answered. "It's always been my plan. I have to take back my throne. I won't allow Kasen to keep it from me."

"That's what I thought." He leaned forward, cupping his hands and hanging his head. "What you said before, about us all growing fond of you, it's true. The problem comes when it's time to say goodbye."

"I know it'll be hard; I've grown to care for all of you in return."

"It's not just that—it's whatever is happening between you and Cam. I know it's more than just a regular friendship. I also know it's growing each day, and it worries Norell; it worries me. When I agreed to be Cam's Kinsman I promised to protect her with my life, and that doesn't just mean in battle."

"There's nothing going on with me and Cam," Rya argued. Her heart dropped into her stomach. No matter what she told Thane she couldn't lie to herself.

"You can deny it all you want, but we both know what's true. I like you Rya, I do, but I've seen this before. I don't want to watch her go through that kind of pain again."

The queen opened her mouth, wanting to ask a dozen questions, but stayed silent as they all froze in her throat.

"There was a girl before, named Hannah. Cam and her grew very close, very quickly, and it didn't end well. Cam wasn't the only one who felt the pain of it; Norell and I did also. We were the ones to pick her up when she fell apart. We had to hold her as she cried, and we had to slowly bring her back to who she was before it happened. In the time you've been here I've come to think of you as a friend, and if you truly want to return to the Obsidian Isles and take back your kingdom, then I support you. All I ask is you try and minimize the devastation it's going to cause. It'll be harder to put Cam back together a second time."

Thane stood up, placing a hand on Rya's shoulder. He hesitated for a moment, lingering long enough for her to see the pain in his eyes. He had always been kind to her, but he was Cam's best friend, and her Kinsman. That would always come first. As he walked away, leaving her alone, his shoulders slumped under the weight of their conversation.

Rya's eyes started to well up, and she could taste the bile in the back of her throat. Her insides were knotted. Her blood boiled, and the rushing liquid burnt every inch of her heart as it pumped through. She reached out, plucking a single flower from the bushes behind her. She held it in her palm, watching the petals turn from pink to bright white. When the entire bulb had frozen, she clutched it between her fingers, and with a shout threw it at the cobblestone. The flower shattered into a hundred pieces, scattering across the ground in front of her, mirroring her heart.

The queen wiped her wet hand on her dress and stood up. She was completely alone in the courtyard, which meant no one to see her outburst. She took several slow breaths, forcing the emotions to recede back into her, hiding themselves away like she always did. Calm and collected, she walked from the courtyard, leaving the slivers of petal to melt in the autumn sun.

FOURTEEN

Thane's arrow smacked into the wood an inch above
Cam's last shot causing the shaft to quake. He threw a
teasing smirk at her as they switched places, but her face
remained stern and focused. Standing at the line in the dirt
she stretched her neck and, with a steady arm, raised her
bow, pulling back the arrow across her cheek and
narrowing her gaze. Rya stood to the side, eager to watch
the release, but before she could follow the arrow across
the ring it smacked into the target, burying itself dead
center.

"Nice shot," Rya cheered from outside the railing.
Cam gave her a little nod before turning to Thane to mimic
the smug look he had before. They'd been exchanging
challenges all morning; it was a way of training they'd
practiced for years. They promised Rya it was always a
friendly competition but she knew one of them would end

the day bragging while the other sat by biting their tongue and cursing themselves for not performing better.

"You're out here again?" Norell appeared next to the queen, resting her arms on the top of the rail.

"It appears so," Rya answered. "There isn't much to do around here, why shouldn't I watch them have some fun?"

"I didn't peg you as an athletic type," Norell shrugged. "It seems beneath someone of your standing to be slumming it in the outer ward day after day. So, which of them is it? Which is the object of your affection this week, Thane or Cam?"

"Ah, I've missed your wit," Rya replied with a sarcastic grin. "I've been so sad since you've stopped waking me each morning with your grumpy face and unpleasant attitude."

"From what I hear, the girl sent in my place isn't as tortured by you as I was. At least you're pretending to be nice to *someone*."

"I'm not pretending," Rya scoffed. "I like Elin, she's a sweet girl and takes great pride in her job. I honestly enjoy her company, unlike the servant I had before."

"I'm *not* a servant," Norell snapped. "You know that now. I expected you'd treat me a little better after learning I'm not some maid you can step on."

"I treat you according to how you deserve to be treated," Rya argued back. "What have you done to earn my respect? Until you show me a reason to give it to you, you don't have it."

The girls' voices had risen enough to disrupt the target practice. Thane and Cam were coming towards them, each looking nervous at what they were walking into, and each prepared to wrangle one of the girls if needed. Thane stopped in front of Norell, but before he could speak his head jutted upwards, watching the sky. Rya had missed the first screech, but with the second they all turned their gaze upwards. A small black hawk circled over the buildings, the sight of it filling her with dread.

"That's not one of ours," Cam worried. "It's too dark, and its head is square compared to the ones we keep."

The bird swooped down, landing inside the roof of the aviary. Thane jumped over the railing and started jogging towards the building while the three girls stood near the ring, wondering what it could be.

"I know that bird," Rya grumbled through the tension.

"Of course, you do," Norell huffed. "You know everything."

"Each of the kingdoms use different carrier birds, and I studied them after becoming queen. It's good for a ruler to know who's sending communication, in case someone tries to keep it from you. The birds the Obsidian Isles deploy are Volcano Hawks; black as the rock that cover the kingdom. There's no mistaking that was one of them."

Thane had reemerged, running at full speed with a small roll of parchment in his hand, and his face white as a ghost. He slid across the dirt, trying to stop but crashed into the wood rails.

"What's happened?" Cam asked, helping to steady him.

"It's from the Isles," he puffed. Rya shot a glare at Norell, smug from her being right but still full of worry. Thane handed the paper to Cam. "It's addressed to your father."

Cam studied the others standing in the library as her father read the note. Thane had been sent ahead to deliver it, as he had always been the fastest runner. When the girls finally caught up Mikkel was already studying the parchment with his brow pinched together and his cheeks as red as his beard. His eyes scanned the lines one at a time, and it was clear he had read the writing more than once. With a growl he crumpled the letter in his massive hand before slamming the other on his large pine desk.

"You and Rya are to stay in this room," he ordered, staring directly at Cam. "You'll wait here until I return. Is that clear?"

"Yes Papa," she mumbled. She wanted to yell and argue, but she'd never seen him so angry, and the last thing she wanted was to stir his rage any further.

"Thane," Mikkel barked while storming towards the door, "find your father, Guthry, and whoever is running the aviary at this time. Have them all gather in the throne room immediately."

"Of course, Your Majesty," Thane replied. He was rarely so proper with the king, but the seriousness of Mikkel's tone was enough to scare him into formality. Thane was once again off running, bursting ahead of Mikkel as he stomped towards the throne room.

The slamming of the door terrified Cam. Her legs wobbled, and she sank into one of the chairs in front of her father's desk. Mikkel had always loved books, and the walls were stacked from floor to ceiling with whatever he could find. The dense air smelled of old pages and leather, reminding Cam of when she'd spent so much time between these walls as a child. Her father would spread out the maps of Kelda over his desk, teaching her all the various kingdoms, and the ways they differed from her own. He would take heavy volumes of ancient stories off the shelves, telling her how the Ashen first came to the forest, matching the Whitebark trees they made their home, and how as the generations protected more outsiders, their features merged together into the tapestry that exists today. Each tale had a lesson buried within, and each of them were to make her a better ruler, but here she was locked away and unable to help. She was sitting in the chair like she was a child again, waiting as her father and the others decided Rya's fate.

"What do you think is going to happen?" Rya's face was stoic but her words hinted at the fear she was trying so desperately to hide.

"I don't know," Cam replied, shaking her head. "Kasen's letter was clear; if we don't hand you over to Nix, he'll station the Obsidian army outside our border."

Norell shook her head in disbelief. "You don't think he'd really attack the Ashen, do you?"

"I wouldn't put it past him," Rya sighed. She sat in the empty chair next to Cam, moving her wrapped wrist as much as she could, testing its flexibility. "How much time did he give Mikkel to reply?"

"A week," Cam answered. "After that, the army will attack from the east."

"Then the men are already on their way," Rya added. "It takes longer than a week to move an army that size across that distance. They had to already be outside the Isles before he ever sent the letter."

"Maybe you can stop them," Norell suggested. "You're technically still the queen; can't you command them to turn back once they arrive?"

"I doubt it. His accusations have poisoned them against me. Even the few who were genuinely loyal prior to this have been corrupted by his lies. If I'm going to turn an army against Kasen, I need my powers. While I'm healing quickly, my magic isn't close to full strength, and without it I'm nothing."

The three of them sat silent, each lost within their own thoughts. The worry on Rya's face tugged at Cam, and the princess found herself kneeling in front of the queen. Her hands grabbed the arms of the chair while her eyes locked onto Rya's. She wanted to make sure she understood the words Cam was about to say.

"I promise, I won't let them take you anywhere." The fear and doubt Cam had before had disappeared and had been replaced by determination. The need to keep Rya safe was stronger than any other feeling. "No one, not even my father, is going to remove you from the Ashen Forest. I promised from the beginning I would protect you, and that's exactly what I'm going to do."

"If Mikkel choses to hand me over," Rya replied, "there will be no way to change his mind. I won't watch you fight your father over something like this. If it's time for me to leave then that's what will happen."

"I know what's waiting for you out there, and I'm not letting you walk out of this castle."

"You can't stop me."

131

"Oh yeah?" Cam scoffed, returning to her own chair. "Watch me."

Almost an hour had passed when the door to the library burst open, nearly slamming into Norell who had been standing along the wall behind it. Both Cam and Rya shot to their feet, startled by the commotion. Mikkel stood in the archway, staring down the length of the room at his daughter and the queen. His eyebrows raised as he glanced down at their hands, seeing the girls' fingers were laced together. Each was keeping the other steady, waiting to hear the verdict.

"I've talked to the head of my army and my adviser," he said, "and I've made a decision. We will not be complying with Father Kasen's demands. Rya will be staying here with us."

Relief washed over Cam like a waterfall. She squeezed Rya's hand in celebration before letting go, aware that everyone was suddenly watching them.

Mikkel ran his hand through his hair, looking exhausted and angry. "For centuries the Ashen Forest has been a safe haven in Kelda and I will not allow some arrogant ass to change that. Who does he think he is? Does he seriously believe I would turn my back on my history, and my vows as king that easy? The Ashen don't fold when it comes to a fight, and Kasen is going to learn that the hard way."

Rya walked towards him, stopping as his shadow enveloped her. She swallowed the lump in her throat, hoping it would release a flood of gratitude, but nothing came. She swayed on the balls of her feet, unsure of what to do. Mikkel smiled down at her, understanding the unspoken thanks she was trying to put into words.

"I need your help," Mikkel added, placing a hand on Rya's shoulder. "You know your army, and I need you to work with my general so we know what we're walking into. I want to be as prepared as we can be for what's coming."

"Of course," she nodded. "I'll start right away."

"You can wait until tomorrow," Mikkel answered. "This has been a taxing day, and I think we could all use a moment to breath. We'll start fresh in the morning."

"Thank you," Rya said, her voice catching. "I can never repay you for everything you've done. I wouldn't know where to start."

"I do," Mikkel smiled. "You can start by taking down Father Kasen."

FIFTEEN

As a child Cam would often sneak out of bed long after everyone else had fallen asleep, fumbling through darkened hallways, and tiptoeing down staircases. Some nights she'd make her way to the second floor, shaking Norell from her dreams to join the adventure. Other nights she chose to go alone, investigating rooms she seldom saw, and exploring the far corners of the castle. The years of late-night excursions made it easy for the princess to navigate the black corridors, and she was soon pushing through the door that opened to the fresh air outside.

The night's chill bit through the light layers she had on, and the cool air stung her cheeks. She'd traveled this path a thousand times before, seeking out her sanctuary in the center of the courtyard, and it had always been done alone. The midnight trips were moments she shared with no one, which made it upsetting to see the figure sitting on the fountain's wall wrapped in a thick quilt. Cam walked towards the body and, as she recognized the soft face framed in the blanket, she smiled, her anger melting away.

"What are you doing out here?" She asked.

"I could ask you the same thing," Rya smirked in reply.

"I'm the princess, and this is my castle." Cam took a seat next to her, playfully bumping Rya's shoulder with her own. "As I remember it, I can do what I want."

"Fine, don't tell me. You keep your secrets and I'll keep mine."

Cam turned her gaze up towards the sky. The moon was only a sliver above them, and the lack of light made the endless sea of stars pop against the black curtain they hung from.

"I come out here to center myself," Cam sighed. "Some nights, I can't get my mind to stop working, no matter how hard I try. My body will ache, and my eyes grow heavy, but my brain keeps running thoughts past me at a mile a minute. It's impossible to sleep when that happens, and so I come out here to calm it."

"That's why I'm here too," Rya nodded. "You said before the fountain was your favorite place. You said it was peaceful, and after today I figured I could use some of that peace."

"It was pretty intense." Cam agreed. She shivered as a swift breeze rolled over them.

"Here, take this." Rya opened the blanket and draped one end over Cam's shoulder, scooting in closer as they closed the gap in the fabric. "You're going to get sick coming out here without a coat."

"I find the cold to be refreshing," Cam replied. "Although, I think I underestimated the weather this time."

Her nerves tingled as her body rested against Rya's, and their breath mixed together in a puff of fog in front of them. Her heart beat faster in her chest, and another shudder ran down her spine. There was a swarm of thoughts she wanted to say, but the ball of fear in her throat was choking out any words she might have had. Rya reached out, taking Cam's hand in her own, and pressed their palms together. A moment later Cam sensed the fire burning under Rya's skin. The warmth of the queen's body was soft and timid, while the heat of her magic felt different; it was hungry and desperate. It spread into Cam's hand, flowing into the tips of her fingers and lighting them with a gentle glow, and she gasped.

Rya smiled. "Amazing, isn't it?" She pulled her hand away, and with its absence the prickle in Cam's palm dulled to nothing.

"When did you first know you had magic?" She asked. She was still gazing down at her now normal hand,

136

but her mind was consumed with the queen's leg pressing against her own.

"The first I remember using it was when I was four. I accidentally exploded a bowl of porridge that I was refusing to eat. My mother was unhappy to find the kitchen walls covered in oats and made me scrub the entire place clean. That night, when my father came home, she told him what had happened, and the next day he rode off to Cira to find me a magic tutor."

"That's sweet. It's nice that he was so supportive."

"It had nothing to do with me, and everything to do with his own plans. My father was born a high lord from a prominent family, but his addictions were slowly ruining us. He spent all his free time in the tavern. He barely payed attention to me until the oatmeal incident. After that he at least spoke to me.

"Each morning he'd come stumbling in around dawn smelling of stale beer and smoke. He'd pat me on the head and ask how my lessons were going. He would always tell me to keep practicing so I could be strong and help him one day. In response I would show him a trick or two I'd learned, or some simple spell. He'd smile from ear to ear, and tell me how proud he was. After being ignored for so long, I was desperate for his praise. All I wanted to do was learn more magic, to train my skills, and be the best. I needed that love from my father, and it seemed the only way I was going to get it was with my powers. It wasn't until years later I learned what his real purpose was."

Cam could hear the fatigue in Rya's words. It wasn't just the late hour, but the exhaustion of her past. She was tired of second guessing everyone's intentions. She was tired of having no one to trust. Cam ached at the pain Rya was trying so hard to hide inside.

"You don't have to worry," Cam said, trying to reassure her. "I'm never going to let anyone hurt you again. Not Nix, not Kasen, no one. You're always going to be safe with me, alright?"

Rya gave a shy smile. "You make me want to believe that."

Cam's heart stopped as the next words come out of her mouth without warning. "You know, you could stay here in the Ashen Forest. You could choose to live here with us."

"What?" Rya asked, taken aback.

"You don't have to leave," she continued. "You could stay here—with me."

Rya cupped Cam's face in her hand, her rich chocolate eyes almost black. "I wish that were true, but trust me, you don't want that. You don't want me."

"Yes, I do."

"You don't know all I've been through, or what I've done. What Nix told you is only a fraction of the stories I have."

"That doesn't matter to me," Cam argued.

"It should. You deserve better."

"I don't care. I don't want you to go back to the Isles. I don't want you to leave. You're happier here, I know I make you happy, and if you stay I can keep you safe forever. Isn't that what you want too?"

"It's not that simple," Rya replied. Before anything else could be said, Cam leaned in, inching her mouth closer to Rya's. She stopped just shy of touching, not knowing if she should continue, when the queen bridged the space and kissed her. She closed her eyes, trying to focus on every detail of the moment. Rya's mouth was warm, a mixture of her body heat and the hint of magic lingering beneath the surface. Her breath tasted sweet, and the tip of her tongue teased Cam's bottom lip. As suddenly as it had begun, it stopped. Rya leaned away and rose to her feet. Cam's stomach dropped as if she were falling, and her body shivered as Rya's warmth was suddenly stripped away.

"That wasn't a good idea," Rya whispered. She took the blanket from her shoulders and wrapped it around Cam's body. "I can't—" she stammered, her teeth chattering in the cool night air. "We can't—I should go to bed. I have a long day of planning a battle tomorrow."

139

"Rya, please." Cam's words stopped as the queen walked away.

Cam was alone in the courtyard. It was what she had expected when she'd climbed out of her bed a short time ago, only now it was wrong. The sound of the trickling water that once comforted her now plunked lonely and cruel into the basin. The peace she'd come out here to find was missing, and she sat in the darkness, cold and empty.

Rya's eyes watched the flames dance in the hearth. The flickering light made her vision grow fuzzy while she wished it would do the same to her thoughts. Kissing Cam had been a mistake. It was the most wonderful mistake she'd ever made, but it was still wrong. Thane's warning trickled in and out of her mind. His words saturated the memory of the brief joy she'd just experienced, twisted it into a sad and forbidden moment.

She moved to the window. The moon had crossed the sky, passing as the time had, growing closer to dawn. Sleep wouldn't come to her tonight, not when she needed it the most. A speckle of black darted across the purple night, and she sighed as the hawk disappeared in the darkness, returning to the Isles with Mikkel's reply. The tears flowed down her cheeks, dripping from her chin. She touched them with a timid hand.

140

"What are you doing?" She asked herself. She looked around to ensure she was alone. "You're stronger than this. You don't give in to any emotions. You don't allow yourself to cry."

The last time she had freely shed tears was when Gerrod ran his sword into Snow's chest. Before that, if she needed to cry, she'd do it hidden in the shadows of her closet doors. Her history, and especially her mother, didn't allow her to express emotion. She was taught it was weakness and needed to be cut out of her heart like a weed growing in the garden. It may reappear now and then, but if she pulled it out and tossed it aside, she would be safe for a while longer.

These feelings she had now, they were born from a spark that sprung to life when she met Cam. They grew to a wildfire, consuming the rest of her until nothing was left but the raw emotion. It was uncomfortable and foreign, and she hated herself for allowing it to happen. No matter how angry she was, she couldn't ignore the part of her that yearned for it. Her skin hummed under Cam's touch, and her heart pounded with the sound of the princess' voice. Her stomach fluttered when she saw Cam's smile, or her eyes, or even the shape of her in the distance. As hard as she tried she couldn't push away those feelings away, and she berated herself each time they rose up.

She had left the door to her room half open when she returned, as a part of her wanted to hear Cam when she came back up the stairs, but as the footsteps climbed the steps Rya rushed to push it closed. She stood with her forehead pressed against the wood. *She's broken you.* She wanted to pound on the door. She wanted to light it on fire and watch it burn into ash the same as the slabs in the fireplace. She wished it would be reduced to nothing so it would match the way she felt inside.

The sound was back. Another set of footsteps pounded down the hall, but these were closer than the ones before. Against her better judgment, Rya opened the door. She expected to see Cam standing in front of her but was met with two other faces instead.

"Why are you awake?" Norell asked, taking a step back. Thane stood in front of her with his hands behind his back. He hung his head, refusing to look at Rya.

"You're awake," the queen answered, "so why shouldn't I be?"

The girl rolled her eyes, then looked at Thane. "We can talk about this later. You should go."

He reached out for her, but she took another step back, placing herself just outside his grasp. Norell rounded the corner and was gone, but Thane stood where he was, running a hand through his hair.

"I'm sorry if we woke you," he sighed.

"I was already up. It's been a rough night."

"I can imagine."

Rya squinted in the darkness, trying to make out if he knew about the scene at the fountain. Maybe he had been watching them. Maybe he was going to lecture her. She was relieved when she realized his mind was busy with some other thought. Her eyes followed this gaze into the darkness of the hall.

"Is she mad again?" Rya asked, nodding the direction Norell had gone. "It's so hard to tell."

"She's worried," he answered. "And she has every right to be. Mikkel is her uncle, and any kind of battle means death is coming. She's lost too many family members in her life, and the thought of another is a lot to handle."

"Her parents aren't alive?"

"No. They left on a journey when she was nine. It was the first one they'd taken together since she was born, and they had decided to leave her behind at the castle. The trip took them to the eastern shore of the Imani Plains. No one knew about the sickness spreading through the land. It wasn't until they were in the heart of Imani that they realized what was happening."

"The red plague," Rya nodded, understanding. "That was a dark time in Kelda's history. I remember my mother being cautious despite how far Asta is from Imani. She wouldn't allow me to talk to anyone outside our home. She went as far as to sending away one of our maids because she'd traveled outside the kingdom the week before. I can't imagine how terrifying that must have been for her."

"Afterwards, when they never returned, she lived here in the castle with Mikkel and his family. He means so much to her, and the threat of Isle's army is tearing her up."

"I can understand that," she answered.

His mouth rose in a half grin, playful and sweet. "I'm surprised you'd say that. I thought anything having to do with Norell would fill you with hate."

"I said I understand her," Rya corrected. "I didn't say I like her."

HOT WATER

The sun had set hours before, and since most were home in their beds, Cora had found the bathhouse to be nearly empty. She lowered her body into the open water with a deep sigh. The steaming wooden tubs nearby would have been better for her aching joints, but the heat had always made her dizzy so she chose the lukewarm pool instead.

It had been two years since she started coming here regularly. The same elderly couple worked the counter, taking her coin and handing her a towel. The same faces passed, either coming or going, each and every night. The scenery was so familiar, and the actions so routine, they blurred together in her mind like one long day stretched to its ends. Each and every night, Cora sat with her eyes shut, allowing the bathhouse to fade away while the water soaked up her pain.

This particular night had felt different from the start. A younger man ran the counter; the son of the owner. A touch of cough had kept the old man in bed according to his wife. The air inside the tiled room was heavier than normal, with a strong scent of something new. Lilac perhaps. Cora payed these changes little mind and was enjoying her bath when a voice interrupted.

"Isn't this lovely?"

The stranger intruding on her night was sitting in the nearby barrel tub. Her arms hung over the side, and she had her head laid back, resting as the hot water turned her skin pink.

"I ask you again, isn't this the loveliest thing in the world?" The woman spoke without opening her resting eyes. Cora tried to ignore the comment a second time, hoping her silence would speak for her. The woman didn't take the hint. "I've traveled all over Kelda, and no matter where I stay, I always make sure to buy a warm bath. It's so hard when you're on the road with the hordes of the little beasts dragging their legs behind you. It's impossible to get a moment's rest unless I pay for it."

Cora shifted her pose, turning her body away from the woman. If she'd had her eyes closed like the stranger she would have missed the new addition walking into the room. The woman was wearing a jet-black corset with a matching skirt which flowed like liquid behind her. Her

146

steps were without sound as she walked across the tile, and Cora had to blink twice, thinking for a moment she might be a ghost. As the woman passed by, she pressed her index finger to her lips, but Cora couldn't have made a sound if she wanted to. The sight of the queen had stolen her voice, and she shivered.

The stranger in the tub was still rambling on about the hardships of her journey, unaware of the danger now standing over her. She must have heard the movement of the dress' fabric, or perhaps being closer the queen's footsteps were audible, either way she knew someone was had joined them, but kept her eyes shut tight.

"Be a dear and refill the warm water," the woman ordered, assuming a worker had come to check on her. "I'll double the gold, just make it last."

"I think I can do that," the queen smirked. She waved her hands over the top of the tub, and the woman's eyes shot open. They were filled with fear, her mouth gasping for air like a fish out of water.

"What have you done?" The woman choked. Cora watched in horror as she struggled to move, but found she was pinned in the tub by unseen hands. "Let me out of here," she shouted.

"I can't," the queen answered. "You haven't finished your bath. I believe you wanted some more warm water."

The queen's palms started to glow as if they were made of burning coals, and she smiled as she shoved them inside the tub. The water sizzled and turned an unearthly orange. The cloud of steam rising around them grew too large, and had blocked Cora's view, but it did nothing to quiet the screams which escaped the stranger's lips. The shrieking echoed off the walls, bouncing around in a symphony of horror. She put her hands to her ears, trying to block out the sound. After what seemed an eternity, the cries became strangled and soft, until they were no more. A sweet, musky smell filled the thick air, reminding her of when the family had roasted a pig over the fire-pit, and she vowed the taste of fresh pork would never touch her tongue again.

The cloud of white hanging in the air was broken when the queen sauntered through looking calm and unconcerned. The fog swirled away to reveal the stranger's face, which had been hidden behind the steam. Her skin was swollen, bright red, and covered in large blisters. Her eyes had turned solid white, and her mouth hung open at an unnatural angle.

Before reaching the doorway, the queen stopped and turned, facing Cora. A sweet smile played on her lips, standing out against the gruesome scene she was leaving.

"I appreciate your discretion," she said. "As a thank you, any baths you take here for the remainder of your life will paid for by me."

Cora's lips quivered, unable to form words. Thankfully, the queen didn't wait for a response and exited. Alone with no one but a half cooked dead woman, Cora stood, clutched her stomach, and vomited into the pool water.

SIXTEEN

The cool autumn breeze rolled through in short bursts, rustling the straw of the hay bales. They had been stacked at the far end of the stables as they waited to be transferred inside, making for an itchy yet sturdy lounge area. Cam was situated near the edge, leaning against one of the tallest points of the stack. Her leg dangled alongside the bale she sat on, swinging back and forth as she picked at the hay, holding the pieces in her hand. Another gust blew past and she opened her palm, watching the hay dance across the air.

"I don't know what to do," she sighed. "She's been so distant the last few days."

"She has a lot going on," Thane grunted, tossing a bucket of dirty water into the weeds nearby. "If I were Rya, I'd be a little preoccupied too. It can't be easy to knowing your own army is marching across Kelda to kill you."

"It never seemed to bother her before. I just worry about her. We haven't spent any time together since Kasen's letter arrived. She's always with your father talking strategy, or in the library with Papa looking at maps. Even at dinner she's only around a short time, then it's off to bed without a word. I wish I could get her alone for a minute, just to talk to her."

"What would you say to her if you did?"

"I don't know," she shrugged. She hadn't told Thane about the kiss in the courtyard, or the aftermath. It wasn't that she didn't trust him, more that she wanted to keep that moment her own for a little while longer. She sighed, "I just—I miss her, and she isn't even gone yet."

"Like I said, she's got a lot going on. I'm sure everything is fine. I wouldn't worry about it if I were you."

"No," Cam scoffed, "you wouldn't, would you? You don't worry about anything."

Thane put a foot on one of the bales and leaned against his knee, staring up at her. She could tell by the somber look on his face she'd hurt him, and in return she was going to receive a lecture. As he began to list off the things and people he loved, and therefore worried about, she leaned her head back and looked up at the sky.

The clouds were wispy and thin, swirling their way across the sea of blue overhead. She watched them dance in slow motion, luring her into a sleepy haze until the shouts from the men snapped her awake.

The yelling was coming from outside the walls, and in an instant the guards were rushing towards the main gate. From her spot on the bales she could see the gears moving, and their clicking beat in time with her heart. The soldiers had spilled out from all the buildings and were lined up facing the opening archway, their swords at the ready. Cam jumped from hay stack landing next to Thane, who grabbed her arm to keep her upright. As soon as her feet were stable she took off like a flash, darting into the sea of guards.

"What's going on?" she shouted, running towards the commotion. No one answered her question, keeping their focus on the entry. She'd reached the front line of bodies when a spear stuck out across her legs, and another at her chest, blocking her way.

"Let me through," she growled.

"Sorry, Your Highness," one of the men answered. "King's orders. If anyone comes through that gate, we are to keep you away. We don't know who they've found."

From the other side of the yard, people were running from the armory to join the growing crowd, and in the chaos, Cam spotted Rya rushing towards her.

"What happening?" Rya asked, grabbing Cam by the arm. "I heard someone say they have a prisoner."

"They've found someone in the woods," Thane answered, suddenly next to them. He stood a head taller than the two of them, making it possible for him to see what was on the other side of the human wall. "They're bringing him in now."

"Do you think it's Nix?" Cam asked.

"I hope not," Rya answered. "If he's been captured it's because he allowed it to happen. The Kael don't get caught."

The portcullis reached the top, and Cam strained to look over the man's shoulder, but couldn't see anything but the back of his neck.

"I don't understand," Thane said, watching the soldiers enter. He was squinting towards the gate.

"What is it?" Cam asked. "Is it him? Is it Nix?"

"No." He shook his head, his face pinched in confusion. "It's a kid."

"A kid?" Rya repeated.

Cam argued with the guard in front of her, but as she held his attention, demanding to be let through, Rya used the moment to push past them. She ignored the protests of the other guards, and the pleading from Cam to wait for her. She stopped short, gasping for air as the solider carrying the prisoner slung him off his shoulder and set in on the ground at his feet. Thane had made it to her side and reached out his arms to grab her, but instead she fell into them, clawing at his sleeves for support.

"What's wrong?" Thane gasped, wrapping his arms around her. "What is it?"

"It's him," she whispered. The words were like a ghost, as all the air had been taken from her lungs and she could barely form the words. "It's Sora."

Thane looked down at the frail body lying in the dirt and then back at Rya's anguished face. He called for Cam who finally broke free of the guard's grasp, and handed the queen off to her as he knelt down, scooping the boy into his arms. It wasn't long before he had pushed past the crowd and was running back towards the castle, the child's head bouncing against his chest.

Gasps and whispers disappeared behind Cam as she tried keeping pace with Rya and Thane. The boy was small and pale, with a tangled mass of thick black hair jutting up in all directions. His tattered clothing hung from his thin body. The large chunks of missing cloth revealed the bruised skin he hid underneath. The soles of his bare feet were shredded and bloody. Each stride Thane took jostled the boy, and left crimson drops from his torn skin trailing behind them. The bright red stood out like a warning on the white stone floor of the castle's entry, and Cam's stomach dropped.

"Who is he?" She asked, still running up the stairs after Rya.

Thane burst into one of the rooms on the second floor and placed the boy on the bed. With his arms now free, he bent forward, his hands on his knees, breathing heavy and wincing at the sweat in his eyes. Rya was already at the bedside, holding the child's hand in her own, searching his unconscious face for something only she knew. Cam hovered in the doorway, feeling alien and uncertain.

"Is he—" she gulped, not sure if she really wanted to ask. "Is he yours?"

"My son?" Rya huffed. "No, he's not mine. Sora is my steward and has been for years."

"He's a child," Thane replied, unable to hide his surprise.

"He's thirteen," Rya answered. "He's small for his age, but that doesn't mean he's not tough. He's a fighter, and he's survived a lot in his life."

That makes two of you, Cam thought, watching the queen allow the tears to drip from her chin. She wouldn't wipe them away, refusing to let go of Sora now that she had hold of him again.

The door had been left open, but the only light remaining in the room was the dull red glow of the fireplace, making it difficult for Cam to see much inside. From her bench in the hallway she could make out the shape of the chair next to the bedside, and Rya's shadow in the same place she'd left her.

Cam took a deep breath and stood up, trying to keep her nerves in check as she walked towards the doorway.

"He won't like his hair this way," Rya whispered as Cam entered the room. "He always kept it cropped short on the sides. Some said it made his ears look larger, but he didn't mind."

Cam placed a hand on Rya's shoulder, giving a tender squeeze. The queen reached out and tucked one of the boy's dark strands behind his ear, allowing her fingers to graze his cheek.

"He's going to be alright," Cam reassured her. "He looks better than you did when we found you, and you bounced back. He will too."

"Right," Rya replied.

Cam could hear the footsteps approaching in the hall, and she knew she was out of time. She'd come to tell Rya her plan, but before she could get the words out, Norell appeared in the doorway.

"Rya," Cam started, "I need to talk to you."

Rya looked back and forth between Norell and Cam, trying to work out what was happening, then frowned. "What's she doing here?"

"That's what I wanted to talk to you about," Cam answered. "We understand you don't want to leave Sora's side, but you have to allow us to help him."

"I can't go." Rya shook her head. "I don't want him to be alone."

"I know, I don't want that either," Cam replied. "That's why Norell's here. Papa and I both thought it was best to have her care for Sora, the way she did for you when you first arrived."

"No," Rya snapped. "There's no way I'm letting that happen."

"Please," Cam pleaded. "My father is still depending on you to help beat the Ashen army, and you can't help us, or be of any use to Sora when he wakes, if you're weak and exhausted."

"There has to be someone else. Why does it have to be her?"

Norell shifted her weight, crossing her arms in front of her.

Cam sighed. "I know you both have your issues with each other, but we have no other choice. There's still a traitor somewhere looking to sell you to Nix. Everyone in the outer ward could see how you reacted when Sora arrived, and they all know how much he means to you. Word is going to spread, and whoever is trying to hurt you is going to take advantage of that. I have no doubt they will try and use him to get to you. We don't know who we can trust, and Papa rather keep the mender out of here until we have more answers."

"And what if it's her?" Rya asked. "What if Norell's the traitor and you're just handing her exactly what she wants."

Norell grunted in disapproval. "If I was going to betray you I'd do it to your face. I wouldn't sneak around whispering secrets to some assassin."

"Sure," Rya scoffed. "I have no reason to doubt you. You've been nothing but truthful and up front since I met you."

"Stop it," Cam cut in. "Norell would never do that. She'd never do anything to hurt me. I trust her with my life, and I trusted her with yours as well. She's my family, and she'll always have my back."

"That's what you're relying on?" Rya stood up, storming out of the room into the hallway. With Cam and Norell on her heals she spun around, shaking her head in disbelief. "Just because she's family doesn't mean she's above suspicion. Her being your blood doesn't make her a good person. Let me tell you what family is; it's watching your father cry over three small mounds in the back

158

garden, wailing over the newborn sons he never saw alive. It's knowing you only survived infancy because you born a girl. It's having a mother who believed a son would never be able to raise her status the way a daughter could and ensuring she got what she wanted. Being family doesn't stop you from being evil, it simply masks it."

Norell's face burned red, and Cam shook her head, silently pleading with her to keep quiet, but it was no use. She stepped forward, getting only inches from Rya's face.

"Now let me tell you what *I* think about family," Norell snapped. "Family is my parents waving goodbye to me as they rode through the gate. It's having an aunt that's willing to step in as a mother to you when you're all alone, only to lose her too. It's watching them burn her body on the pyre after she's gone.

"All I've ever wanted was to keep my family close, and yet death keeps snatching them away from me, and here we are again, on the verge of tragedy. Mikkel, the man who stepped in to be my father when I had no one, is preparing to fight a war that doesn't need to happen. My cousin, who's more my sister than anything else, is ready to lay down her life to protect you. I hate that they are facing danger, and I hate you for making it happen, and yet I keep agreeing to help you. Do you know why? Because Cam asked me to. Because I love my family that much. I'm not going to do anything to hurt her, and that means I'm not going to hurt you either. I know it's hard for you, but you're going to have to trust me."

Cam was frozen, unsure what to do. Norell was standing like a wall, waiting for Rya to reply. The queen was fuming, clenching her good hand into a fist, and Cam could see a bright green glow illuminating from between her fingers.

"Fine," Rya said, breaking the silence. "I'll let you take care of him. But know this, everything you feel for your family, I feel for Sora. He's all I have."

"Understood," Norell replied. "I promise, I won't let anything happen to him, and I don't make promises I can't keep."

SEVENTEEN

The boy stirred behind her, and Cam turned to watch him. All night he'd moaned and twitched, responding to whatever dreams had invaded his sleep, but he never woke. She waited for him to calm as he'd done each time before, but instead his eyes flew open and he sat up with a shriek.

"Where am I?" He asked. His eyes searched the room, confused and scared. "Who are you? What have you done with my queen?"

He threw back the covers, intending to jump out of the bed, but halted when his feet emerged from the blankets. They'd been wrapped to twice their size with bandages and smelled of the plants Norell had rubbed against his wounds. His hands moved around his torso, trembling over the fresh fabric of the nightshirt he wore.

"You're in the Ashen Forest," Cam explained. She kept her voice calm and sweet, hoping to ease his worry. "You're in my father's castle; you're safe, and so is Rya."

"What?" He scooted up the bed until his back hit the headboard, then pulled his legs to his chest, hugging his knees. "You know the queen? And you've kept her safe?"

"Yes," Cam nodded. She held out a hand to stop Norell who had come running inside, scaring him even more. "My name is Cam, I'm the princess of this kingdom. This is Norell, she's my cousin and she's been tending to your injuries. We're friends of Rya's, and I promise we aren't going to hurt you."

"You're lying," he frowned. "My queen doesn't have friends."

"If she doesn't have friends," Norell questioned, "then what are you to her?"

"I'm her steward," Sora answered with pride. "I've spent years serving her."

"Being a steward is a lot of responsibility," she replied. "She must put a lot of trust in you. Does that not make you some sort of friend to her?"

"No—I don't think so," he stammered.

"She's put trust in us as well," Norell continued. "Even if that doesn't make us friends, she left you in our care and that means something."

"I guess."

Cam could see the boy getting more aggravated, and she tried to diffuse his anger. "Tell me, how did you and Queen Rya get to be so close? You said she saved you, what did she save you from?"

He glared at her, obviously sizing her up. He kept his arms wrapped around his legs, and his mouth closed.

"We save people also," Cam offered, trying to coax him a little more. "I found Rya at our border. She was hurt so I brought her here to the castle, and we've been helping her heal. Is that what she did for you?"

"Sort of," he mumbled.

"I've come to care a lot for Rya. It happens when you save someone. It's why I have no doubt she cares a great deal for you as well."

"She does." His muscles relaxed just a fraction. He took one more look at Cam's face, then began. "I was born to a poor family from the northern tribes. They had left the mountains looking for work in the Trava fields, but the drought made things difficult. By the time I was four my parents had decided they could no longer take care of me.

"My keeper had been trading children in Kelda for years before me. She was cunning and convinced my parents that selling me to her would be in my best interest. She would pay them a hefty amount of gold, and in return I would live in a nice home with a rich family. It was all a lie of course, but they bought it, and I never saw them again."

"That's horrible," Norell gasped. "I thought the child slave trade had been annihilated in Kelda."

"That's what the kingdoms want to believe, but I can tell you first hand it's not true."

"I'm so sorry," Cam whispered.

"It could have been worse," he shrugged. "For some reason my keeper, Lady Wilma, took a liking to me. Instead of selling me outright as she did most of the other children, she rented me to various people as we traveled. We would set up camp in a new village, and she would hand me over to whoever offered the most coin, and when she'd collected enough new children, we'd leave and start it over in the next town. That was my life for years. Thankfully, Lady Wilma refused to allow anyone to defile me. Under her orders I was to be kept pure. She did not object, however, to people beating me. That's how I ended up meeting Rya."

"She paid to hurt you?" Norell gasped.

"No, she would never," Sora snapped. "There was a general in the Isles' royal army who liked to unload his anger on innocent people. He paid a sack of gold to use me as a whipping boy, and had me tied to a post in the guard house. He had laid out a handful of tools to beat me with. I don't remember much else, except the warmth of the blood running down my back, and the sound of my queen's voice when she came to rescue me."

"Rya found you?" Cam asked.

Sora nodded. "Yes. I heard her shouting at the general and then there was this horribly loud crack in the air. Between the blood, the tears, and the bright light that somehow swallowed the room, I never saw what happened. When the light faded, the general was dead on the ground, and it was just me and my queen alone. She untied me and took me inside to clean my wounds. She talked to me, asked me questions about my life, and in the end, she promised to keep me safe. She made me her steward so I would always be close to her. Some people objected, but that never mattered to my queen. She does what she wants."

A few stray tears ran down Cam's cheeks as Sora finished his story. She could imagine Rya cradling the young boy in her arms, trying to calm his fears. She could hear Rya's voice whispering a promise to him, the same as Cam had done for her.

"What happened to Lady Wilma?" Norell asked. "If she only rented you out, how did Rya manage to keep you all these years?"

"I told My Queen about Lady Wilma's love of the bathhouse, and how she would most likely be found there. My Queen went and convinced her to release me. After that she told me I belonged to no one. I was free to leave her service at any time if I wished, but I knew could never do that. She needs me as much as I need her."

"You're a wonderful steward," Cam smiled. His breathing had calmed down, but the hesitation still lingered in his eyes. She knew the one thing that would break through his wall completely. She stood up and said, "I'm going to get Rya for you right now. She's down the hall, it will only be a minute."

Sora looked taller than she remembered; Rya could tell he'd grown, even if he was curled into himself. She found him sitting in a ball on the bed, his limbs tucked in close to his body. It was the way he always retreated when the bad dreams became too much, and she knew by the look on his face that his sleep hadn't been a peaceful one. When he saw her in front of him the fears melted away, and his body unfolded.

"My queen," he whimpered, trying to reach her.

His bandaged feet stuck out over the bed, and Rya stepped closer, falling onto the edge at his side. She pulled him in tight, pressing his face against her shoulder while she rocked him back and forth. He was closer to being a man than a child, but in her eyes, he was still the starving ten-year-old she'd found cowering before one of her guards.

"It's alright," she cooed, "it's going to be alright now."

Cam and Norell had slipped out the door as she came in, thankfully leaving the two of them alone for their reunion.

"I had to find you," he cried. His words warmed the fabric of her shirt. "I thought you were in trouble. These people here, they told me they are your friends. Is that true?"

"Yes," she nodded. "Sort of. They saved me when I thought no one would, and they've kept me safe here in their castle. I'd say you could call them friends after all that."

He leaned back, staring at her as if she were some sort of impostor. She watched his eyes scanning her features, stopping at the scab near her eyebrow for a moment before continuing. He was searching for something, but she didn't know what it was or how to give it to him.

"You always told me be wary of people." He whispered. "You said giving your trust to someone is handing them a way to hurt you, and that I should never be too free with my heart."

"I know, but it's different with them. Cam and Thane have been nothing but kind, and even Norell has managed to prove her worth. You're in good hands here. We both are."

"Were you going to come back?" He asked. She expected the words to be sad or angry, but there was nothing harsh about them. "Were you going to return to the Isles?"

"Of course," she nodded. "I told you as I left that I'd come back for you. I hope you never doubted that."

He shook his head. "No, but now that I'm here, are you still going to fight Father Kasen?"

"Yes," she replied quickly. "I can't let him keep my throne. I can't let him win. I sacrificed so much for so long to become who I am today. I'm the rightful Queen of the Obsidian Isles, and I will not stop fighting for what's mine."

"I'm only asking because if you're happy here, if you're happy with this new life you've been living, maybe you don't have to go back."

"That's not an option," Rya answered. "When they placed the crown on my head I promised myself no one would control my life again. I refuse to be anyone's puppet, and I won't be anyone's tool. If I don't return to the Isles then I'm failing myself. I'd be allowing Kasen to decide my future, and I can't do that. The time has come to leave this place, and you've arrived at just the right moment. You can come with me, and we'll fight together."

"If you're sure," Sora sighed. "You know I'll follow you anywhere. There are some whispers and rumors that

Kasen had planned on bringing Prince Gavin back. He wanted to put him on the throne to replace you."

"I'm aware," Rya nodded.

"That's why I'm here, though, to tell you that's no longer his plan. He's decided with everyone believing Prince Gavin is already dead, the best thing for him to do would be to take the crown himself. Once he has you killed, he'll be the next in line to rule the Obsidian Isles. I escaped so I could find you and warn you."

"That's absurd," she shouted. She jumped off the bed, pacing the space beside it. "He has no claim to the throne. He's not even born of nobility. What makes him think he can just take the kingdom like that?"

"He's telling the people that since you stripped the other elders of their titles, and you have no child to be the heir, he's the only remaining choice for king. He's the highest-ranking member of the court at this point."

"And no one has a problem with this plan of his? The people are just accepting his grab for power?"

Sora shook his head. "A few argued in the beginning, but they were publicly punished. After that, most decided following Kasen was the lesser of two evils. You being the other option."

Rya chewed on her thumbnail while the thoughts ran through her mind. She had to find a way to beat Kasen and bring the people back to her side. The fight back was going to be hard before but knowing the people were equally afraid of Kasen as they were her made it worse. Even with her magic it would be a difficult battle, as he would still hold power over the army.

"That's not all," Sora added. "These people, the Ashen, you said they are friends to you—they're in danger."

"I know," Rya sighed. "Kasen sent a hawk a few days ago telling us the army is marching this way. He threatened to send a portion of the soldiers to retrieve me by force if Mikkel didn't hand me over to the assassin he's hired."

"He's lying," Sora frowned. "He demanded any male over the age of ten was the join the army. They are nearly double the size as before, although most of old men and children. He's sacrificing all of them, and all the Ashen, in order to have your head. He's doesn't care if King Mikkel complies or not. He's commanded them to burn the entire Ashen Forest to the ground."

Rya dropped her hands to her sides. The faces of everyone she'd met flooded her mind. She saw Mikkel falling in battle, and Eirik being caged like an animal for slaughter. Thane would die fighting as a Kinsman, and she couldn't even begin to imagine what would happen to Cam. Even the faceless Obsidian people crossed her mind, the ones too old or too young to be fighting such a war. They would be the first to fall, and hundreds of innocents' lives would be lost. It was all too painful. The moment she'd been dreading was before her now, and she knew exactly what she had to do.

"Mikkel plans on sending his men out a few days from now," she explained. "We'll have to leave sooner than that. We can sneak out the night before and put some distance between us and the Ashen. Hopefully, with me gone the Obsidian army will leave them alone and try tracking me instead."

"And if they don't?" Sora asked, his voice washed in fear.

"Then I hope Mikkel is as great a fighter as I believe him to be."

Sora looked shameful as he asked his next question. "Will you be alright leaving your new friends here? Can you handle not saying goodbye to them?"

"I've always known my place is in the Isles," Rya replied. She sat on the edge of the bed again, pressing her palm against his soft cheek. "I've got you and that's all I need. I won't have a second thought about leaving all this, and all of them behind."

She hadn't noticed the door was open until the sound came. Heavy, loud footsteps tore away from Sora's room and towards the staircase. As they faded into silence, Rya's heart sank.

EIGHTEEN

The sun was sinking into the forest, ending another long day for the princess. The excitement of Sora waking and learning of his story had worn her down, and Cam decided to spend the late afternoon in her room, curled on the bed with a book. Her eyes had closed, and the words in front of her were lost in the blackness, when the door crashed open. The sound startled her, and Cam jumped to her feet with her fists raised, ready to start swinging. The book dropped to the floor, landing with a thud on her foot. The pain throbbed until the sight of Norell's face erased it all. She stood in the doorway, hunched over and panting.

"What's wrong?" Cam asked, guiding her inside and sitting her on the bed.

"I came as quick as I could," she puffed. "I had to."

"You're starting to scare me. Just tell me what happened."

"I was going to check on Sora when I heard him talking to Rya. He said something about Kasen's plan changing and—and Rya, she—she told him they were leaving here. She's going to run off during the night before your father marches to meet the Isles' army. She's going to leave without telling you."

"That can't be true," Cam replied. "I'm sure you heard wrong. She wouldn't disappear like that, not after everything we've been through."

"I'm telling you what she said," Norell snapped back. "I wouldn't make it up, and you know it. She told him she doesn't care about anyone here, and she's not upset about leaving. She's not worried about it—or you—at all."

Cam couldn't respond; she couldn't find the words.

"I warned you from the beginning," Norell continued, "and here we are. I couldn't stand by and allow her to run off on you like Hannah did. I couldn't let you go through that again."

"You're wrong," Cam replied. "You heard wrong."

"I know you wanted her to be different. I admit that I wanted to believe that myself these last few days, but she's not. She's gotten what she wanted, and now she's going to leave."

If Norell kept talking Cam didn't hear it. She had bolted from the room, taking the stairs down two at a time until she landed on the second floor. Her heart beat pounded in her ears as she ran to Sora's doorway. She burst inside, her eyes searching for the brunette's face, but she wasn't there.

"She's in her room," Sora told her. She turned to leave when he stopped her. "Princess," he said in a sad tone. "I know it's hard to watch her go. I've lived it. I also know this is something she has to do. I told her we could stay here, but she said no. I'm sorry."

Cam didn't reply. She left him and walked the short distance to Rya's door. She raised her hand to knock, but stopped, holding her fist in the air in front of her. She didn't know what to do, she didn't know what she'd say, she just knew she needed to hear it from Rya's own lips. Taking a deep breath, she turned the doorknob and stepped inside.

Rya stood staring out the window with her arms crossed over her chest. Usually her stance had an air of confident defiance, but not this time. She was watching the clouds pass; the portrait of a lonely young woman desperate to comfort herself in her own embrace. Cam imagined that's how Rya had looked most of her childhood, alone and trying to be brave.

"Is it true?" Cam asked. She didn't have to explain what she knew, Rya's refusal to meet her eyes was validation enough. Her face grew red with anger. "You're just going to sneak off in the middle of the night, without saying goodbye, without leaving an explanation?"

"It's time," Rya answered. Her words were short and tense.

"I know you had plans to return to the Isles," Cam argued, the tears stinging her eyes, "that was never a question, but you could have at least told me when you were going to leave. You spent every day with me since you woke, and we—I mean, you don't think you owe me at least that?"

Rya faced her now. Her cold, dark eyes were hard and unyielding, but Cam could see the quiver in her lips before she spoke.

"I came to the Ashen Forest for safety while I healed. That's what I got, and now I'll be leaving."

"Stop it," Cam yelled. "Stop acting like you don't feel it, that you don't know what's happening between us. I've been denying it as much as you have but I can't now, not with you threatening to throw it all away."

"I'm not throwing anything away," Rya shot back. "I wasn't looking for romance when I ran away from the Isles, I wasn't expecting any sort of friendship, and I will not give up my life for either of them. I am the Queen of the Obsidian Isles and I will regain my crown. There is nothing, and no one that will stop me. I thought that was understood?"

"Oh, I completely understand. I was told they call you the Black Queen because it's the color of your heart, but that can't be true. You have to have a heart for it to turn black, and it's clear you don't."

Cam spun around and stomped out the room, slamming the door behind her. She fell back against the wall, sliding down to the floor in a puddle. She couldn't believe it, even after hearing Rya's words she couldn't accept that what she felt wasn't real. Her hands trembled in her lap, and she stared down at them, remembering the tingle of Rya's magic as it seeped into her skin. Her mind clung to the moment of connection, and the way a piece of the queen had been a piece of her as well.

She took several deep breaths. She had to try and compose herself before the long walk back to her room. Norell would be waiting for her. She would be sitting on Cam's bed, ready to hold her as she fell apart, but first she'd have to make it back up the stairs. Wiping the tears from her cheeks, she stood up and placed her palm on Rya's door. It was one last attempt to feel her, a final chance to be close to her. A faint noise came from inside; she removed her hand and pressed her ear to the wood. It was a sound she'd never heard before, one she didn't expect, and she knew in that instant there was still hope. The sobbing of a shattered queen hit her ears, and Cam gasped. Rya was as broken as she was, and that kind of pain couldn't be forged.

NINETEEN

The stars had appeared outside the queen's window, signaling the end of her last day with the Ashen. It had passed too quickly, and while she watched night fall over the buildings she tried to ignore the emotions gnawing at her.

She pulled the dark green cloak over her shoulders, securing the buttons just under her chin. The guilt from before hit her again as she stared at her reflection. The dark gray pants were thick enough to keep her warm, and the boots Elin had brought her were practically new. The outfit had been given that morning after Rya lied to the girl, telling her she was going riding and would need a suitable outfit. When she'd fled the Isles in a heavy gown she didn't consider it wasn't made for running. This time she wanted to be prepared, but it meant taking even more from the people who had been so kind to her. She almost returned the clothing, feeling better about stealing from another traveler as she'd done before, but in the end, she couldn't do it. She wanted to take a piece of the Ashen with her, even if it was in the form of a cloak.

While Elin thought she'd gone riding, the truth was Rya never left the castle. She'd locked herself inside her room, only opening the door for Sora when he brought his meals to share with her. She couldn't fathom running into Thane, knowing he would be upset at the hurt she'd caused Cam. Avoiding Norell was another advantage of hiding. She didn't want to see the girl's smug expression taunting her, knowing Rya was as heartless and cruel as she expected. The thought of seeing Cam was the worst kind of torture. She wanted to make sure the princess was alright, wanted to comfort her somehow, but at the same time she knew leaving was the right decision. Facing Cam would only destroy them both, and she needed every bit of her strength to move forward.

She tugged the last bit of bandaging off her hand, and flexed her wrist, testing the movement. The wrapping fell to the floor, and she held her hands in front of her with her palms pointing to the ceiling. The ball of blue light started the size of a cricket, quickly growing in size. It hovered over her hands like a lightning filled cannonball, casting an eerie glow on her skin. She smirked and clapped her hands together, dissolving the orb into nothing.

A small wooden box stuck out from under the bed, and Rya squatted down to retrieve it. She lifted open the lid and stared down at the dagger inside. The white bone handle had a faint gold inlay that had been worn in some areas, and as she picked up the assassin's knife she wondered the number people he'd killed with the small blade. It was the same blade Nix had thrown at Cam, the same one that almost took her own life, and she would use it to end his.

The moon had pushed itself above the trees, and Rya sat on the edge of the bed awaiting the signal. Three light raps on the door, followed by a kick on the bottom. The time had come. She stood and glanced one last time around the room. She took a deep breath, grabbed the handle, and pulled open the door.

Rya gasped, "What—no—" She stammered with wide eyes, glaring at the boy in front of her. He had followed the plan exactly as he should have with one small error, he wasn't alone. Cam was dressed in dark, heavy clothing. Her bow was in one hand and she had a quiver of arrows across her back, and another strapped to her thigh. The front of her platinum hair had been braided across her brow, then tucked into the tight bun twisted on the back of her head.

"I'm coming with you," Cam clarified, not waiting for Rya to argue. "I don't care if you won't admit you have feelings for me. I don't care if you deny needing my help. I don't care if you never talk to me again. I'm going to be by your side no matter what, because that's what friends do— it's what people who love each other do."

Rya grit her teeth together, glancing back and forth between Sora and Cam. She raised her hand to the princess, feeling the magic gathering in her palm, but Cam didn't flinch.

"You can do anything you want to me," Cam said with no hint of fear or anger, "I'm going to get back up and find you. I promised to protect you, remember?"

The queen dropped her arm, cursing herself for not only failing to follow through, but for thinking she could ever harm Cam to begin with.

"Fine," Rya sneered. "You can help me escape the Ashen Forest, but that's it. Once we reach the border you return home."

"We'll see," Cam smiled. She turned and started off down the dim hallway with Sora and Rya following behind.

"I'm sorry," he whispered to the queen. "She wouldn't let me leave. I didn't know what else to do. I figured you would be angry if I killed her."

Rya smirked, amused by his comment. "You're right," she agreed. "That would have upset me greatly."

The trio tip-toed through the halls and down a staircase Rya had never seen before, until it spit them out into a narrow corridor. It was exactly like the one Cam had led her down that first day, only instead of heading to the kitchens this one ran the opposite direction.

"Where are we going?" Rya hissed in the darkness.

"This leads to the storeroom," Cam answered. "There's a hatch in the floor that leads to a passageway out of the grounds. It was built for the royal family in case anyone ever attacks the castle. Of course, the Ashen haven't been threatened for hundreds of years so it's been forgotten. It's the perfect escape."

Guilt tugged at Rya as Cam finished her sentence. Hundreds of years without worry was a legacy that was going to be ended because of her. It was her fault Kasen was marching on them now.

The hall ended and Cam pushed against the thick wooden door with her shoulder, grunting as it slid open. Inside they found shelves stocked full of excess dry goods from the kitchens, piles of tools tucked into corners to avoid rust, and stacks of extra bedding for upcoming winter months. It was exactly as Rya thought a storeroom would look except for one big difference—the man standing in the middle, glaring at them over his ginger beard.

"Papa," Cam gasped.

Mikkel stood with a massive foot placed on the escape hatch, his arms crossed over his barrel chest. To his right stood two figures in the shadows; Thane and Norell leaned against the wall looking defeated and pained. Cam slouched next to Rya, shocked and shamed under the gaze of her father.

"What were you thinking?" Mikkel asked. "Did you really think you could slip out of the castle that easy? Even if I hadn't caught these two trying to sneak horses out the main gate, I would have discovered you were gone eventually. Did you honestly believe I wouldn't come looking for you?"

"It's my fault," Rya answered. Sora was hanging on her arm, cowering under the angry king. "Cam was only trying to help me."

"Cam knows better." He pinched the bridge of his nose, his eyes closed in disappointment. "I thought we had agreed to fight Kasen together."

"We can't." She replied, shaking her head. "I need to leave. I need to be far from here."

"But why?" He asked.

Rya knew everyone's eyes were on her. She owed them an explanation, but she was afraid to say it. She didn't want to watch the kindness in their eyes dissipate as the truth came out. She knew she had to leave the Ashen Forest but volunteering to go and being ordered to leave were completely different.

"I was leaving to protect you," she said. "Kasen plans on attacking your kingdom whether you comply or not. He's recruited more men and double his numbers. I was

182

hoping I might draw the army a different direction if I ran. I never intended on Cam trying to come along, and I never wanted any of you to be in any danger."

Mikkel's shoulders sank and he dropped his arms at his sides. "It sounds like we're in danger either way. If you leave and they don't follow you, they will still attack us. If they split the army, they will be after you and still be pounding on our doors. If what you say is true, Kasen won't be deterred by you fleeing. He'll be angry that I allowed you to leave." He sighed, taking a beat before asking, "did you even have a plan for after you left us?"

"Yes, but it's a little crazy."

"That sounds right," Cam said with a weak smirk.

"I said before that Kasen knows Prince Gavin is alive, but it's more than that. He knows exactly where Gavin has been hiding these past years—and so do I. I'm heading to the Ivory Cape to find him and bring him back with me. Only with the two of us together do we have a chance at beating Kasen. I can't do it without his help."

"That *is* crazy," Norell snorted. "Why would he help you? He should hate you after everything that's happened."

"If he doesn't join my side," Rya replied, "then he'll be Kasen's next victim. If he wants the crown, he knows he'll have to kill anyone who can challenge him. After I'm gone, Gavin is only threat Kasen has."

"So, it's either help you or die?" Thane laughed. "You don't leave him much choice."

"I'm hoping he agrees," Rya nodded.

Mikkel looked around at the rest of them, and ran a hand down his beard. "Alright," he said. "If that's the plan, then that's what we'll do."

"What?" Cam asked. Her mouth hung open in shock, matching the same expression on Norell's face.

"If Rya needs to reach the Ivory Cape, we'll help her get there. We still have a spy among us so it needs to be done quietly. You two," he barked, pointing to Thane and Norell, "head back to the stables and take three horses. I think any more than that would draw attention. Meet them at the tunnel's exit when you're done."

"Uh—right." Thane stammered, rushing out the storeroom door. Norell was on his heels, disappearing in the dark night outside.

"Papa?" Cam was still lost in surprise. "You're going to let us go?"

He stepped forward, putting his hands on her shoulders, and leaning down to her level.

"I don't know how I could stop you," he smiled. He pulled her into a tight hug and kissed the top of her head. "I love you."

"I love you too, Papa."

Cam's face was hidden behind his arms, but Rya didn't need to see her to know she was crying.

Mikkel stepped back, and stooped down to the floor, lifting up the hatch he'd been standing on.

"Climb in," he said to Cam. "I'll drop the boy down to you since he shouldn't be jumping down with those bandaged feet."

Sora blushed bright red but limped forward and allowed the king to lift him by the armpits, sinking him into the black of the hole. Once he'd disappeared, Mikkel turned to Rya and huffed.

"We're going to give that army a fight," he said in a low voice, trying to keep it from reaching Cam below. "Head north to the Craken Peaks and then along the coast to the Ivory Cape. I'll do my best to keep Kasen's forces distracted as long as I can."

"Don't forget about Nix," Rya added. "And we don't know who the traitor is who's helping him."

Mikkel laughed. "I think the five of you can handle one Kael assassin. I have faith."

"I— "she faltered "—thank you. I don't know what else to say."

"Just keep Cam safe."

The passage was washed in black. Unlike the ones that led to the kitchens or storeroom, this narrow space was rough and unfinished. Every few steps someone would

185

trip over a rock, or dip down into a sunken dent in the ground. Tufts of roots hung from the dirt above, brushing their hair as they passed underneath. More than once, Rya swatted at an unseen object touching her cheek, panicking that it was something more sinister than a vine.

After walking in the pitch black, Rya was pleased to notice the pale glow of the night showering down from somewhere ahead. The exit to the tunnel was above them, blocked by a rusted metal grate, and through the holes she could see a pair of black boots facing away from them, kicking at the grass.

"It's going to be rough," Thane hissed, ignorant to their arrival. "Maybe it's better if you stay here."

"No way," Norell spat back, trying to keep from yelling. "You're not going to run off with Cam and leave me here to sit here with my hands in my lap waiting for your return. I'm going with you and that's the end of it."

"But it's dangerous," he argued.

Norell swung around the spear she'd been leaning on, showing the sharpened tip to Thane close up. He took a step back, holding up his hands in defeat.

"I might not use a sword," she grumbled, "but I'm not completely useless."

"A little help here," Cam interrupted, wiggling her fingers through the grating.

Thane dropped to his knees and grabbed one end while Cam pushed from underneath. Slowly the metal disk slid aside, allowing room for them to crawl through. Thane had collapsed on his backside with a grunt, and Norell pushed past him, her hand outstretched to help each of them from the hole.

"Thanks," Rya mumbled as she took the girl's hand.

Questions filled Rya's mind, but she was forced to keep quiet until they'd reached the cover of the thick woods. Hidden behind the trees and the brush, she was finally able to speak.

"Where are we?"

"Outside the back of the grounds," Thane whispered in reply. "It's where we were supposed to meet you before Mikkel caught us."

She scoffed. "And how long did it take Norell to sell us out?"

"I didn't," Norell answered. "As soon as he saw me and Thane, he knew something was up. Even without our help he worked out what was happening. It seems you and Cam are the only ones ignoring what's going on between you two."

Rya's face grew hot, but the cover of night hid the pink of her cheeks. Cam kept her head down, watching her feet as she walked, obviously trying to hid the same blushed skin.

187

"Here we are," Thane grinned. The horses stood between the trees, their reins wrapped around low hanging branches. Rya immediately recognized Rainy who shook her head upon their arrival. Behind her, Zara looked bored as she waited, and Eclipse nipped at the leaves of the tree he was secured to. Rya smiled as she saw him.

"Alright," Cam nodded. "Norell, you ride with Thane. You've been on Rainy before, so it'll be easy for you. Rya, I had them bring Eclipse for you but if you're not comfortable you can ride behind me instead."

Rya glanced at Thane, and he returned the look. They both knew that in the end Rya would still be leaving, she'd still be breaking Cam's heart, and riding half way across Kelda pressed together wasn't going to make that any easier.

"I'll be fine," she nodded, "and Sora really should be riding double with me."

"If you're sure," Cam replied, failing to hide the twinge of disappointment in her voice.

The group mounted the horses and with a silent nudge, led them further into the forest. The thin moon was overhead guiding them north as they moved in a single file line. All around them the trees stood like shadow creatures, their arms stretched overhead, their fingers twisted and gnarled trying to grab the sky. The sounds of the forest, the rustling of leaves, the break of a twig, a mysterious croak, all seemed amplified in darkness.

The horses came up over one of the hills and Rya looked into the distance. The shadows of the Craken Peaks swallowed the border of the forest, consuming the barrier and leaving no trace. The snow-capped tops laughed down at the group, taunting them with the promise of cold weather and icy terrain. With no other way to reach the Cape without Kasen knowing, they had no choice but to ride straight into the white winter of the north.

The moon had settled behind the horizon, and although the sun was still hiding the sky had begun wake. The dim light of the morning showed the exhaustion on all their faces. Rya could feel Sora slumped against her, either sleeping or close to it. The night had crawled by once they set their course, the world passing in a mix of grays and blacks. The daylight was a welcome sight, but it also meant their cover was fading away.

Thane and Norell had gone ahead to check for shelter while the others lagged behind. Eclipse and Zara were still moving steady, but it was obvious they were just as worn. They took slow steps between the trees for almost half an hour when Thane finally reappeared. His mouth grinning from ear to ear.

"You've found a place to camp?" Cam asked, hopeful.

"Better," he smiled.

TWENTY

The abandoned cabin they had stumbled upon consisted of four rotting walls held together with a shabby shingled roof. Each of the two shorter sides had a single window that was covered in a thin film of dirt and grime. Thane opened the door and Rya winced as its hinges squealed in protest.

Sadly, the inside wasn't any better than the exterior. A single bed was pushed against one wall, and the few blankets they found had been chewed up from various rodents trying to find warmth. The fireplace was nothing more than a small niche in the wall that hugged a mound of old ash. It was obvious that no one had called this place home in years.

"Lovely," Rya breathed, her nose scrunched up.

"It's better than sleeping outside," Thane shrugged. "We'll have plenty of nights under the stars later, we might as well take advantage of the shelter while we can."

Cam was quick to volunteer to gather wood from the surrounding area, and sensing Rya's eagerness to join her, Norell offered to help first. The queen was left behind and tasked with sweeping away what she could to create a place to sleep, while Thane dug out the powder from the fireplace they'd soon be using. Sora sat against the wall, pouting while he watched them work.

"You should let me help with that," he grumbled as Thane dumped another handful of ash out the window. "I'm not useless."

"You're still recovering," he answered. "You need more time to heal, and shoveling dirt isn't going to speed that along."

"He doesn't like to be still," Rya teased. "Sora needs to feel useful. He hasn't taken a day off since I've known him."

"I had nothing but days off while you were away," the boy muttered. It wasn't clear if he meant to wound Rya, but if so, the comment had done its job, striking her hard in the heart. She tried to mask the hurt before anyone could see what he'd done.

"I feel a little faint in here," she lied. "I think I'll step outside for a minute."

191

"Are you alright, Your Majesty?" Sora asked, trying to stand. She motioned at him, forcing him to sit back down.

"I'm fine. I think the combination of no sleep and this stuffy shed is getting to me." She pulled back the weathered door and left, allowing it to slam shut behind her. The guilt of leaving Sora was growing harder to shoulder each hour that passed. She couldn't erase the image of him lying in the bed with ratted hair and bloody feet. The faded scars he'd received as a small boy were covered in fresh marks. They were a sign he'd been tortured in her absence. She knew Sora would never complain to her. He would never admit if he was angry that she had left him, but she also knew she had let him down. All those years ago she had made a promise to protect him, and she'd failed. It didn't matter if he ever confessed what Kasen did to mark his body, she would make that man pay for those new wounds.

"Everything alright?" Cam asked. Her arms were full of small branches and bits of wood. It was enough kindling to get them through the night.

"Yeah." Rya forced a smile. "I just needed some fresh air."

Cam watched her for a moment, studying her. "I'll take these insides to Thane," she finally said, accepting Rya's answer. "The sooner we get the fire going, the sooner we can eat. That should make us all feel better."

She nudged the door open with her foot and slipped inside. Norell however had lingered behind.

"I want to apologize," Norell said, almost too low to hear. She cleared her throat, trying again at a normal volume. "I want to apologize. I shouldn't have teased you about Sora before. It was wrong, and I'm sorry."

"Are you?" Rya asked, rolling her eyes.

"I just said I was."

"You might be saying that to appease Cam. You admitted yourself you do things for her that you hate."

"I'm trying to apologize to you," Norell snapped. "I'm admitting I was wrong, which doesn't happen often."

"You being wrong?" Rya asked. "Or admitting it."

"Why are you so difficult?" she shouted. "After hearing about how you saved Sora, I thought I could change my mind about you, but you make it so hard."

"It doesn't matter what you think of me." Rya could feel the anger and guilt swelling in her chest. "It's not going to change anything. It's not going to erase the rumors and stories that travel Kelda about me. It's not going to change what I've done, or the damage it's caused. Right now, Sora is sitting inside burying his feelings deep inside him, refusing to admit he's hurt. He wants to ignore that I fled the Isles without him. He wants to forget that I left him behind in that hell. He won't tell me what happened once I was gone. He won't talk to me about the punishment he endured because of me. He's going to hide his resentment away inside him until it bubbles up and one day explodes."

Norell cocked her head to the side. "Like you're doing right now?"

Rya's chest heaved with her heavy breathing as she tried to calm herself. "He'll leave me. He'll run off once it becomes too hard to look at me any longer."

"I don't know you very well," Norell continued, "and I don't know Sora, but I don't believe he's going anywhere. He's your family, and that means standing by each other even when you think they are crazy, or stupid, or making the biggest mistake of their lives."

"You don't sugarcoat things, do you?"

"The point is, you and Sora chose each other and you're bonded for life. Stop worrying about what he's thinking. He'll talk when he's ready."

For the first time ever, Norell's tone was without anger or hate. There was no taunt hiding under the surface, no backhanded remarks, and no suspicion. She was being honest and sincere, and it made them both uncomfortable. Norell nodded her head, then ducked inside the cabin, eager to leave the awkward moment outside.

Rya had to admit that having the others along on the journey did come with some advantages. Thane had come prepared with a good amount of food, the best of which was a slab of salted meat he had cooked over the fire for them all that night. It was the big enough that even after they took their share, they'd have scraps of dried meat for the next few days. She thought back to her time running from Nix, and the lengths she had gone to in order to survive. Stealing from the villages in the dead of night was one thing but being trapped in the wilderness foraging for berries was worse. They were never filling and hard to come by, making her desperate for something more. It'd been days since she'd had more than a handful of food when she found a carcass lying in the dirt. The rabbit had been torn apart by some small predator, but the bottom half remained fairly intact. Rya would never admit to anyone that she stood in that spot a little too long, staring at the rotting flesh, trying to decide if it was worth eating. In the end, her pride was stronger than her hunger, and she left the body behind and continued on her way.

"You're sure Gavin's in the Cape?" Thane asked, stroking the small fire. "I don't want to get up there and find out he's hiding down in Asta."

"As sure as I can be," Rya answered. "The last rumors I heard were that he works a fishing vessel."

"If he's been alive this whole time," Norell added, "why wouldn't he just come back to the Isles? Why would he stay hidden?"

"If you'd met Gerrod you'd want to stay away too. I'm assuming when he was taken, Kasen fed him some story that's kept him from returning. Gavin was only fifteen when he disappeared, and he was a sweet boy. Everything about him contradicted who his father had become. He was gentle and caring, but he was also naïve, the type that would believe almost anything you told him. It's why Kasen wanted him, he was an easy target to manipulate.

"That's good," Thane nodded. "If what you're saying is true, we shouldn't have a hard time convincing him to come with us."

"I wouldn't be so sure," Rya replied. "I can tell you from experience that a few years can do a lot to alter a person. We have no idea what kind of man he's become."

"Alright," Cam nodded. "All we have to do is travel to the Cape, find the lost prince, talk him into trusting us, return to the forest, stop a war, and take back your crown. Anything else?"

"Nope," Rya answered. "I think that's all of it."

Cam smiled at her, the same sweet gentle smile she always had reserved for Rya. "Sounds easy enough to me."

TWENTY-ONE

Limbs overlapped and twisted around each other as the bodies sprawled out across the bare cabin floor. Full bellies mixed with the warm glow of the fire had lulled them all into a deep sleep, making them unaware of the danger lurking just outside. They failed to wake for the footsteps in the brush, or the whinny of the horses that were tied up nearby. It wasn't until the door's noisy hinges cried out that anyone moved at all.

Cam was the first to rise, bolting upright as the door smacked into her ankle. She blinked twice, unable to register the face staring down at her. As her mind caught up with her eyes she gasped.

"What are *you* doing here?" She cried out.

Her shout woke Thane, and his hand was on the hilt of his sword before his lids had opened. He pulled the blade free, but Rya had been quicker. Her hand shot out in front of her and a blazing ball of orange light flew at the man's chest, knocking him onto his back. He landed with a thud, rolling side to side, gasping for air while the magic dissipated over him.

Cam was on her feet now, weapons in hand. Her attention shifted to the glimpse of movement in the bushes outside, and a familiar voice screamed at the accomplice.

"You idiot," Nix yelled from somewhere among the trees. "I told you to wait for my signal."

She was out the door in a flash, with Rya on her heels. The girls stood back to back in the clearing in front of the cabin, searching the surrounding area, only to find it empty. Leaves rustled from the branches above, and Cam released an arrow towards the sound. Then another shuffle from a nearby tree, followed by another arrow. Both failed to hit their mark, and they were left with only silence. Once again, the assassin slipped from their grasp and disappeared into the forest without a trail.

The anger burned in Cam's cheeks, and she huffed short quick breathes as she stormed back inside. Thane had the man pressed against the wall next to the door, his blade resting against the traitor's fat neck.

"Ruben," Cam growled. She squatted down in front of him, her eyes burning into his. "What are you doing here? And what are you doing with that assassin?"

He remained silent.

"Explain yourself at once," she shouted.

Thane's sword hovered above the man's flesh, brushing his stubble with each breath Ruben took. Despite the weapon kissing his neck, he didn't seem bothered by the situation, or the dangerous way they were staring at him. It was only when Rya returned to the cabin that he showed any fear, and his eyes grew wide at the sight of her.

"I knew she would hurt us with her magic," he stammered, pointing a pudgy finger in Rya's direction. "She's tried to kill me, you all saw it. She's dangerous and out of control."

"You were teaming up with a Kael assassin," Cam barked back. She couldn't control the rage in her voice, nor did she want to. "You led him right to us. You've been working with him the whole time, haven't you?"

"I was doing what was right for the Ashen people. I was protecting my kingdom as I swore to do when I took the armor."

"No," Cam shouted. "You swore to follow your king, and you betrayed him. You betrayed us all. A real man of my father's army would follow his king's decision. He would obey the orders of his princess. You only did what you wanted. You stopped being one of the Ashen when you sided with Nix."

"That's not true," he argued. "I'm loyal to King Mikkel and all the Ashen people. You've just been blinded by her magic. You've been made to think she's worth saving. We can still make this right. We can take her to Nix, or Father Kasen. They'll be happy to take her, and they'll leave the Ashen alone."

"How much did they offer you?" Rya asked, stepping forward. The man's lip quivered as he tried to think of an answer. "That's why you're really here, isn't it? If it was about doing the right thing, you would have simply given our location to Nix and washed your hands of it. If you're out here actively hunting us down with one of the Kael, you've been promised a portion of the prize. Tell me, how much is your betrayal worth in gold?"

Ruben stammered through some sounds, unable to form real words. Thane pressed the cold tip of his blade to his skin, and a small dot of red formed on the surface.

"It doesn't matter," Cam said, shaking her head. She stood up, turning away from the man she once trusted, speaking only to the others now. "He'll never get whatever they promised him, and he'll never return to the castle."

"You can't—" he screamed. He jumped upwards, grabbing for the princess as she turned to face him once more. He'd forgotten Thane's sword was still pressed against his flesh until it was too late. He'd barely reached his feet when his hands clapped against his throat, covering the stream of blood that ran down the front of him.

Thane took a step back, looking to Cam with sorrowful eyes, but she was unwavering in her anger. Ruben gargled incoherent sounds with his hands desperately clasped around his neck before falling back to the floor, this time face down and unmoving. The red liquid spread, outlining the motionless form that rested at their feet.

"I didn't—" Thane stuttered. "I was just—"

"I know," Cam replied. She stared down at the man, remembering the dozens of hunts they'd been on together. Looking at his limp body she could only think of how she pitied the animals' lives they'd taken more than she did his. "He killed himself, one way or another. Once my father found out he was working with the Kael, he would have been marked for death. If anything, he got off lucky; this way he didn't suffer long."

No one said a word. They all stood looking down at the crimson puddle.

"We need to get moving," Cam said, breaking the silence. "Nix knows we're here. We can't stay any longer."

Snapped from the stillness of Ruben's death, Rya grabbed Sora by the arm, dragging him around the blood and out the door to ready the horses. Thane walked over to the torn-up bedding and wiped the red off his sword before returning it to his sheath. Norell was still frozen, her wide eyes transfixed on the body.

"Come on," Thane whispered, wrapping his arm around her shoulders. "It's time to go."

Left alone, Cam knelt next to the body, and with a grunt she rolled Ruben over onto his back. She studied the creases of his face before glaring at his cold dead eyes. She'd known him all her life. He'd eaten at their table. He'd sent his daughter for schooling with Norell. He had been a regular soldier in the army until he was promoted to the royal guard, making him one of the men trusted to protect her. Now, he was dead.

"Rya's fate wasn't your choice," she sighed, knowing his ears would never hear her. "I made that decision when I brought her to the castle, and no one is changing my mind."

Miles passed without a word spoken between the group. Each of them silent as they got lost in their own thoughts, each processing what had happened in their own way.

Rya felt Sora's arms around her waist, tighter than they'd been before. He was no stranger to witnessing death, and she knew it wasn't the body they'd left behind that caused him worry. It was the thought of letting her go again. His embrace was a silent promise that he'd always be by her side. Part of her wanted him to hold on forever, but another piece of her heart wanted to send him away. She needed to protect him like she couldn't before and sending him back to Mikkel would keep him safe, but she knew it would never happen. He'd follow her to the ends of Kelda now that he'd found her, and she couldn't deny him the one thing he so desperately wanted.

The sun disappeared into the western sea, and night was falling on top of them. Camp would not be in the safety of a cabin, but under the open sky and nestled between the crowded trees. The blankets were huddled around a small fire Thane had started, each begging for the bit of warmth the logs put out. Dinner had been a few scraps of leftover meat and a roll toasted over the flames; it was just enough to keep them full until morning.

"I think we need to sleep in shifts," Cam suggested. "I don't want to give Nix another chance to surprise us like earlier."

"Do you think he'll be back so soon?" Sora asked.

"I think if he has a chance to get to Rya, he'll take it. The only upside is he knows he's heavily outnumbered and has lost the only ally he had. Even a Kael assassin has his limits."

"They've always scared me," the boy admitted. "I grew up hearing stories about how horrible they are, and Lady Wilma would threaten to sell us to the Kael when we were misbehaving. I had never seen one though, until that one showed up in the Isles dressed in all black from head to toe. The only thing I could see was his cold eyes piercing into me. It was frightening."

203

"I didn't realize he was following you from the beginning," Cam said, looking at Rya. "I thought Kasen hired him after you fled as a way to track you down."

"Kasen knew he could never attack me on my own ground, even with some of soldiers backing him. He set up a ruse, having me summoned to the guard house to break up some fake dispute. Nix was lying in wait on the roof and, as I approached the building, he dropped down on top of me. His dagger had been knocked from his grip, so I reached out to fire some magic at him, but he was ready for it. He grabbed a nearby log and swung hard at my arm, shattering my wrist. After that, I was defenseless. I was only able to escape because half the army was unaware of the treason and, in the confusion of who was fighting who, I slipped away. Nix wasn't far behind and tracked me all the way to the Ashen Forest. You know the rest."

Rya hung her head. She was tired, but it wasn't physical. Her head and her heart were in a constant battle, and the internal war was wearing her down. If it was this hard for her, she couldn't imagine the conflict brewing inside Cam.

"I'll take the first shift," Cam offered.

"I'll sit with you," Rya added. She rolled her eyes at the other's surprised faces. "It'll be easier for us to stay awake if we're in pairs. Sora still needs to heal, so I think he

204

should be allowed to sleep the whole night. Thane and Norell can take the second shift."

"Alright," Thane nodded. Try as he might, he couldn't hide the sly smile from Rya. "You two wake me and Norell when the moon reaches overhead. Sora, I want you to sleep as much as you can." The boy opened his mouth but Thane was quick to add, "and no arguing. Just rest."

The girls positioned themselves against the trunk of a nearby tree, ready for a long night. They were beyond the reach of the fire's light, but Rya could see the glow reflecting in Cam's eyes, and the familiar flutter she tried to suppress rose up again.

"Thank you," Cam whispered, not wanting to disturb the others. She laid her head against the bark, her hands resting on her bow and arrow.

"For what?" Rya replied. Her weapons were hidden, waiting under the surface of her skin until they were needed.

"Sitting with me. You didn't have to do that."

"It's my fault you're out here. It would make me pretty evil if I had you sit up all night alone?"

"You're not evil." Her voice had switched to the smooth tone she got when she was going to say something serious, and Rya braced herself. "I know you want people to think you are. You want them to believe you're tough and powerful, which is true, but there's more to you than that. I've seen the parts you keep hidden, the ones you're so scared of. I've seen that soft caring center you guard behind your hard edges. I could never consider you evil."

Rya dropped her gaze, staring at her hands folded neatly in her lap. It was the way she'd been taught as a child, the way pretty girls sat and obeyed. "There's a lot you don't know." She sighed. "If you heard it all, you wouldn't feel the same way about me as you do now."

"Would you feel different about me?" Cam asked. "If I told you that I wasn't sad to see Ruben dead on the ground, would you think differently of me? If you knew that I'd never considered taking a man's life before that moment, would it change the way you feel?"

"No, never," Rya answered without missing a beat. "But you wanting the man who betrayed your family and your kingdom to die isn't the same as what lies in my past. Not all my actions were honorable, and what's worse is that I don't regret the last few years. If I could take it all back, or change all the choices I made, I wouldn't. It might make me a monster, but I believe the people I hurt got exactly what they deserved."

"Then we aren't that different after all," Cam shrugged. "Because I believe that's exactly what happened to Ruben."

TWENTY-TWO

With each day that passed, the wind grew colder. The leaves overhead barely clung to the naked branches of the trees. Winter grabbed hold of the north much earlier than the rest of Kelda and lasted well past its welcome. Just as Rya expected, the group had left with only the clothes on their back and none were prepared for the dropping temperatures. The thin coats they'd expected to make for better travel did little to shield them from the icy currents that made their home around the mountain range.

Food was growing light, and the wildlife had retreated underground, or slept burrowed in the tree trunks as they prepared for the long snow. The group still had some dried meat strips, but the bread was gone and the fruit they'd managed to gather was running low. Thane and Cam had taken off into the thinning woods to try and find an animal to hunt, leaving the other three alone at the camp.

"You're nearly healed," Norell smiled, inspecting Sora's feet. "The herbs did better than I thought they would. I'd say you'll do just fine with a single bandage now, just to keep your boots from irritating the fresh skin."

"Thank you," Sora smiled.

"Where did you learn to do all that?" Rya asked, watching as Norell finished wrapping his foot. "If you're the king's niece, why would you train to be a mender? You shouldn't have to work at all with your status."

"Not everyone wants to sit around doing nothing," Norell answered. Rya rolled her eyes at the girl's response, and Norell sighed. "After my parent wrote to say they were sick, I spent a lot of time with the castle's mender. I thought if I could learn what he did, maybe I could go save them. It was a stupid thought of a child of course, and by the time the letter reached us they had already passed. That didn't stop me, and the more time I spent with him, the more I learned. I swore I would be useful, that I would have the skills to help the ones I loved, and that I would never lose anyone again. Of course, when Eirik was born, I discovered there would always be some sickness I can't cure. Death takes us all in the end, whether we want it to or not."

"You might not be able to save everyone," Rya replied, "but you saved us."

Sora smiled and nodded, but Norell kept her eyes on his wrapping, avoiding both his and Rya's gaze. The queen grew flush, feeling too exposed to them both, and cleared her throat.

"I mean," she stammered, "not that it matters to you, since we hate each other."

"Right—" Norell smirked. "—since we hate each other."

The days continued to blow by, and the group's spirits were getting lower. Nix was still hiding in the shadows, and the idea of him was enough to keep them tense. They'd been vigilant since their day at the cabin, raising weapons for each snap of a twig or shuffle of leaves, but thankfully they were all false alarms. Rest was becoming as scarce as food and warmth. Each of them was exhausted and struggled to keep their eyes open during their watch, and when time for bed finally came, the ground was as cold as ice and made sleeping through the night difficult.

Rya had all but given up hope, watching their fallen faces as they rode along, when the light shifted and the trees opened up ahead of her. A blinding white glowed behind the trunks, calling to them.

"We've reached it," Thane cheered. "It's the northern border."

The Ashen Forest had reached its end, and as if the trees themselves knew their boundaries, they stopped at the invisible line, unwilling to cross over. The world outside the forest looked barren and vacant without the woods towering overhead. The idea of stepping into the void was terrifying, like being stripped naked and left on display.

"I can't believe it," Cam breathed. She stopped next to Rya and dismounted. Taking tentative steps from the shelter of the trees she walked from her kingdom and into the unknown. "We've made it," she smiled back at them. "I can't believe we made it."

"This is your chance to turn back," Rya announced. "It would be easy to go home. You could return to the castle and stay safe and warm. No one would think less of you for leaving me here."

"You're joking right?" Thane replied with a grin. "If we proved anything on this journey, it's that you need us. We aren't giving up on you; we're in this together."

Cam smiled back at her. "You can't get rid of us that easy."

"Let's get this over with," Norell added.

Rya couldn't reply. When she voiced the offer, she never expected them to stay. With the frozen nights and empty stomachs, she would have sworn they'd bid her goodbye and return to the comforts of their home. She didn't have that luxury. She had no home to return to. She knew she could only move forward, and the fact that they were going with her was almost too much to bare. She jumped down from Eclipse and joined Cam in the empty space ahead of them. The jagged cliffs stood before them like stone giants exploding from the earth. They looked alien against the landscape, while simultaneously appearing to have belonged there from the start of time.

"We can't take the horses," Cam sighed, staring at the snow-covered peaks. "The pass is rocky and slick with ice at this time of year. It'd be easier to navigate without them."

"What does that mean?" Thane asked. "We just leave them here?"

He wasn't the type to be easily shaken, but as he laid his hand on Rainy's neck his words wavered. "I won't do it."

"I'm not a fan of the idea either," Cam replied, glancing at Zara. "But if you ride her there's a chance she could slip off the side and you would both be lost forever. Is that better?"

"We can send them back," Rya added. "We can have Norell and Sora take the horses back to the castle. Then they'll all be safe."

"No way," Sora argued. "I'm staying with you. I'm healed and ready to fight."

"You shouldn't have to," she sighed, rubbing the spot between her brows. "You're just a child and this isn't your battle."

"I'm thirteen," he shouted. "Think about what you were doing at thirteen, and stop treating me like I'm a kid."

"Everyone stop talking," Norell interrupted. They all stopped bickering as she slowly took in the whole of the horizon. Rya knew the wheels were spinning in the girl's mind. She was always doing that, weighing options against each other, calculating the outcomes. Rya guessed that Norell spent most of her life trying to find a balance between her emotions and doing what was necessary. She was always trying to be practical and calculated, two qualities Rya had little experience with.

"We'll go around," Norell nodded, satisfied with her decision.

"It'll add days to our trip," Cam retorted. "If we head straight over the pass it'll be faster."

"Not if we're on foot," Norell replied. "Leaving the horses here and taking the direct path will put us just as far behind as skirting the bottom, and when we finally get to the other side, we'll be without them. How long do you think it will take us to walk all the way to the Ivory Cape? We don't want to keep King Mikkel waiting for us any longer than he has to."

Cam opened her mouth, but her words never came. From what Rya had seen, Cam and Thane rarely had a good argument against Norell.

They walked back to the trees, climbing up into the saddles once again. Rya watched Norell scoot closer to Thane, and his lips whispered his gratitude to her. With Norell's arms wrapped around Thane's waist and her head resting on his back, Rya was hot in the cheeks. She felt foolish that she ever believed Norell had feelings for Cam. If she had looked a little harder, she would have seen the sly glances and soft touches Thane and her passed back and forth.

Walking the horses through the open space between the towering mountain and the dense forest was unsettling. Cam caught Rya checking over her shoulder every few minutes, half expecting Nix to be strolling behind them with a smug smile on his face, but she knew he wasn't that stupid. If they were exposed, he would be too.

"He's not there," she said, trying to ease Rya's mind.

The queen looked once more behind her. "I know," she sighed. "It's silly. I just keep thinking about the tracks in the snow, they'll lead him right to us."

"I'd bet half my fortune he's taking the pass instead of following us. He wouldn't risk being seen."

Rya frowned. "Betting is a dangerous hobby."

"Come on," Thane laughed. "It can be loads of fun when you're winning."

"No." Rya shook her head. "I've seen first-hand the damage it can do. My father spent his life drinking and gambling away his inheritance. It's what caused his death."

"What do you mean?" Cam asked.

"It's the reason he had me train my powers. I was twelve when he woke me in the middle of the night and dragged me by the arm down the street to the tavern he spent all his time at. He was drunk again, stumbling his way through the horde of people inside. A door in the back opened and he shoved me through. I remember the men staring at me as I stood in my night shirt, shivering from the cold air and fear. They were laughing. My father shouted something about them cheating, saying they stole his money. They ignored him and went back to their game, but he couldn't let it go. He ordered me to use my magic against them. It was the moment he told me would come. He wanted me to hurt them, but I couldn't. I was terrified.

"When I finally managed to make my body move, I ran out of the room, through the tavern, and into the street outside. My father caught me. He screamed at me for letting him down. He grabbed my arm again, trying to drag me back inside. He kept saying I was a failure, that this is what I was made for. I was so angry and afraid; the magic just came out. I knocked him backwards about five feet

214

where he landed on his back. The last memory I have of my father was him cursing me as he left me and returned to the tavern. I went home alone, and never saw him again. A week later a man came to our door and told my mother they'd found his body. He had been beaten to death and left in an alley. I never said anything, but I knew who did it. I knew it was the men from that night. I just didn't care."

No one spoke. The pity and sympathy the others were feeling was kept silent, and she was thankful for that. She had endured a great deal in her childhood, but she'd made it through. She was a queen now. She was strong and feared and most importantly, she was alive. The people who'd fooled her into believing they loved her—they hadn't been as lucky.

THE DUNGEONS

The pebbles and hard clay cut through his flesh as his face slid against the dirt. His cell was nothing more than a hole carved into the ground, with the rough floor and walls made of packed earth. The corner he did his business in was only feet away, and from his position he could smell the stench of the fluids that lingered, waiting to seep into the soil.

Meager bits of stale bread and leftover meat sat in front of him, shoved through the opening in the bar's hours before, and dumped onto the floor like trash for him to eat. He'd gulped down the single cup of clean water as soon as it entered the cell, leaving the tin sitting empty in the dirt, mimicking his own body. It was the same every day, he was given just enough to keep him alive, just enough to keep him hopeful.

"You're not dead are ya?" A voice chuckled. "We've been placing bets on how long you'll last, and I'm not up for another two weeks."

"You wish," he coughed, inhaling the dust around him.

"Yeah, that's what I thought," the guard answered, still laughing. "You're a fighter."

"That he is," another voice added. He knew that tone; that sick, sinister song that came from her lips. He cringed as it rang in his ears.

He put his hands to his sides, pushing against the ground. His arms trembled, and the muscles in his shoulders ached, but he'd managed to get to his knees. His vision was blurred and faded, but he could see her standing just outside the cell, her face framed by the bars that held him captive.

"Happy to see me?" She asked, her smile the only sharp image in his vision. "I was walking around the castle, allowing the fresh air to wash over me, and I thought 'I wonder what my friend is up to', and so here I am to check on you."

"Leave me alone," he cried. "Just—leave me."

"I'm afraid I can't do that," she answered. "You see, I've come here with good news. You've been locked down in this dungeon for a year now. It's an anniversary and those are worth celebrating."

He couldn't reply, only weeping as his body swayed weak and unsteady.

"I have a special gift for you," she continued, ignoring his pain. "Tonight, at sundown, you'll be taken from this cell, and you'll be released into the world once again."

Still no words escaped him. It was too much to hope for, and he wouldn't allow himself to believe it.

"I thought you'd be happier about the news." She shrugged. "Of course, if you'd rather stay down here until you die, I'll allow it."

"No," he begged. "I want to go. Please."

"Please what?" Her twisted smile returned, making him ill. If he had anything left in his stomach he would have vomited that second.

"Please, Your Majesty, my queen, allow me to leave this place."

"That's more like it. I expect respect from you going forward. Otherwise we'll have to arrange another stay here."

He whimpered and she leaned in closer. Her hands wrapped around the bars of his cage, and she pushed her face against the cold metal.

"There's one more thing you should know," she whispered. "Someone in Kelda, for some reason or another, has been spreading horrible stories about you. From what I hear, you travel to different lands, luring people into a false sense of ease, and then when they finally drop their guard, you attack. Rumor is that you prey on the elderly and the weak. You like knowing they can't fight you off as you torture them to death, and after you're done you steal all their processions.

"Once you've stocked up your cart with whatever you think is worth anything, you take the objects back home and display them in your shop. They say you sell the dead people's belongings to innocent customers who are completely unaware of the horrific ways you acquired them. I'm sorry to tell you, but these rumors have driven your father out of business, and they've had to take your family's home to pay his debts."

"My parents," he sobbed. "What happened to my parents? Where are they?"

"I don't know," she shrugged, standing upright. "I don't really care either. Finding them is something you'll have to figure out when you leave here. I do hope you can find a way to pull yourself together now that your name's been dragged through the mud. I would hate for this reputation you've been given to ruin your life. That would be disastrous."

The queen turned her back, fading into the darkness beyond his cell door, followed close behind by the faceless guard. The young man fell back to the ground. His face slid once more against the rough flooring, but he felt nothing. He was numb, never knowing if he'd ever feel again.

TWENTY-THREE

Camp was made in the shadow of the looming mountain, but the size of the stone did little to shield them from the weather. As night began to fall so did the snow, weighing down their blankets with a cold, wet touch. Rya and Cam sat shoulder to shoulder, pressed together with one blanket wrapped around their torsos, and the other over their laps. Even with their efforts, Cam shivered in the cold night air.

"Here," Rya smirked, taking Cam's hands between hers. The heat came easily enough, but Rya had to keep her focus to make sure she didn't burn her.

"Thanks," Cam whispered. "I forgot you're a human flame."

"I can't do it too long, unless I want to wear myself out. But it's worth it to keep you from freezing."

"Does it feel the same to you as it does me? Is the magic warm like fire in your veins?"

"It's a heat," Rya replied, "but different. I've always thought of it like a thunderstorm growing inside me." She envisioned the energy humming within as charged tendrils that stretch throughout her body. Once it reached her hands the magic would build as it waited to strike forward in whatever way she willed it to. "A single bolt of lightning can start a fire to burn down an entire forest, and with a quick snap of my fingers I could do the same."

"That's a dangerous gift to have in the wrong hands. Literally."

"You're right." Rya smirked. "I've spent so many years training and honing my powers to reach the level I'm at. Most people don't get that far. There's a lot of physical pain that comes from exercising magic, and many have a low threshold for injury. They stop when it gets to be too much, but I kept pushing through. I had nothing to lose, and so I suffered the agony and aches to gain the reward."

"Nothing to lose," Cam repeated. "That's such a sad concept. I can't imagine growing up without anyone to care about you."

Rya huffed. "Neither of my parents did anything for me that wasn't motivated by their own selfish reasons. My mother was more cunning than my father, and she groomed me for years without me knowing. Each day since

I was born, she would tell me that I would be her star. I was to be her way up society's ladder."

"Your father was a lord, wasn't that enough?"

"That was just the start for her. My mother was born a farmer's daughter, with little money to her name. The one quality she did have was natural beauty. She knew the value of that beauty, and as she came of age, she used it to her advantage. My father wasn't shy about his wealth, and as he was usually drunk and stupid it was easy for my mother to lure him in. It wasn't long before he believed he was madly in love with her. Only after they were married did she realize how serious his habits were, and how quickly he was able to drain the gold from their accounts. Her plan to raise her status was failing, and she needed another way out of her inferior life.

"I was five when they cut the servants by half, and by ten they'd reduced that number again. I would notice furniture from the upper rooms disappear, learning later they were sold to keep the lower levels looking lavish. It was important to her to keep up appearances. If anyone had discovered the poverty we were sinking into, I would never have made a wealthy match for marriage. That was my only reason for living. She planned on selling me to the highest bidder like a pig for slaughter, collecting the gold for herself as some reward for birthing me."

"That's horrible." Cam squeezed her hand, giving the smallest gesture of concern.

"She always told me that a boy could only rise to the level of his father, but that a girl had assets that would raise her to the top. She said no one would love me if I weren't beautiful. No one would ever want me if I weren't perfect. I tried so hard to be everything she wanted from me, but inside I was dying to be free. I never wanted to use my looks to trick a lord into marrying me or sleep my way into a castle. That was her life, her way of getting by, not mine. I fought back in small ways where I could, but in the end, she won. I could do nothing to stop her. She had convinced Gerrod to take me to the Isles where I was to be married to Gavin. I turned fifteen on my way to his kingdom."

"Ouch," Cam gasped. She had yanked her hands free and was waving them outside the blankets, the bright red of her skin glowing in the darkness.

"I'm so sorry," Rya apologized, shrinking into herself. "I guess I forgot to concentrate, and let the heat get away from me."

"It's alright," Cam smiled, still cooling her palms in the night air. "It's my fault for drudging up your past. If you don't mind me asking, where's your mother now?"

"Dead," she answered. "She caught an illness shortly after I left with Gerrod. It was a cruel fate for her to die before I ever made it to the Isles, before she could collect on the money she'd been promised. I was told she'd passed from contaminated food, the result of her buying cheap cuts and rotten produce. I could never prove her death was due to magic, but a part of me that feels I played an unknown roll in it all. Even if I hadn't, there's comfort in believing the lie."

"Did she really do what you said before—the thing about burying the babies?"

"Yes."

Rya hung her head. It was the one part of her family she had any sadness towards, and she hesitated about telling the story. She had blurted it out before in a moment of rage and worry, but somehow the idea of whispering it now was terrifying. The intimacy of the moment was one she wanted to avoid and grab onto all at once.

"I had always suspected something was wrong," Rya continued. "I only knew my brothers existed because of my father. When he was drunk he would stumble out back to lay next to one of the mounds. He'd cry this awful wailing sound, and mumble about his lost boys. My mother never spoke of them at all until I was older. We'd had a fight about one thing or another and she threatened me. She told me if I didn't learn my place she'd bury me out back like she did the others. She said she could take my life as easy as she gave it, and no one would be the wiser. Combined with her feelings on the financial prospects of men, I knew that she had killed them."

They sat in the darkness, not speaking, not moving. The air around them was heavy with the revelation, but Rya felt lighter. The secrets she'd held onto for so many years had rested on her chest like a boulder, and by speaking the words the stone had rolled away, leaving her able to breathe again.

"Thank you." She spoke so softly she wasn't sure Cam could hear her. She could feel herself crying, but for the first time she didn't want to brush away the tears. She wouldn't hide the feeling she had right now, sitting in the snow, next to the girl she was falling for, bearing her heart for her to see. "I—needed to get that out. I'm sorry you had to hear it."

"I'm not," Cam replied. She placed her hands back in Rya's and smiled. "I don't ever want you to hide who you are, or where you came from. I want to always see you—the real you—no matter what."

Cam leaned in, resting her lips on Rya's cheek, kissing away a tear that had rested on her skin. The touch was soft and light, the same as the kiss of the snow that began to fall over them.

TWENTY-FOUR

Three days had passed since they'd started the trip around the mountains, and Cam was beginning to doubt their decision. They could have climbed over the pass within a day, she was sure of it. The snow had grown thick on the rocky terrain, and while they were still able to ride, the horses were forced to walk across the icy ground. Her attitude was made worse by the fact that they seemed to be lost.

"I know it was on this end of the range," Norell argued. "I swear it."

The plan had been to find the tribe that owned the land near the Craken Peaks, and hopefully secure a night's shelter with them. As they reached the other side of the mountains, they couldn't see anything but the harsh landscape.

"There's no one out here but us," Cam replied. She was trying to keep calm but the cold nights of restless sleep had taken their toll.

"It should be here," Norell snapped back.

"I'm not arguing that," Cam said. "I've studied the maps more than anyone, and yes there's supposed to be a tribe here, but there's not."

"Which one was it again?" Thane asked. "The Uhan?"

"No, the Ebez," Norell answered.

Cam was just about to call it quits, to order them all to start east. She thought their only hope would be stumbling across a village before the Cape, when she spotted a thin white ribbon rising into the air.

"Look," she shouted, pointing towards the smoke. "It's got to be from a fire, right?"

"But where's it coming from?" Thane asked, squinting through the light flakes of snow. "I only see the mountain side."

"Wait," Norell said, grabbing Thane's arm. "Do you hear that?"

They all stopped. Five pairs of eyes searched the horizon as the deep growling grew louder and multiplied. Suddenly they were coming from all sides- long sleds being powered by a crew of dogs. The riders were bundled up in thick pelts, and cloth kept their faces nearly hidden. As they trapped the gang between them, one of the riders jumped off and walked forward, pulling down her face wrapping. She had the same brown skin as Norell, and the same stubborn look on her face.

"Who are you?" The woman shouted. Her words were in the common tongue, but her accent reflected her true heritage. "Why are you here in our land?"

"We are simply passing through," Norell answered before anyone else. "We ask for your help in sheltering us for a night, allowing us to escape the cold. After that, we will be on our way."

The other riders mumbled through their masks, each speaking a language Cam couldn't translate. The woman nodded at their words and turned back to Norell.

"We have no safety to offer you," the woman scoffed. The thick hood of her coat couldn't mask the disapproval she had for them. "Be on your way and leave us in peace."

"We need your help," Thane added. "If you could only—"

"I have already given you our answer," she snapped. "I suggest you keep moving."

Norell jumped off the horse and ignoring Thane's protests charged up to the woman. The dogs jumped and yelped with excitement, and the other riders all shouted, ready to move on Norell. The woman held up her hand to them, and waited with her mouth pinched tight. In the mix of the wind and the sound of the dogs, Cam could only see her cousin mouth two words. A heartbeat later, the woman nodded her head, shouted to the other riders, then mounted her sled and took off.

"Follow her," Norell ordered, pulling herself back up onto Rainy. In a flash they were off, trailing behind the group of sleds as they followed them closer to the mountain side.

Cam pushed Zara faster, riding alongside Thane's and Norell. "What did you say to her?" She yelled over the distance.

"A phrase my mother taught me before she left. The one she said would mean the most. The Ebez words that mean *always family*."

It was clear why they couldn't see the tribe's camp the second they rode up to it. The side of the mountain towered over them, but once they looked closer they could see it was different than its backside. Round holes had been carved from the rock itself, creating deep rooms for the people to house in. Ledges and pathways connected the different levels, and thick animal hide blankets hung in the openings. Some of the chambers had small holes above the doorway, allowing smoke from an indoor fire to escape the space. The Ebez had used the natural elements around them to create a secure and serene village of their own, and the result was amazing. Cam couldn't help but stare in awe at the ingenuity and dedication of their work.

The flattest part of the camp was in made into a sort of village center, with most of the action taking place in the big open area. A group of men and women worked on skinning a few deer that had been recently killed, throwing the meat into several large pots that hung over the fires. All around them the dogs sat with tails wagging, eager for the scraps that didn't make it into the meal. Children ran in circles, pretending to shoot each other with dull tip arrows, while a younger group sat staring wide-eyed at an elderly woman. She was telling them a story, and Cam didn't need to know the language to suspect it was full of suspense and intrigue.

The mysterious woman stopped them near the edge of the camp and tied off the horses. Without speaking, she waved at them to follow her up one of the ledges. Cam's hand ran across the wall while she walked, tracing the intricate designs they had carved into stone. Some were swirls and patterns. Along another ledge was etchings of animals and stars. The Ebez had not just dug out holes to live in, they had decorated the nature around them with their culture.

"This place is beautiful," Cam breathed.

They climbed one more ledge, stopping at the highest point that Cam could see. The woman reached out and moved back the bear skin flap of one of the homes.

"Inside," she grumbled, gesturing to them. "You'll need to ask permission to stay."

Cam hesitated, but Norell nodded and walked past her, disappearing behind the curtain. Cam tried to size up the woman, unsure if they were wise to trust her. She was one to follow her gut, but the strangers stone face and blank expression left Cam's intuition wanting. If there was one thing that made Cam uneasy, it was not being able to follow her feelings.

"We have no choice," Rya whispered, passing her by. Sora and Thane were already inside as well, leaving Cam alone on the ledge with the grumpy woman. She sighed. If she couldn't trust herself about the Ebez, she could at least trust Norell.

The interior wasn't what she'd expected. The cold hole in the side of the mountain had disappeared behind thick blankets that hung on the walls and covered the ground, draping every inch of the space in warmth. Cam thought it wasn't a pit but a cocoon that she could snuggle up in and forget about the snow falling outside.

A middle-aged man stood at the end of the room, his honey colored eyes glowing golden in the flicker of the candles that lit the space. He wore a bronze medal emblazoned with the face bear pinned to base of his jet-black ponytail. The eyes of the beast stared down at them over his head, and his aura held the essence of the animal as if they were one.

"I'm told you are looking for some help?" He said in the same accent as the woman. "Which land did you come from?"

Cam looked to Norell. The girl was standing tall, her shoulders back and her head held high. Some piece inside her had awoken as she faced the leader of her mother's people. Her eyes were lit and vibrant. The air around her seemed to shudder as she spoke. Cam could only believe that they were meant to arrive here. A force had guided Norell to her other home.

"We are from the Ashen Forest to the south of these mountains," Norell answered. "We are asking for shelter for one night, maybe two if you're so kind. We are traveling to the Ivory Cape and need to rest before we continue."

The man looked past her at the rest of them, who were all trying their best to hide behind her narrow frame. His eyes took in each of their faces, one at a time, studying their features with great interest. When he'd finished, he looked back to Norell with a suspicious frown.

"You're all from the Ashen Forest?" He asked.

Norell thought for a moment before answering. "We were born all over Kelda, but that is where we come from

233

now. My mother was from the Ebez, and so my roots are split between here and the Ashen. Sora," she said pointing to the boy, "also has family from the north, but he was never lucky enough to know them. We come to you with nothing but respect and hope you will find it in your hearts to help us."

He looked at them all once more, his eyes lingering a little longer on Rya's face, and Cam grew nervous. The Black Queen was a name known all over Kelda, and Cam assumed that included the northern tribes. If they felt the same way about Rya as the other kingdoms did, she wasn't sure they could convince them to give them shelter.

"You may stay one night," he answered. "Winter's already begun, and we can't spare more than that for outsiders."

"Thank you," Norell said with a bow. "Your kindness will be repaid."

She turned around and ordered them with her eyes to go, but before they could escape the cave, he stopped them once more.

"You said your mother was from the Ebez, what was her name?"

Norell paused, her cheeks turning pink under her bronze skin. "Yukie," she answered. "She left here many years ago."

The man's eyes lit up. "Yukie is your mother?"

234

"Was my mother. I'm sad to say she passed away some time ago."

His face shifted to sudden sadness. The light that had just burned in his eyes was snuffed out. Cam dropped her eyes to her feet, uncomfortable being in the middle of this moment.

"You must know," the man continued, "my name is Aero, and Yukie—your mother—was my sister."

"Oh," Norell gasped. It was clear she had no expectations of meeting family, and she was upset to have broken the news of Yukie's death in such a way. Norell's mouth kept moving, but no sound came out, leaving them all standing in an awkward silence.

The man called out without warning, and the sudden noise startled Cam. She hadn't realized he'd yelled a name until their guide from before appeared again in the doorway. She peeked her head inside, still hard faced and pouting.

"Take these ones to the spare tent." He held out a hand towards Norell. "This one I need to spend more time with. I'm afraid we have much to discuss."

Cam watched as Norell took his hand. They sat on the fluff of the blankets, legs crossed, facing each other. She wanted to demand to stay, to keep her cousin safe in the company of this outsider, but she knew she couldn't. He was no stranger to Norell, not really. With a heavy heart

235

she followed the woman back onto the pathway and down to the hole on the farthest end. The blanket covering the opening wasn't as thick as the other, and inside only the ground was lined with hides. Still, it was a thousand times better than sleeping exposed to the chill of the night.

"It'll be alright," Thane whispered as they rested on the ground. "Norell's in good hands. Her mother always spoke highly of the Ebez."

"I hope you're right," Cam sighed.

She laid back, resting her head on a bunched-up portion of bear skin. The ceiling of the cave glittered with specks of minerals. If she unfocused her eyes they looked like the stars, and soon they were guiding her to sleep.

TWENTY-FIVE

Rya was knocked out almost the second she hit the ground. The long sleepless nights, and cozy feel of the cave was comforting, and she drifted off without a second thought. She had no way to telling how long she'd been dreaming, since the only natural light was hidden behind the cave's covering. All she knew as she opened her eyes was that she wasn't the only one awake.

"What did you tell him?" Cam whispered. Rya could see her outline in the darkness. Her form a shade darker than the air around her, and at her side was another.

"I told him I'd have to think about it," Norell answered. She was twirling some object in her fingers. "I didn't know what to say."

Rya closed her eyes again but kept her ears open.

"How long does he want you to stay?" Cam asked, her voice sad.

"I don't know that either. He wants me to know the family I have here. He wants to teach me about the Ebez. He thought maybe my mother was ashamed of them and where she'd come from. She sent a few birds with news over the years, but when they stopped he thought it was because she was too busy living her new life in Kelda and wanted to forget her past. I told him how proud she was of her tribe, and about how she would tell me the Ebez stories as I fell asleep. I know there was more she would have shared with me had she not died, and now I have that chance. I just—how do I say no to him? All I've ever wanted was my family, and here they are welcoming me with open arms, how do I turn that down?"

Cam sighed. "Remember the stories you used to tell me, the ones where you said you owned me?"

"Yes," Norell laughed. "I told my parents since I could talk that I wanted a baby brother or sister. They never gave me one, but then your mother announced that she was expecting and we moved into the castle to help take care of her. When you finally came, I truly believed you were mine. You were the baby sister the queen gave to me, since my own parents would not, and I refused to leave your side."

"You bit the mender," Cam added.

"I didn't like what he was doing, poking at you like that. He needed to learn that no one would harm you while I was around."

"You've done a great job in making sure that's true." Cam's voice softened. "I know you're always trying to protect me, but I never want that to be at the expense of your own destiny. If this is where you want to be, I'll support your choice. You will always have a place in the Ashen Forest, no matter how long you're away."

No more words were spoken, the only sounds were hushed sniffles of their tears. Rya opened her eyes once more and looked to the figure sleeping across from her. Thane's body trembled as he forced himself to remain still; he too had heard them.

The morning had come and with it the inevitable goodbye. The cold air stung Rya's lungs, and she pulled the thick cloak tighter around her shoulders. They had all received one as a final gift from Aero before they departed. She bounced on Eclipse, eager to get moving, but she understood the delay. If she'd found a secret family that was desperate to love her, she might have the same feelings about leaving. She watched as Norell hugged her new uncle one last time before climbing up behind Thane.

"Are you sure about this?" Cam asked once they were outside Aero's earshot. "You don't have to leave them."

"I made my decision the moment I talked to you," Norell answered. "I'm happy to have come here, but Aero and the Ebez will be here after our journey is done. They share part of my blood, but you have always been my family. I won't turn my back on that for anything."

Cam nodded, exchanging a look with Norell that Rya could only describe as pure joy. After the moment had passed, Norell stared at the back of Thane's head, her cheeks glowing red.

"I couldn't leave him either," she said in a softer voice than Rya had ever heard from her. "Before we left the castle, he promised to marry me when we return, and if I let you run off and get yourselves killed, that can't happen."

"Is that true?" Cam gasped. "Thane, did you actually propose?"

He nodded, his cheeks burning as much as Norell's. "I may have done something like that."

Norell nudged his shoulder, and they both laughed. Rya couldn't help but stare at them, watching the casual way they toyed with each other, the way their touches seemed gentle and full of promise. They were already one being, and yet remained themselves at the same time. It was exactly what love should be and watching it made her ache.

She found her eyes wandering to Cam, watching the breeze tinge her cheeks pink. Her hands were dry from the cold, and her hair had lost its shine. She laughed at some joke that Rya had missed, and she noticed the princess' smile was crooked, rising a little higher on the left side than the right. Everything about her in that moment was plain and ordinary. She'd was stripped of any royal imagery and had left behind all privileges. She was just a girl on a horse, and to Rya, she was the most beautiful person she'd ever seen.

"You alright?" Cam had caught her staring.

"Yes," Rya choked. "Yes, I'm fine."

"It's making you nervous, isn't it?"

"What is?" Rya's face lost all color.

"We're getting closer," Cam replied. "We'll be at the Ivory Cape in days, and then it's on to confront Kasen. I'm sure the resolution of all this is exciting, but it's got to be nerve-wracking also."

"Yes, of course." Rya was relieved that she hadn't been found out, especially with the others so near. "It's all going to be over soon."

Sora leaned forward, whispering into her ear as they watched Cam pull ahead.

"I know you love her," he breathed, "but will you be able to leave her?"

"I will always do what I must," Rya answered with a sigh.

The landscape shifted from the rocky jagged ground of the mountains to rolling hills and low bushes. The area beyond the Craken Peaks was desolate, with poor soil for farming, and the grass held little nutrients for livestock. With no homes to block the view, the border of the Ashen Forest could be seen on one side, and the coastal cliffs on the other, giving the stretch of land the informal name—the gap. The best part about the gap was that with no large trees to maneuver through, and no rocky terrain making the ground unstable, the horses were able to gallop across at full speed, making up for any time they'd lost traveling around the mountain's base.

Back in the open, Rya's mind moved once more to Nix. He was still out there, she could feel it. The Kael were skilled at tracking, even at night, and she knew he was hiding somewhere, waiting to strike. The others weren't as worried, joking that he'd be a fool to attack them with no cover, and bragging about him being outnumbered. One thing Rya had learned while running before, was never to underestimate a Kael.

TWENTY-SIX

The days flew past as quickly as the scenery around them, and the horses pushed forward. The cool breeze that came up and over the cliff side kept the chill from fading, but at least the snow had disappeared, making the ride easier to handle. The gap was flat with the exception of a scatter of prickly shrubs that dotted the browning grass. The dull colors blurred together like swirls of marble until the sun had ended its journey and disappeared, taking the light with it. Still they rode, pressing forward until they recognized the shimmer of the moonlight on the water's surface. The horses slowed to stop, and the five them all stared at the vast expanse of black ahead of them.

"We've reached it," Cam cheered. "Veil Lake."

Their arrival had given them all a second wind, and they worked together to put the camp in place. They moved as one unit, finding wood, starting the fire, and laying the blankets. Rya stopped for a moment and watched the rest of them. A smile tugged at her lip as she realized it was the first time in her life that she was part of a team. In fact, it was the first time she'd felt included at all. The happiness that tickled her was quickly pushed aside by guilt and fear. Sora was the only one of them who knew the real plan. The others were blissfully unaware that in the end it would be her, and her alone.

The fire was still flickering as they finished their dinner. Thane had taken Sora to the lake and when they'd returned, they brought with them a couple large fish, making the night's meal rather filling. Rya sat back and watched Sora chase lightning bugs on the outskirts of the camp, while Thane and Norell played some game that involved a board drawn in the dirt and the capturing of each other's rocks. Thane had just mumbled some curse words at Norell's move when Cam stood up.

"Come with me," she said, waving to Rya.

"Where do you think we're going?" The queen scoffed.

"To the lake. It's been ages since I've had a proper bath and I think a swim will make up for that nicely."

"Absolutely not. That water will be ice cold, and I'm not getting in there."

"Are you scared?" Cam teased, backing away.

"I'm not scared of anything," Rya replied.

She was on her feet, following Cam from the warmth of the fire. The lake wasn't far, but with the slope downward and the small trees that lined its edge, they could no longer see the others. Standing on the bank Rya reconsidered her decision.

"This is insane," she pointed out. "You know Norell is going to throw a fit if she finds us. We should just go back."

"No way. I came to swim and that's what I'm going to do." Cam stripped off her shirt, and Rya looked away, catching only a hint of the moonlight on her pale skin. Next were the boots and then the pants. Her clothes in a pile on the shore, Cam took a running jump into the water.

"It's not that bad," she laughed. "Get in here."

This is a bad idea. Rya removed her boots, kicking them next to Cam's stack of clothes. *Thane will have my head for this.* Her arms crossed in front of her, grabbing the bottom of her shirt and pulling it over her head. *This is only going to make things harder.*

She jumped.

"You're a liar," Rya shivered. "You said it wasn't cold."

"I know," Cam smirked. "I wasn't going to be stuck freezing in here alone."

The queen shook her head, then fumbled through the water with her arms outstretched. When her hands found Cam's, she pulled the girl towards her. They were naked—

hidden under the darkness of night, but still naked. She wrapped her arms around Cam's body, the cold water pushed aside by their forms. The heat was almost instant, and the orange glow surrounded them both. Rya closed her eyes, trying to keep her mind on the magic, and not focusing on the body pressed against hers. Her senses tingled as every part of her skin came alive. She was aware of Cam's knee slightly above her own, dangerously close to her thigh. Her fingertips traced the dip in Cam's lower back, and she steadied them from moving lower. Cam's hair was over her shoulder, tucked between them now, tickling the soft skin of Rya's chest. Every nerve was awake and eager, wanting and waiting for the princess' touch.

"Rya?" Cam's voice brushed her ear. She paused, and then louder than expected, the princess yelped. "Okay, something just touched my foot."

Rya smiled until the slimy skin of some hidden creature brushed against her leg. With a squeal she released Cam and the two of them started kicking wildly towards the shore. Their arms flailed and splashed in all directions until they reached the bank and clambered onto the cool ground. Lying under the light of the moon, soaking wet and shivering, the two broke into laughter.

"That's not what I expected," Cam smiled. "Sorry I dragged you out here."

Rya smirked. "It was worth it."

With the moment passed, and their skin turning blue, the girl's started to put their clothes back on. With their backs to each other, they tried to hide their stolen glances and curious looks, and each of them pretended not to notice the other's. Rya's shirt clung to her wet back, and her pants fought against her when she pulled them up. Winning the battle, Rya sat down to shove her feet into her boots when Cam appeared next to her.

"I love the stars," Cam smiled. She was leaning back on her hands, looking up at the night sky. Her own outfit was crooked and wrong, as if the clothing wanted to be free from her skin as much as Rya wanted them to.

"Yes," she nodded. "They can be beautiful."

Cam's hand moved towards her, the light touch caressing Rya's fingers. She closed her eyes again, but this time she allowed her thoughts to be of nothing but Cam.

TWENTY-SEVEN

The queen looked gorgeous in the light of the moon. The silver glow washing over her olive skin, highlighting the contours of her face. Cam had almost let herself go in the water, almost giving in to what she knew she shouldn't have. The sudden magical heat mixed with their bodies, and it was too perfect, until some mysterious water monster ruined it. Sitting on the shore next to Rya, she couldn't help but wish she could go back and recapture that moment, turning it into something more.

"Can I ask you something?" Rya whispered. She'd pulled her hand away from Cam's, resting her arms on her knees. The sudden distance was heavy and wrong.

"Of course," she nodded.

"Can you tell me about Hannah?"

Of all the questions Cam expected Rya to ask, that was not one of them. Hannah's name should never have spilled over her lips. She'd never wanted to talk about her, not to Rya, but it was too big a piece of her heart and her past. She didn't want to lie.

"She was from a kingdom beyond the Halton Sea," Cam answered. "She came here looking for safety from some bad people, and we took her in. She was given a room in the inner ward, and we worked hard to keep her safe. She was always so grateful, and so sweet." The memory of Hannah's laugh pounded in Cam's head. It would burst from her lips before fading to a giggle at the end. She could see the curls of her auburn hair hanging over her shoulders, burning bright like fire when the sunlight hit it.

"You loved her." Rya added. It wasn't a question.

Cam nodded. "I did. I fell for her—hard. That had always been her plan. After a few months of luring me in, she told me the truth. Her father was a king and planned to attack the Ashen Forest from the sea. She was sent as a spy to gain information on our port, our army, our castle, and anything else. She said playing with my emotions was just part of the fun, and that it made it easier for her to get what she wanted. My heart wasn't just broken, it was shattered."

Rya's hands kept clenching and releasing, the way they did every time she grew angry. She couldn't tell if Rya's reflex was from hearing about Hannah's betrayal, or the simple fact that Cam had loved her.

"What happened to her?" she asked. "I'm assuming you punished her after learning the truth."

"She left," Cam replied. She knew it wasn't the answer Rya wanted, but it was the truth. "She ran off that night, escaping into the woods. I could have stopped her, but I didn't. I could have sent the guards to try and find her, or shut down all boats leaving our port, but I said nothing. I allowed her to flee with the information she'd gained. In a moment of weakness, I forgot to put the good of the Ashen before myself, and it could have cost us dearly. Thankfully, nothing ever came of it. I never saw Hannah again, and no one has ever tried to attack us. I mean—until Kasen, but that's a different story."

"Is it?" Rya had that look, the same one she'd had each time she tried to push Cam away. "I came to you looking for safety. I used you for my own reasons, and in the process, I've drawn you too close to me. I've done horrible things to people, and I can't guarantee that you won't be one of them."

"I can," Cam replied. She shifted her body and knelt down in front of Rya.

"You aren't safe with me." Rya was shaking her head. "I'm tainted. My heart is as black as they say, poisoned by my past and my actions. You can't know who I am based on our time in the forest. I forgot my true self since I've been with you, and now you've been deceived again."

Cam lifted Rya's chin, forcing her to look at her. "Will you stop saying that I don't know you. They call you the Black Queen. They say you're evil. You don't get a reputation like that for handing out puppies to orphans. I know exactly the type of person you are, and I think that scares you. You say you lost your true self when you appeared in my kingdom, but I think the truth is the opposite, I think you found it."

Rya's dark eyes bore into hers, burning with either rage or desire. Cam took a breath, waiting to see which would come forward, knowing either reaction would burn her in one way or another. In a flash, Rya's lips were on hers, and Cam melted into them. Both pairs of hands grasped fistfuls of clothing, desperate to eliminate any barrier between their flesh. The ground was cold against Cam's lower back, and Rya was over her, their lips parted and their tongues dancing together. The queen's fingertips grazed her stomach, moving upwards under her shirt. Her mouth moved to Rya's neck, nipping at the curve that met her shoulder and then kissing it gently.

"Wait," Rya gasped, and Cam froze.

"I'm sorry," Cam panted. "I shouldn't have—"

"No, not that. Listen." They both waited, trying to calm the quickness of their breaths. Cam was confused, and opened her mouth, wanting to ask what she was expecting, when the awful shriek cut through the air.

"Norell!" she yelled. "We need to get back to the camp!"

The scene Cam imagined as she ran back up the hill was nothing compared to the reality in front of her. Norell was on one knee on the far end of the campsite, holding herself up with her spear, ignoring the blood that ran from her busted lip down her chin. Her free arm was stretched out, shielding a terrified Sora behind her. Both of them were staring in horror at the bodies in front of them.

On the ground near the fire the two men struggled against each other. Thane was on his back, both his hands holding the hilt of the large dagger, trying to keep the tip from plunging down on him. Nix was on top, doing his best to force the knife closer to Thane's throat. They were so focused that neither noticed the girls had returned.

A growl escaped Rya's lips followed by the bolt of white-hot lightning that stretched from her hand to Nix. The electricity hit him square in the shoulder and the force of it thrust him backwards. He landed with a thud on the dirt, still holding his weapon in his hand. Cam rushed to Thane's side, helping sit him up as he gasped for air. Rya stood over them, teeth clenched together, and a ball of blue energy growing between her palms. With another grunt she pushed both hands out in front of her chest, throwing the orb towards the assassin with all her strength.

"You'll never win," he laughed, watching it coming towards him. He'd barely spoken the words when he rolled across the dirt and scurried into the low brush, completely dodging the attack.

Cam was just helping Thane to his feet when Rya glanced back at her. The queen looked over at Sora who was cradled in Norell's arms, trying to stop his hands from shaking. Without a word, she darted off into the darkness after Nix.

"Rya, no!" Cam shouted.

She was quick on her feet, but Rya was fueled by rage which made her just as fast. Cam pushed her legs harder than she had before. The queen's shadow was ahead of her, growing closer with each step she took.

"You coward," Rya screamed into the night. "I'm right here, come get me."

Cam slowed down as she approached, taking timid steps towards her.

"Rya," she said, her voice quivering. She gave no reply. "Rya," Cam repeated, this time with a hushed voice. "Rya—you need to come with me. This is what he wants. He wants you alone and vulnerable. It's the only way he can get you."

She screamed again, this time a vicious, haunting sound that sent a chill down Cam's spine. She reached out with trembling fingers, hesitating for a moment then wrapping her hand around the queen's arm. Her body was on fire. Instinct told Cam to let go, as if she was grabbing a hot coal from the oven, but she couldn't. She could feel Rya's fury, her hurt, her pain, all in that touch. The burning inside her spread into Cam's fingers, pumping through her blood until it reached her heart, connecting them.

The pain was overwhelming as the raging inferno that burned in Cam's veins consumed her. Still she held on, not wanting to break free from Rya, fearing that if she did they might lose her forever. Her vision was turning white, and the world spun around her. She didn't know what to do next, but she knew that she needed to protect Rya. She needed to keep her safe.

"What the—" Rya gasped, looking down at Cam's hand. Her fingers were still wrapped around her arm, but now they were outlined in a cobalt light. A blast of cold energy flooded from Cam's flesh, soothing the fire that inflamed them both. Cam fell to her knees, and as the connection between them broke, the glow on her palm disappeared.

Rya dropped to her side, holding Cam's arms to help steady her. Cam was drained, like she could fall asleep and never wake again. She looked at Rya with heavy eyes.

"What happened?" She asked.

"You saved me," Rya cried. "I've heard of it happening before. People unleashing dormant bits of magic in a moment of emotion. I've never seen it myself until now."

Cam shook her head, not wanting to admit the truth. She'd felt everything Rya had. It wasn't only the physical pain, but the emotional scars that she'd developed over the years. She had crawled inside Rya's skin, had become her in that moment, and all she wanted to do was help her. She wanted to take Rya's pain away. She wanted to stop her hurting. She wanted to protect her and heal her. Then all of a sudden it was like someone dumped a bucket of ice water on her, and extinguished it all.

"Cam," Rya whispered, staring into her eyes, "if you hadn't stopped me, I don't know what would have happened. I was overcome with my emotions, and I could feel it ripping me apart from the inside out. If you hadn't— I'm afraid I would have lost myself in one way or another."

"Your welcome," Cam joked in a hushed voice. She was so tired, she could barely form the words.

Rya gave a light chuckle, then leaned Cam forward resting her head on the queen's shoulder. Her soft lips pressed against Cam's forehead, while Rya's hand stroked her hair.

"If it weren't for all this," Rya sighed. "If I didn't know how this was all going to end, I could really let myself fall for you."

A tear drifted down Cam's cheek and hang under her chin, desperate not to let go. She understood the feeling.

"That's a shame," Cam replied. "Because I already have."

TWENTY-EIGHT

The look on Thane's face as they appeared was nothing short of pure relief. Rya held Cam up as they shuffled along, the same way she'd been carried to the cave during Nix's previous appearance. Other than a little fatigue, the princess was unharmed, and thanks to her so was Rya. Thane rushed forward and took over, using much less strength to keep Cam upright. Norell was on the ground with Sora, but he was no longer cowering in her arms. He sat next to her with knees pulled to his chest, and his arms hugged his legs, still looking like the little boy Rya remembered.

"Are you alright?" Rya asked, sitting next to him. She smoothed down a piece of his hair. "Tell me what happened?"

"He almost had me," Sora answered. His words didn't match his posture. He was in a ball, scared and small, but his voice was sharp and hard with his anger. "He grabbed me, put a knife to my throat, and said I was his key to getting to you."

Thane spoke next, his tone so much lower it started her. "Norell saw it happening. I grabbed Nix from behind and pulled him off, but he started swinging at me with the dagger and I had to let go. When Norell tried to run off with Sora, Nix turned and smacked her in the face, knocking her to the ground. That's when I jumped back on him. We'd just hit the ground when you two came running back."

"Good thing you did," Norell added. "I wasn't sure Thane could hold him off much longer, and I knew I wouldn't be able to keep Sora safe on my own."

"You *are* safe though," Rya sighed, looking back at Sora. "You're alright now, and we're all here. You don't have to be upset anymore."

"It's just—" Sora faltered, "—I know him."

"What?" Cam asked. Her body was still weak but the revelation had renewed her mind. "What do you mean? You know him from where?"

"I didn't know it was him—not before—but seeing his face so close to mine. His name was Nicolas when I met him. He belonged to Lady Wilma for a while before he disappeared one day."

"She was selling children to the Kael?" Thane growled. "What kind of monster does that? Who gambles with a child's life like that?"

"Wait," Rya interrupted. "You said he belonged to Lady Wilma, and I know she didn't keep kids past a certain age. So that would make him—"

"—Fifteen maybe," Sora answered. "He was always tall and skinny like that, older looking. Everyone thought he was nice, but he made me nervous. It was like I could see the wheels moving in his head as he watched people, like he was sizing us up for some unknown reason. I guess Lady Wilma found the right buyer for someone like that."

Rya thought back to the face that haunted her dreams. The sunken eyes and gaunt cheeks that stared at her through her nightmares. She would never have imagined that the monstrous grin that terrified her belonged to a child.

"We're being hunted by a kid," Thane huffed.

"He may be young," Rya replied, "but he's still a member of the Kael. He's spent years training, the way you and Cam have, only his goal is to murder without feeling. He's not a boy anymore, he's a killer."

"But he's still a person," Norell added.

"Is he?" Rya asked.

"Are *you*?" Norell crossed her arms. "You want us to believe that because his path took him to the Kael, that he trained to be an assassin in order to survive, that makes him less than human. What about your past, and your mistakes. You deserve to live don't you, so why doesn't he?"

"The actions I've taken were to serve justice to those who deserved it. I will admit I've made some poor choices, but they will never amount to the horrible things Nix has done."

"None of this matter," Cam interrupted. "Nix doesn't care what we think of him. He isn't torn between what's right and what's wrong. He's plotting his next move, and he's desperate to kill Rya. That's what matters. If and when he comes for us again, I will be there to fight him, and if he dies in the process—so be it."

Dawn had caught up with them, and most of the others were curled under their blankets, lost in their dreams. Cam rested against her rolled up bedding, staring at the dying embers of their fire. She had taken the first watch against Rya's wishes, wanting some time to herself to process what had happened. She ran her fingertips over her open palm, swearing she could still feel the chill beneath her skin. Glancing at a sleeping Rya, she wondered if it would ever happen again.

"Mind if I join you?" Sora's voice startled her. He was standing with his tiny frame blocking the sunrise behind him. "I couldn't sleep."

"Of course," she nodded. He sat at her side, tucking his legs against his chest. His hands toyed with the straps on his boots. She asked, "Are you really alright?"

"Yeah," he sighed.

"It's okay if you're not," she added. "What Nix did was horrible, and no one would think less of you for being upset."

"It's not Nicolas that's upsetting me," he answered. "I'm unhappy seeing *her* this way."

"Who, Rya? You don't like seeing her what way?"

"Tormented." He paused, still watching the queen sleep. "She's usually so strong and confident. She doesn't let anyone shake her, but this is different. It hurts me to see her so torn."

"You love her very much, don't you?"

The boy nodded. "As do you."

Cam rubbed the back of her neck. Sora had been at Rya's side for years. He was as much her Kinsman as Thane was to her, and she knew he would have the answers to the questions she was afraid to ask Rya.

"Can I ask— "Cam stammered, "—has Rya ever had anyone else that was special to her?"

He shook his head, still staring at his feet. "She's had a handful of young men and women who caught her attention. They would usually disappear into her room and be gone by morning."

261

Cam blushed. She didn't know what she expected him to say, but the image of Rya leading someone else behind closed doors made her stomach drop.

"She was never in love with them," he added, sensing her unease. "My queen says she doesn't believe in love, but I think it's more than that. It's like she believes she's not worthy of love, or that she doesn't deserve it. I'm pretty sure she believes she's destined to die alone."

"Why would she think that?" Cam asked. Her heart cracking at the image of Rya in a cold empty room, closing her eyes and allowing death to take her.

"You've heard her stories. You know everyone in her past has only used her for their own benefit. Love always came with strings attached. It was no surprise that she fell so hard when Victor came along."

"Who's Victor? She's never mentioned him."

Sora blushed and rested his forehead on his knees, hiding his face as his continued. "He was the son of a local shopkeeper. They met when she was thirteen and he was barely a year older than her. He spent years promising to marry her when she turned sixteen. He told her they were going to move into the house next to his father's store, where they would grow old surrounded by a bunch of children and grandchildren. She was days away from fifteen when Gerrod came and dragged her off the Obsidian Isles. She waited and waited for Victor to come rescue her.

She thought when he found out what happened, he'd ride to the Isles and steal her back, but he never came."

"Why not? Did he not really love her?"

"He did," Sora replied, "or at least that's what he told Rya after she had him brought before her in chains. I stood in the corner watching him on his knees in front of her, begging her to understand. He kept saying he was young and naïve, and that her mother was a skilled liar. He claimed he had shown up at Rya's home the morning after she left, demanding to know where she'd been taken. Her mother told him that Rya had gone with Gerrod willingly, and that she was desperate to marry Gavin because he was a prince. By the time he returned home he hated Rya, and cursed her name for fooling his heart."

"Did she believe him, that he didn't know any better?"

"She might have," Sora replied, "but she had returned to Asta after Gerrod had died, hoping that her new status as a queen would allow her to marry her true love. That's when she learned how big Victor's hatred had grown.

"The Isles' soldiers told stories of that visit. She had walked into the town center ready to reunite with Victor, only to find him seething and bitter. He spat at her. He called her names and accused her of sleeping her way to the throne. He attacked her in front of whole town while she stood in silence. The soldiers thought she would explode.

They expected her to turn him to ash where he stood, but instead she walked away. If I had to guess, that was the day the Black Queen was born. She returned to the Isles a darker version of the girl who left."

"What happened to Victor?" Cam asked. "If I've learned anything about Rya, she would not have allowed him to get away with insulting her in that way."

Sora nodded. "She got her revenge. Masked guards had gone to Asta to retrieve him, that's how he ended up begging her for his life. She let him talk without listening, and when he was finished, she answered with only a wave of her hand. The guards locked him in the dungeon in the Isles. For a full year she kept him alive, but miserable. She said it was how she'd felt when Gerrod held her captive. During the months that passed she spread false rumors about Victor across Kelda. By the time he was released his name, his reputation, and his family were ruined. He walked away from the Isles with nothing but the clothes on his back, and no honor to his name. It was the best punishment she could think of to match what he'd done to her."

"Oh, Rya," Cam sighed. Her chest hurt, and her eyes stung.

"'Oh, Rya' what?" The queen was standing in front of them, her head tilted to the side, her eyes searching their faces. "What have you been telling her, Sora?"

264

"Nothing," he lied, scrambling to his feet. "I think I should try and sleep again." He shuffled to his blanket, and pulled the fabric up to the top of his head, hiding his face.

Rya took the seat next to Cam. She ran a finger over Cam's cheek, wiping away a tear that had broken free.

"I would say whatever Sora told you is a lie," Rya huffed. "But he doesn't have that in him."

"He was telling me about Victor," Cam admitted.

Rya flinched at the name. "He was another disappointment in my life. He tricked me into loving him. He made empty promises knowing he'd never keep them. I was a fool for ever thinking I could have a life like that."

"What about what Victor said about your mother, about her lying to him?"

"I'm not an idiot. I know my mother would do such things, but he should have known better. I loved him and had told him a hundred times. He chose to believe her words instead of mine."

Cam wanted to defend him. She wanted to say that the betrayal came from her mother, and not Victor himself, that he was only reacting to the lies she had told, but Cam knew that wasn't entirely true. She imagined someone trying to say Rya didn't love her. She thought of how Rya herself had tried to hide her feelings from Cam, but Cam's gut was stronger than any words. She knew what she felt, and she knew how Rya looked at her. If she had been in

Victor's place, she would have done all she could to get Rya back.

"I promised you I would always protect you," Cam said, taking Rya's hand in hers. "That wasn't a lie. Those weren't empty words."

"I know." Rya nodded. "But some things you can't protect me from."

"Like what?"

Rya sighed. "You can't protect me from myself."

TWENTY-NINE

The Ivory Cape was the smallest of the kingdoms, tucked away at the northeastern edge of Kelda. The harsh winter storms that formed over the Nestian Ocean made harpooning dangerous work, and with blubber oil and large fish their main export, it left only a small number of people willing to live in such a cruel environment.

The snow had started to fall as the road turned north again, forcing them to walk against the strong winds that swooped down from the shore. They slowed the horses to crawling pace, and even with Aero's cloaks the cold gusts caused their teeth to chatter.

"It should be easy to find Gavin here," Thane smiled. He was always smiling. No matter how bad the situation got, he could find a way to be happy. Rya was going to miss that.

"I think we should start there," Cam said, pointing ahead. The shabby building was barely visible in the distance, masked by the flurries of white that zipped around the air. A sign swung back and forth just below the roof. Squinting, Rya could make out the word *tavern* in bold yellow letters. Cam continued, "Maybe someone will know him. If anything, we can see about renting a room and sleeping inside for once."

"Sounds good to me," Thane nodded.

They jumped off the horses, guiding them through the pressing wind. Their footsteps moved a little quicker the closer they got, powered by the idea of a warm meal and soft bed. Rya noticed the lack of footsteps leading to or from the stoop, and that the windows were boarded up. The roof drooped in the middle, and the door to the side stable knocked against the wall with each gust that blew. Without any sign of life, frustrated and angry, she was about to scream when the front door burst open. The sound of voices and clatter exploded from the opening, and a cloud of warmth swallowed her.

"What are you doin' out there?" The man standing in the doorway was tall with thin shoulders but a round belly that stuck out between the straps of his suspenders. His beard was salt and pepper in color, and the bits of face that stuck out were worn from the sun and the sea, reminding Rya of the people in the Isles. He squinted at them through the snow. "Get in here," he ordered. "Unless ya plan on freezin' to death."

A muffled shout inside produced two young men behind him. One of them took the reins from Rya's hands while the other guided the other two horses towards the stable. Another gust stung her cheeks, and she rushed inside behind Thane.

The building had four different fireplaces burning, one on each wall, filling the large open space with warmth. The bar sat in the corner, while the rest of the room was filled with tables and chairs. Men and women were scattered around, laughing and drinking, their cheeks pink from either the cold or the beer, and none seemed to notice the group that just entered.

"Harold," the kind man shouted. "Get these folks some drinks, would ya? They've been wanderin' outside."

The man behind the bar nodded and pulled out five mugs and began pouring a steaming liquid into each of them.

"The name's Clint," the man informed them. He walked to an empty table, waving a hand for them to have a seat. "I take it you all aren't from around here."

"What makes you say that?" Norell asked, sitting across from him.

"No one from these parts would be caught outside durin' the winds. Don't worry, though, they only last a few hours and then they peter out 'till the next day."

The barman set the mugs on the table, and Rya took one of the handles, peering inside at the amber foam under the steam.

"It's not goin' to kill ya," Clint laughed. "It's hot cider, best cure for the winds. O' course, once you're warmed up, ya should try Harold's ale; he brews it himself."

"Thanks," Cam smiled.

"What brings ya this far north?" Clint asked, watching Thane drain his cup.

"Vacation," Rya answered. The man laughed again. He seemed kind enough, but she knew better than to trust just anyone.

"We were hoping to find a room for the night," Cam added. "Do you know if your friend Harold rents here?"

"He does," Clint nodded. "I know he's got a couple free, but some o' ya might have to share."

"That's not a problem," Cam replied.

Clint rose from the table with a smile and made his way across the room, stopping to talk to Harold at the bar. Thane had his head tipped back, trying to get the last few drops of cider from his mug. Rya pushed hers towards him.

"Here," she said, shaking her head. "I'm not going to drink mine."

"I don't know why not," he smiled. "It's delicious."

"I prefer not to drink anything that will impede my judgment." She was watching the men, trying to decipher their words but with the jolly atmosphere around her, she couldn't hear any of it.

Another minute passed before Clint nodded to Harold and returned to the table. He placed two keys in front of them, each marked with a scrap of leather that had a number burned into it.

"Rooms 5 and 6," he said. "They're yours as long as ya need them."

"What's the cost?" Rya asked, suspicious. "For the rooms and the drinks."

"It's on the house," he answered. "As long as ya promise to tell me why the Black Queen is lurkin' around the Ivory Cape."

His words froze Rya's insides more than the cold winds that howled outside. She narrowed her eyes at the stranger. "Who told you we were coming?"

"It's my job to know who's in the Cape. I'm in charge around here, and I can't have just anyone comin' into the village to make trouble."

"You're in charge?" Sora asked, nose scrunched in disbelief. "You're the King of the Cape?"

"The one 'n only," Clint smiled. "We're a small kingdom, and I take pride in workin' these waters next to the men that serve me. The sea is tough, but we're tougher."

"My apologies," Cam replied with a bow of her head. "I'm Princess Camreigh of the Ashen Forest."

"I know who ya are," Clint interrupted. "I know all your names; King Mikkel mentioned it in his letter. What I don't know is why you're here, and what ya need from us."

"My father wrote you?" Cam gasped. Clint reached into his coat pocket and placed a folded piece of parchment in her hand.

"Ya should read it," he urged. "I think you'll find some things have changed since ya left your home."

Cam's eyes scanned the words in silence. Rya could hear each beat of her heart as the seconds ticked by. She searched Cam's face for any sign of the contents. Had Gerrod already won? Had the war been that brutal?

"Oh—" Cam said, laying the note on the wooden tabletop. "That does change things." She looked at the rest of them. "Gerrod was tipped off that we were heading to the Cape. He pulled the army back from the Ashen border, and he's ordered them to surround the Isles' castle. He's barricaded himself inside, waiting for an attack."

"He knows what we came for," Rya added. "He's figured out the plan."

"And what plan would that be?" Clint asked, injecting himself back into the conversation. "I still need to

272

know what ya want with Gavin." His eyebrows raised at the shock on their faces. "Ya don't think I know there's a prince hidin' in my kingdom? Who do you think is the one keepin' him safe all these years? Now you lot show up and the King of the Obsidian Isles is hidin' behind an army and stone walls, I'm not an idiot."

"We need to speak with him," Rya answered. "It's a matter of urgency."

"I'm sure it is," he snorted. "Thing is, I don't know if he's goin' to want to listen. Tell you what, tomorrow I'll meet you down here and either I'll have Gavin with me or I won't. His choice."

Rya's head pounded, and her hands grew warm. It wasn't the way she wanted it, but they had no other choice and Clint knew it.

"Fine," she agreed. "Tomorrow morning."

THIRTY

The two rooms would have been unremarkable to anyone else, but given that the five of them had spent the past nights outside in the cold, the single bed in the middle of the plain space was a dream come true. Vents on the floor allowed the warm air from the bar below to flow upwards. It made the blankets smell like stale cigars with a hint of firewood and ale, it kept the place cozy without the need of a chimney of its own.

The group knew they'd need to share the rooms, but it had been Norell's bright idea to put the boys in one and the girls in the other. Her intention had been to keep an eye on Rya and Cam, but the result was her sandwiched between them on the narrow bed.

"I can't believe this," Rya grumbled, clutching the edge of the mattress.

"Move over," Norell huffed, follow by a shout of pain. "Something just burned me!"

"Sorry," Rya smirked to herself, pulling her hand back from behind her.

That's how it went the whole night. Each of them growling as they yanked back the blanket to fight the chill, then kicking it away again when the combined body heat made them sweat. Shins were kicked, knees dug into another's back, and on at least three occasions Rya gained an extra inch of space by *accidently* using her magic. By the time the morning came, it was clear that none of them had a decent night sleep.

Thane stood in the open doorway, watching them put on their boots, and tuck in their shirts, his face rested and bright. It made Rya bitter to see him so shiny and renewed.

"Come on," he smiled. "We promised to meet Clint after breakfast."

"What if we skip it," Rya frowned. "We could just search the Cape ourselves."

"We need his help," Cam argued. "I know you don't trust him, but he's all we've got. If he wanted to harm us he could have done it last night. It would have been easier to attack you when you were exhausted."

"I'm still exhausted," Rya replied, "only now I'm also agitated."

275

Cam shook her head, and led Rya up by the hand, holding it as they descended the staircase to the main level. The chairs were still scattered around the large room, but the amount of people occupying them was far fewer than the previous night.

The smell of food wafted over the tabletops, and the gnawing hunger in Rya's stomach grew louder. She took a seat at one of the center tables while Thane spoke to the woman behind the bar. It wasn't long after his return that a younger man came rushing through the side door with platefuls of food, placing them in front of the group and then disappearing as quickly as he had appeared. No one spoke as they shoveled the food into their mouths, forgetting the years of table manners and proper dining etiquette they'd learned. They had almost finished when the door swung open.

"I see you lot are off to a good start."

Rya hadn't noticed Clint's limp the night before, or perhaps he hadn't had one when they'd met, but he did now. He pulled up a chair, and swung it around, leaning over the back of it as he smiled at them all.

"I hope ya slept well." He said, polite enough.

"Did you talk to Gavin?" Rya asked, ignoring the attempt at small talk. "Is he coming here to meet with us?"

"That I did," Clint replied with a nod. "He agreed to talk to ya, but I warn ya he ain't happy about it. Also, he

276

doesn't want all y'all gangin' up on him. I promised him it'd be you and the princess. No one else."

Thane shook his head, trying to speak through the mouthful of food he was choking on. "Cam stays with me."

"I understand the concern," Clint frowned, "but that's the way Gavin wants it. There's a meetin' room under the stairs we can use. You'll be right out here, only an arm's length away."

Thane tried to protest again but Cam held up her hand.

"It's fine," she said, shutting Thane down. "Rya and me can handle ourselves."

Clint gave a nod then rose from his seat. The two girls followed him to a door that sat under the staircase, almost a half-foot shorter than they were, forcing them to duck to enter. Inside was completely bare, having no windows and only the one exit, which was now blocked by the King of the Cape standing in their way. Cobwebs gathered in the corners, and the ceiling creaked as someone walked down the steps above. A thin table was squeezed between four weathered chairs, and Rya eyed Clint with caution as they all took a seat.

It wasn't long before the tap on the door broke the tension in the air. The wood groaned as it opened and then shut, guided by the hand of the young man that had entered. He stood for a moment, contemplating if he should sit before pulling out the chair next to Clint and plopping himself down.

If Rya had been searching the faces of the crowd she still wouldn't have recognized him. He'd grown taller and thinner, leaving his high cheekbones protruding from his face. His once brown hair had grown a few shades darker and was longer than he'd kept it in his youth, the lush curls hanging over his forehead and ears. He was dressed in a common fisherman's coat, nothing like the lavish outfits his father made him wear. The soft emerald green of his eyes was the same though, as was the vertical scar that ran over the right side of his plump lips.

"Gavin," she said, smiling at him. "You look well."

"I look well?" He winced. "That's all you have to say to me?"

"Well no—"

"What are you doing here?" His voice was calm but she could hear the rough edges of his words. The years had obviously turned him against her. "Have you come to try and kill me again?"

"What?" Rya had guessed that Kasen would make up some lie to tell Gavin, and it wasn't a shock that he blamed her for the prince's exile, but she was surprised that Gavin would believe it. "I never tried to have you killed. Whatever you've been told is a lie."

"And I'm supposed to just believe you? How do I know you're not lying to me now? You can't think I'm that stupid."

"I would never think that of you," she sighed. "I remember the brief time we spent together before you disappeared, and I'm hoping you do also. I never did anything to hurt you Gavin. Why would I orchestrate such an elaborate plot to have you killed, when I could have done it myself years ago?"

Her choice of words didn't sit well with him, and he hung his head, fuming and refusing to look at her.

"Gavin—" Clint's voice caught and he had to clear his throat before the next words could be spoken. "I've kept ya here as I promised Father Kasen, but I haven't been truthful with ya over these years. I've found out things about that man, things that lead me to believe he isn't who we thought before. I think ya should hear her out. I think she might be able to offer some answers that both of us need."

Gavin nodded, keeping his eyes on the table.

"Kasen lied to a lot of people," Rya sighed. "If you ask anyone in the Isles where Prince Gavin is, they'll tell you that he was kidnapped and murdered years ago. Only Kasen and I knew that wasn't the truth."

"My father?" the young man asked, finally looking her in the eye. "He doesn't know I'm alive? You haven't told him?"

Cam glanced at Rya, a pained expression on her face.

"King Gerrod," Rya continued, "passed away three years ago, not long after you disappeared."

"He's dead?" Gavin's voice held no sadness. No hint of sorrow or loss, just surprise. "Three years, and I've heard nothing about his passing."

"That's my fault," Clint admitted. "Father Kasen told me to keep it from ya. He said there was still great danger for ya out there. I was trying to protect ya."

Gavin stood up, kicking back his chair. The soft spoken, shy boy she'd known those years ago, the one he pretended to be when he'd walked into that small room, had been replaced by the young man he was now. He was raging, angered by the lies and betrayal, fueled by the hatred of his father and his exile. He was feeling it all now, and he was too close to Rya for her to be comfortable with it.

"How did it happen?" He asked. "How long after I left did you wait before marrying my father? How many nights did you spend with him before his death, hiding my whereabouts and plotting your next move?"

"It wasn't like that," Rya shot back. "I married him as he lay dying, and only because Kasen made me. He said it was the only way to save the kingdom. He said others were waiting for Gerrod's death to make their move on the throne, and I had to become queen to keep the Isles safe. You know I never wanted that."

"But you took it, didn't you? And what's become of my father's kingdom—my kingdom? If the rumors I hear are true, you've done horrible things while playing queen."

"I did my best," she replied, attempting to keep her tone calm against his rage. "I tried to rule, but I chose to use fear and pain to keep the people in place. I see now that I was wrong to go that route, and in doing so I've handed Kasen the means to take the kingdom from me. He has attacked me in my own home and driven me out. He has named himself the ruler of the Obsidian Isles and plans on having my head to solidify the title."

"And now you're here? Let me guess, you want me to help you keep your crown, which is my birthright, and which you've stolen from me. You knew I was here, you've admitted that, but you never told anyone. You never sent anyone to find me. You never intended on returning me to my home—my home, not yours— and instead kept quiet the same as Kasen in order to serve your own agenda. You're no better than he is, so what makes you believe I would help you?"

"You're right," Rya shot back. "I didn't want you found. I didn't want anyone to challenge my place on the throne, and I was scared of what your return would mean. I made my choices, and whether or not I believe they were right, they have led us here. You have a choice to make, and I can't tell you what to decide. All I can say is that if you think staying here will keep you safe from Kasen, you're wrong. He'll come after you next. He'll do everything he can to make the rumors of your death true."

"I'm not afraid of Kasen, and I'm not afraid of you. I won't aid you in taking back something that was never yours to begin with."

"You're right," Rya nodded. "I should have never been on that throne, so I have a deal to make. You help me defeat Kasen, and take the kingdom away from him, and I'll step down and hand you the crown. The Obsidian Isles will be yours and yours alone.

Cam's mouth hung open in shock, and Clint's eyes grew twice as wide. Gavin, however, kept his face stony, weighing the offer in his mind.

"I'll accept your offer," he answered, "under one condition."

"What is that?" Rya braced herself.

"After I'm crowned king, I will hold court to decide your punishment for the actions you've taken."

Her mouth went dry. Cam's hand reached for hers under that table, but Rya kept hers folded in her lap where her magic could do no damage.

"I told you I'm not an idiot," Gavin explained. "I know what you've done, and I know the way the people feel about you. If I'm to be a great king to those people I need them on my side and holding you accountable for your actions is the perfect way to accomplish that. You'll answer for it all—torture, theft, treason, murder, and whatever else I learn about along the way."

"You can't be serious," Cam scoffed. "You expect her to hand you the crown and then stand in front of you while you sentence her. Any one of those charges could result in death, why would she ever agree—"

"You have a deal," Rya answered, cutting Cam off.

Gavin held out his hand, and without hesitation Rya took it, shaking their agreement into permanence.

THIRTY-ONE

The silence that followed Rya's deal with Gavin was harder to bear than the deal itself. Cam sat quietly in her chair as Clint and Gavin left the small room under the stairs. She held her tongue while Rya gathered the others from the tavern, and led them up the steps to their rented room. Even as they argued over what to do next the princess didn't say a word, but instead sat on the edge of the mattress with her head in her hands, completely still.

"You have a plan, don't you?" Thane asked. He was leaning against the far wall, stroking the edge of his chin with the back of his fingers. The worry in his eyes had pushed away the constant spark of optimism he'd always held. He was afraid.

The queen glanced down where Sora was sitting against the foot board of the bed, with his legs crossed under him. His hands were fidgeting with the straps of his boot, trying to mask the dread he was feeling as well.

"I do have a plan," Rya replied. "I wouldn't agree to something like that without one."

"Well, what is it?" Norell replied. She was standing next to Thane, their arms brushing together. The closeness made Rya jealous. "There's no telling how many years he'll keep you imprisoned," Norell continued. "Or he could decide to kill you. Have you thought of that?"

Rya shrugged. "Then we'll simply have to convince him not to. He'll be traveling with us all the way to the Isles, we can use that time to change his mind about me."

"What makes you think you can do that?" Norell huffed.

"I won *you* over didn't I?" Rya answered. Norell started to argue, but Thane interrupted.

"She's right," he nodded, finally regaining the light that had briefly gone out. "Gavin must remember Rya from before he came to the Cape, we just need to remind him of that. If we can keep his mind off all the reasons he hates you, he might go easy on you later."

"And what if that doesn't work?" Cam asked, finally breaking her silence. She lifted her head, her red puffy eyes staring directly at Rya. "What if he decides to punish you? What if he chooses to kill you to make himself more popular?"

"Then I run," Rya replied. They were all staring at her now. She knew what they were thinking. She knew the shock they were feeling at her words, but it was the only way to make them feel better. "If we can't convince him to spare my life, then I'll leave Kelda altogether. I'll take Sora, and whatever gold we can manage, and we'll sail to another land. We'll start over, living free like we were always meant to."

"You can't be serious," Cam scoffed. "If you're going to run you need to return to the Ashen Forest. We can protect you."

"No," Rya said, shaking her head. "That's the first place Gavin will look for me, and I won't put you or your father through another war on my behalf. Father Kasen wasn't shy about hiring the Kael to come after me, and I can't promise that Gavin won't to the same. It's too risky."

"This is insane," Norell added. "But it's the best plan we've got."

"That's the spirit," Rya mocked.

Cam stood up. "Alright," she sighed. "If convincing Gavin to like you is our only way, then that's what we'll do. I just want you to know, I don't like any of this."

"I know," Rya frowned. "Me either."

The princess came forward, drawing her into a hug. Her arms tightened around the queen until was no space was left between them. In a shaky voice, she whispered into Rya's ear.

"I won't let him hurt you."

Cam let go and gave one last squeeze of Rya's hand, then left the room. Thane and Norell followed closely behind, and with their footsteps fading down the hall Sora stood up and took the spot on the bed.

"You lied to them," he frowned. "You lied to Cam. You told me you were going to be honest with her from now on."

"I know what I said."

"Then what happened?"

"I can't," she sighed. She dropped down next to him on the mattress, staring at the ground. "I don't want her to look at me the same way everyone else does. I want to keep pretending for a little longer that I could be the person she thinks I am. If I tell her the truth, if I tell her I have to kill Gavin, then her mind will change in an instant. I'll become nothing more than the Black Queen, and her hatred of me will be the same as everyone else's."

"Then don't do it," Sora replied. "You told her you'd run, and you still can. We can leave just like you said, and start again somewhere new—somewhere warm and beautiful."

"That isn't an option. It's not who I am to run. I only fled the Isles the first time because I knew I couldn't win without my magic. I'm tired of my life being guided by someone else's decisions. If Gavin insists on holding court to decide my fate, then I will have to end his life. There's no other way."

Sora dropped to the ground, kneeling before her with her hands in his.

"I'll do it," he said in a stern voice. "If he needs to die, then let it be by my hand. You don't have to be the one to kill him, and then when it's over, Cam will never need to look at you with anything but love. You'll be innocent and you can have all you ever wanted."

"Absolutely not." Her hand moved to his face, cupping his soft cheek in her palm. "I can't put that weight on your shoulders. You've never killed a man, you don't know what it does to your soul, and I won't be the reason you learn. I want to hope that Gavin will change his mind, but if it doesn't, I'll have to take his life."

"I'm sorry," he cried. He rested his forehead on her knees, the tears dropping onto the tops of her boots. "I'm sorry it has the end this way."

The tears came to her eyes, and she blinked them back. "I'm sorry it has to end at all."

THE BEACH

The air swept in over the sea and Gavin winced. The gash had split his lip into two uneven parts, and the salt and sand from the ocean's breeze stung the open wound. The blood was still wet on his chin, and his tears had stained his cheeks. It was a sight he wanted no one to see, and yet he found he wasn't alone.

A girl was walking along the edge of the crashing waves, heading right for him. Her dark hair danced in the wind, and her dress clung to the form of her legs. Gavin put his head down, hoping she'd ignore him. The last thing he wanted was company, especially from her. Unfortunately, she had made her way to his side, and without asking sat on the rocky ground next to him.

"That looks painful." Her voice was kind but without worry. Talking about his pain was as casual as discussing the weather, and he wasn't sure if he was upset or grateful for it. "Here," she added, handing him a small handkerchief. The cloth was soft and white, but Gavin waved it away.

"No thank you." He mumbled.

"Take it."

"No, Rya, it's too nice. If you allowed me to use it, you'd never get it clean again. It'll be stained forever."

"It's not mine, so that's not a concern," she replied.

A playful smirk lifted the corner of her mouth, and he took the cloth with a nod. He placed the fabric to his lips and winced. The silk was cool to the touch and felt nice against the cut. He left it for a moment before pulling it away, finding it had turned pink with his blood. He held it out for her to see, but she shrugged him off, so he put it against his lips once more.

Rya had only been with them for a couple weeks, brought up from the Deserts of Asta to become his bride. He had known nothing about her before she arrived, and even now he had little knowledge of who she was, or what her life was like before the Isles. She was always stoic, and had the aura of a quiet storm growing over the sea. As a child he would watch those clouds form from the tower of the castle, growing and swirling in silence, gaining strength until they rushed towards the shore to unleash their fury. That was how he imagined Rya, and it both excited and terrified him.

"Is he always like that?" She asked, her voice sweet against the sound of the ocean.

"Like what?"

"Angry? Is he always lashing out on you like he did?"

Gavin shrugged. He had always been a target of his father's rage, but few had seen it first-hand. He hadn't known Rya was watching through the open door when his father grabbed the vase and swung it at Gavin's head. He didn't see her eyes fixated on him until after the blood from his lip dripped onto the clean floor. She was to be his wife, and now she had that image in her head, the sight of him cowering like a little boy.

"He shouldn't get to treat you like that," she continued. "He shouldn't be allowed to treat anyone like that."

"I deserved it," Gavin replied out of instinct, just the way his father taught him.

"How so?"

"I'm not the son he wanted. I'm not the strong fighter he deserved to have. I'm weak and I can't do anything right. It's my fault he gets so mad."

"That's idiotic." She shook her head. "I've seen the way you talk to the people around here, and how much love they have for you. Everyone has a kind word and a smile when you come around. If every man were born a fighter, the world would fall apart. It's men like your father that bring the wars, and men like you that talk them down. You'll be a great king, and you won't be anything like Gerrod."

"If I even live long enough to be king," Gavin sighed. He turned to Rya, her dark eyes searching his for his meaning. "He's said things," he continued. "He's made threats that make me believe my future isn't as certain as his own. I know he wants a different heir. I know he would love to get rid of me and give the thrown to a better son."

"He's insane," Rya scoffed. "How would he even do that?"

"By marrying someone younger, someone that could birth him a stronger son in the future. Promise me something, Rya—"

"What?"

"Promise me that if something happens to me, and I'm suddenly gone, promise you'll get out of here. Promise me you'll run away from the Isles and never look back."

She nodded. "I promise."

Gavin sighed, looking out over the sea. He couldn't know whose life would end first, his or his fathers, but he could count on one thing—Rya would never have to deal with being Gerrod's next target.

THIRTY-TWO

The sun's light was barely a sliver on the horizon as Rya sat mounted on Eclipse at the edge of the Ivory Cape's border. Clint had promised to ride with them until his kingdom ended, and now that they had reached the invisible line that started Trava, he dismounted to say his goodbyes.

Gavin jumped off his horse, and allowed the man to wrap him into a tight hug. The corners of Clint's cracked eyes were wet with tears, and his hand gently held the back of Gavin's head, like a father comforting his young child.

"I'll see you again," Gavin promised. Clint released him, looking into the young man's eyes, and Gavin smiled. "Only the next time I'm up here we will both be kings."

Rya's eyes dropped to her hands on the reins.

"I have to thank you—" Gavin added. "—for everything you've done for me, and everything you taught me. I wouldn't be the man I am today without you."

"The best way to thank me," Clint replied, "is to be the best leader you can be. None o' that bullying stuff ya pop did, hear me?"

"I promise."

One last hug and Gavin mounted his horse, pulled away from the man who had stepped in as his family when he had no one, and joined the group heading towards the Isles.

"Should be an easy ride," he sniffed, wiping away a tear of his own. "The road through Trava and the Imani Plains is pretty smooth."

"We can't take Centrum Road," Norell answered from her seat behind Thane. "It's too dangerous."

"Not taking it will cost us days. I say we risk it."

"No," Rya snapped back. "We stay off the road."

"Kasen knows we're coming," Cam explained. "He's already done all he can to stop Rya from challenging him, and when he hears that you've joined us, he'll only become angrier and more desperate. Taking the main road puts all our lives in danger and removes our element of surprise."

"I guess you're right," Gavin huffed.

Norell nodded. "Not to mention Nix is still after us, and if he's lost track of us he'll be watching the main road as well."

"Wait—" the prince looked over at Rya riding next to him. "Who is Nix?"

"Oh, I can't believe I forgot," she answered. "There's a Kael assassin that's been hired to hunt me down and kill me. He's supposed to return my heart to Kasen on a plate."

"What?" He gasped. "You forgot to mention the murderous lunatic that's chasing you? How does something like that slip your mind?"

"In case you haven't noticed I have a lot going on right now. Besides, he's failed so far and I'm hoping he continues to do so."

"Great," he scoffed. "You realize that even if we stay off Centrum the chance of us making it to the Isles unnoticed is minimal."

Rya frowned at the truth of his words. Trava was the main hub of trade for Kelda. The fields were expansive and grew every edible plant they could. Each plot was equal in size and with a Council controlling the land instead of a single ruler it was easier to gain a piece of it for yourself. People from all over Kelda and beyond flocked to Trava at a chance to escape their station in life, which meant that it was always crawling with people.

"At least the traders coming and going has one upside," Rya replied.

"What's that?" Cam asked.

"Trava has inns and taverns at every turn. We shouldn't have to spend a single night on the ground as long as we're passing through."

The path Thane chose for them took them east from the central road towards the coast. It was winding and rocky, with wild vines of fruit trying to strangle it in places. Rya could see the heads of workers bobbing between the rows of growth, making their money by plucking the ripe pieces to take to market. Homes dotted the edges of the fields, signaling where one man's plot ended and the next began. She was staring at one of the modest buildings when Gavin rode up next to her.

"Thane is one of Cam's guards, isn't he?" He asked, nodding ahead to the young man.

"He is, but it's more than that. Did your father ever teach you about the Kinsmen?"

"Yes," he nodded. "He said if we ever went to war with the Ashen you must kill the Kinsman first. The rest of the men might fight to protect the kingdom, but the Kinsman will fight to the death protecting the king, and you can't take a land when a king still sits in their throne."

"Charming," Rya grimaced, "but not wrong. Thane is Cam's Kinsman. Wherever Cam is you'll find Thane right behind her."

"Or in front," the prince snickered. "I understand know why he's leading our little caravan."

"What does that mean?" Rya frowned.

"He's a sacrifice. I couldn't understand how you of all people could fall in line behind someone else, especially if he isn't of noble blood. Now I get it. If we come across a trap or a line of soldiers, Thane will reach them first. He's going to be the first to fall, and you stay protected back here behind him and the princess. Seems like a safe position for you to place yourself in."

"You don't know anything," Sora grumbled. She had almost forgot he was riding with her until his angry voice rose behind her. "Thane is leading the way because he's a great hunter, which means he is good with directions and navigating the terrain."

"Sure, kid," Gavin nodded.

"He is!" Sora shouted. "And even if he wasn't, you would never have to order Thane to ride in front to protect anyone, he would just do it, because that's who he is—and it's who I am. I would put myself between Queen Rya and any kind of harm without question."

"I bet you would." Gavin's smirk had faded, and his eyes sharpened as he studied Sora's face. "I'm sure you'll get a chance to do just that. From what I understand, there is no shortage of people wanting to hurt Queen Rya."

Sora's chest puffed up against Rya's back, and she knew his rage was boiling inside him. There was no use fighting Gavin now, not while they had so far between them and the Isles. She placed a soft hand on Sora's arm wrapped around her waist, and she could feel the tension leave his muscles. He knew she believed him, and that was all that mattered to the boy.

Rya addressed Gavin in a calm voice. "I know what you must think of me, and I don't blame you for feeling the way you do, but these people are my friends. We protect each other, and I wouldn't sacrifice any of them. You however—" she smirked "—you might be expendable."

Gavin slowed his horse, falling in line behind her without a retort. Sora's breath tickled her ear as he whispered to her.

"Your trying to get him to spare your life, remember? I don't think comments like that are going to win him over."

While Rya knew her tongue might be the cause of her death, she didn't care.

"I don't trust him," she whispered back. "If he believes the rest of you don't mean anything to me, he might try and use you for his own gains. Now he knows that he tries to harm any of you he'll be dealing with my wrath. I'm sure he's heard how terrible that can be."

THIRTY-THREE

The large river that flowed from Veil Lake through the middle of Trava split into two, each arm snaking its way across the fields and stretching towards the Castil Sea. After two days of trudging down the side paths that wove themselves back and forth they finally reached the top of the two forks without issue.

The Riverside Inn sat on the edge of the water, overseeing the slow current that flowed past. The exterior of the two-story building was constructed of the tan brick Trava was known for, and stood out against the green crops growing behind it. The top of Council Castle could be seen in the distance, it's large turrets a beacon to the middle of the town they called Danek. Even this far from that bustling village travelers hurried around the inn like ants. Some were traders trying to unload product, others were foreigners looking for a bit of work, then there were the mysterious ones that hid their business. That's the category Cam found herself in now.

The leather bag was soft in her hand, and the coins clanked together as she shook the weight of it once more.

"You said two silver pieces, right?" She asked, peering at the man behind the counter top.

"Two per room," he corrected. His eyes passed over each of them, counting silently in his head how much he was going to make.

Cam glanced at Rya standing nearby, then shifted her gaze to Norell. Their first night in Trava was spent with all six of them crammed into a single room. While it proved to save them a bit of money, it ended with none of them getting a good night's sleep. The idea of a bed of her own was tempting, but it was a chunk of their coin that she couldn't justify.

"Three rooms please," she replied, handing over the silver. She'd have to settle for sharing, but one roommate was far better than five.

He handed over three brass keys, and directed them down a narrow hallway to a staircase.

"Who's sleeping where?" Thane asked as they ascended the darkened second story. "I assume Rya and Sora will be in one room."

"I'll bunk with Cam," Norell offered. "I think if anyone's going to be alone with Gavin, it should be you Thane."

The prince chuckled at her caution, but didn't argue. Cam handed over each of the keys, then watched as Rya disappeared inside the room down the hall. Norell tugged on Cam's arm, guiding her towards their doorway.

Inside, Norell wasted no time getting a fire started in the small furnace tucked into the wall. Cam sat on the edge of the mattress and watched her work. She imagined herself inside Rya's room, cuddled together on the soft bed, watching the sunlight fade and night turn the room dark. It was a dream she knew wouldn't come true.

"I know this isn't what you wanted," Norell huffed. She stepped away from the crackling logs and sat next to Cam on the bed. "I promise, it's for the best."

"Sure," Cam pouted.

"I have to ask, what happened back at the lake? Did you two—you know?"

"No," Cam answered quickly. "Not that it's any of your business. It might have happened, but I heard you scream, and the next thing I know we're chasing Nix into the night."

She couldn't control the tremble in her voice, and the sound prompted Norell to wrap her arm around Cam's shoulders. Her comfort was always appreciated, but Norell was not the one she wanted holding her in that moment.

"Time's running out," Cam said with a tear on her cheek. "I mean that in a few days we will be marching into the Isles, and once that happens me and Rya won't have a moment alone together. None of us knows what's going to happen. The army might throw down their weapons at the sight of Gavin, or they might come charging after us with their swords drawn. If that happens no one can promise we'll all survive, and even if we do, we still have no idea what Gavin's going to do to her when he's king. Too soon this will all be over, and I won't be able to tell her how much she means to me, or how much I love her."

Cam watched the orange and red smolder of the wood. The flickering embers reminded her of the sparks from Rya's fingertips, and how they singed anything they touched. Her own heart had been scorched around the edges, charred by her touch and left forever marked. If Cam placed her hand on her chest, she could almost feel the heat burning beneath her flesh.

Norell never responded. The few silent tears she let out meant more to Cam than any words she could have said.

✕

The tavern seemed quaint and calm when they'd spotted it from the inn down the road, but as they entered the air was alive with chatter. Rya followed behind Thane and Gavin, searching the faces of the patrons, looking for Nix's hard eyes. She pushed passed a pair of young me bickering, and then moved around a young woman laughing a little too hard at a man's joke, finding her way to an open table on the far side of the room.

The chair was hard and uncomfortable, and the table rocked back and forth as Gavin and Thane joined her, each holding three mugs of ale. Gavin pushed two of them towards her, shaking the tabletop with the movement.

"No thanks," she said, pushing the glasses back.

"I didn't poison them," he laughed. "It's only a bit of beer."

"I'm not a fan, but thanks anyway."

Gavin wiped the thick foam from his upper lip. "If you don't drink then why did you come with us?"

"Because we're good company," Thane answered before chugging his drink.

"To protect you," she replied, her boredom coming through her words.

"Right," he nodded. "You're extremely concerned about my wellbeing. I could tell by the years of you ignoring my existence."

"I've already explained that. If you can't accept what's happened, that's fine, but there's no point in talking about it every five minutes."

Gavin said nothing, downing the rest of his drink instead.

A dozen mugs of ale later and the pair of boys were just as unsteady as the old table they sat at. They had gone through a course of laughter and then tears, hugging and claiming to be best friends, then wanting to fight each other for dominance the moment after. The entire ordeal irritated her. She had hoped for a quiet night alone with Cam, but instead the princess was being guarded by her cousin, and she was stuck babysitting two drunk idiots.

"I have a question," Gavin slurred, leaning in towards Rya. "I'm going to be a great king."

"That's not a question, that's a statement."

"I'm not like my father, I will be better than him." His voice was tense but his eyes were soft and moist. "Don't you think I'll be a good king?"

She pitied him in that moment. He seemed so sad and lost, like he had been when she last saw him. "To be honest I have no clue. I think that as a boy you wanted to please everyone, especially your father. Now you can see how horrible a man he was, but I don't doubt there's a part of you that still wants to make everyone happy, and I'm certain that won't end well for me."

305

The last of her words had been lost, driven away by the snickering of Thane and Gavin's snorts of laughter. They were once again drowned in the alcoholic euphoria, and Rya was practically invisible.

The night was half over, and the patrons that remained were quiet and somber, or entirely passed out on the tabletops. Gavin and Thane were trying in vain to help each other walk out the door, leaning on the other for support. The pair swayed from right to left as they shuffled down the road. Another tip to the side and an unseen force grabbed them and held them upright. Behind them, Rya walked with her hands stretched out, using her power to keep the boys on their feet and not face down in the dirt.

"You," a voice growled from behind. The man had burst from the tavern, and was now staggering after her with heavy steps. His face was bright red, and his eyes were glazed, but she could see the rage fueling his drunken temper. "You killed my brother."

Rya rolled her eyes, dropped her hands, and turned towards the man. "I've killed quite a few people. You'll have to be more specific."

There was a loud thud and she turned to see Gavin on the ground passed out with Thane standing over him looking confused. She faced the stranger again and sighed. His eyes were wide and the vein in his neck swelled as he fought for words. Unable to voice his anger due to lack of vocabulary, or the alcohol altering his mind, he did the next best thing and reached into the back of his belt. The blade he pulled out was six inches long, and rusted around the handle.

"I think not," Thane shouted in a heroic voice. He reached for his own sword, only to find the sheath missing. He failed to remember that he'd left it behind, and began spinning in a circle, like a dog chasing its tail, searching for the weapon.

The man roared, and charged full speed at Rya.

"I'm not in the mood for this," she grumbled, thrusting her hands out in front of her and swirling them around. Vines growing up the side of a nearby building ripped free of the brick and threw themselves at the man, twisting around his limbs and holding them still. His body kept moving forward while his feet locked together, and he crashed to the ground. The sound of his nose cracking was immediately followed by his muffled screams.

Rya placed a boot on his side and kicked, rolling him onto his back. Blood poured from his broken nose, mixing with the dirt and caking his chin in a red mud.

"You'll pay for this," he spat through the blood.

"No, I don't think I will."

"You murdered by brother, and you'll die for what you've done."

"Again, I have no idea who your brother is—was, but if I killed him, he definitely deserved it."

The stranger thrashed from side to side, struggling against the bindings.

"Was he the man stealing from my crops?" Rya asking, tapping her chin as she thought. "Or maybe the one cheating on his wife? Or the man who I caught abusing his animals. You know, beating a donkey isn't going to make it move any quicker. He learned that the hard way because no matter how much I beat him, he didn't work any faster. At least the donkey lived."

"Whatever he did wasn't worth being run over by your own horses and left for dead. Did you know he was still alive when we found him? He was broken all over, but still breathing. He felt every ounce of pain until he passed."

"Oh," Rya gasped in excitement. "That was *your* brother? I'm surprised you're so upset, he was not a nice man."

"Take that back," he shouted.

"I can't," she shrugged. "Did you know he was a thief? He would steal people's horses in the dead of night, then convince them he could retrieve it for a small reward. A scam artist like that has no place in my kingdom. He needed to be removed."

"You're a monster!" He pushed against the vines until he could move his hand. In its new position he was able to place his blade against the plants, wiggling until it cut through them. Suddenly free he stumbled to his knees, then lunged for Rya with the knife still in his grip.

A gargling gasp escaped his lips as he knelt, frozen. The knife fell to the ground, and his hands moved up, pawing at his neck. His face paled, turning blue while his lungs begged for air. Her magic was strangling the life from him, and he was powerless to stop it.

"Rya," Cam voice whispered. She was suddenly at the queen's side, her gentle touch cooling Rya's arm. "Let him go."

"He attacked me," she argued, still holding him by the throat.

"I know, but there are other ways to deal with it. You don't have to kill everyone who wrongs you."

"I disagree." Rya shook her head, but released her invisible grip.

The man collapsed, gasping for air. His hands shook, and his body was weak, but he wouldn't be beaten. His trembling fingers wrapped around the handle of his knife once more, but he was too slow. The rock collided with the side of his head, and in an instant, he was unconscious with Cam standing over him.

Rya crossed her arms, glaring at the princess. Cam shrugged.

"I said you didn't have to kill him, I said nothing about knocking him out." She looked down at him, cringing at the blood that covered his face. "What did you do to make him so angry?"

"Why is it always my fault?" Rya asked. "It's possible he came at me without a reason, and I'm the innocent one in all this."

"Are you?"

"Not completely. Apparently, I killed his brother."

It was now Cam's turn to look annoyed. Rya hung her head back, groaning. "The world is better without him."

"How so?" Cam asked.

"He took advantage of the poor and weak, and when he did return what he'd stolen he would up the price for his service. A man like that doesn't deserve to be free. Besides, I hadn't intended on killing him in the beginning. That was a happy accident."

"It doesn't matter what happened back then, but you can't kill this man for being related to another. That hardly seems fair."

"I told you, I was attacked."

Cam looked down at the man once again, this time with distain. Rya smirked.

"So, can I kill him now?"

THIRTY-FOUR

Thane rubbed his temples with his fingertips, trying to push away the pain that pounded against his skull. Gavin was on the floor next to him, his face buried in the pile of blankets while he moaned while Sora stood over the pair, offering each a cup of water.

"You need to drink something other than beer," Rya smirked. She was looking down at them from her seat on the bed, trying to contain her laughter at their expense. "Water will make it better. I promise."

"How do you know?" Gavin groaned. "You don't drink."

"True, but I've spent many years in the same house as someone who did. Every night he'd come home as wasted as you two, and each morning I watched him go through the pains of the hangover. You need lots of water, and a good breakfast."

"I swear I had a dream you were going to kill a man," Thane added, forcing a small laugh.

"That wasn't a dream," Gavin replied. "She was attacked in the street."

"What?" Thane gasped. The excitement making his brain hurt more.

"I'm surprised you could remember that," Rya laughed. "You were face down in the dirt at that point."

"My ears still worked," Gavin winced at his own voice.

"What happened?" Thane asked. "Did you actually kill him?"

"Don't worry," Rya sighed. "Cam took care of it, and he is still very much alive. She found a pair of traders, showed them her tattoo, and convinced them the man was a danger to the Ashen people. They jumped at the chance to help a princess and bound and gagged him. They vowed to take him to the port in Cira where he will be put on a boat and shipped across the Halton Sea, hopefully to die over there somewhere."

"You don't sound happy about that," Gavin pointed out. "You would have rather killed him yourself?"

"Yes. It's easier that way, but Cam doesn't care for the violence, so I let her send him away."

"I get it now," he exclaimed. "You're in love with her. That's why you let her tag along. I've seen what your magic can do, and if anyone else had tried to follow you they would have been frozen on the spot. Then you consider last night. I have never seen you take orders from anyone, not when you'd made up your mind, and yet you just let her have her way. How did I not notice that you're in love with Cam?"

"Honestly," Thane replied, "I don't know how you missed it. It's super obvious."

"That's enough," Rya snapped. "You two need to get downstairs. Some food in your stomach will help get your head right."

Gavin pushed himself up from the floor, brushed off the front of his shirt, and laughed. He was just walking out the door when Rya's keen ears caught his whispered words.

"The Black Queen falling for the Ashen Princess," he chuckled. "Like that could ever work."

Thane managed to stand, still holding the side of his head.

"Sora," he winced. "Could you give me a minute with Rya."

"Of course," the boy nodded, setting Thane's glass on the nearby table, then promptly rushed from the room.

"He's wrong, you know," Thane said, sitting beside her on the bed. "It could work between you and Cam, if you wanted it to."

"I'm not returning the Ashen Forest."

313

"I know you're not. We could ask you a million times to do so and I know you'd turn us down each time. But we're only days away from the Isles, and we haven't done much to change Gavin's image of you."

"I'm aware." The tingle of fear and anxiety was stirring within her.

He took her hand in his, squeezing it gently until she looked at him. His eyes had always been so kind, and so calm, just as they were now. His hair had grown past his shoulders since she'd arrived, and the journey from the Ashen Forest had put a blond fur on his jaw. She didn't want to look at him any longer, she wanted to turn away and pretend she didn't care, but she couldn't.

"I'm smart enough to know you have more than one backup plan," he added. "I don't want to know what it is since I'm sure it's something I would never approve of."

"I do," she replied. "Because of that, when we reach the Isles' border, I want you to take Cam and return the Ashen Forest."

"What—no. We're with you until the end."

"You can't be. You've seen yourself how hated I am, and how many people want me to pay for the things I've done. Gavin is not one to stand up against a crowd, and when his own people are chanting for my head, he'll want to give it to them. I won't go out like that, and whatever

314

happens next, I don't want Cam to see it. I don't want any of you to see it."

Thane wrapped his arms around her, his hug absorbing her. The bristly hair on his cheek tickled her forehead, and the tears stung her eyes. She knew that she loved Cam, but she knew she loved him too. In way she loved Sora, and in the way, she would have loved the brothers she never met. He had wiggled his way into her stone heart, and helped drive out some of the poison. She could never tell him what he meant to her, or how much she cared, so instead she just squeezed him tighter.

A few moments later she took a deep breath, and stepped away from him. His eyes were red and his cheeks were wet, but so were hers.

"You know she'll never go," he sighed. "Cam's not going to just leave you."

"I know," Rya nodded. "That's why I'm telling you this now. I'll need your help when the time comes. I'll say my goodbye, then you'll need to take her, even if she fights you. When we talked before you said you would always protect Cam, and that didn't just mean in battle. This is part of that. If you want to keep her safe, you'll drag her far from me, and far from the Isles."

Thane nodded, and wiped away the last tear clinging to his eye.

"Now," she smiled, forcing the smile she had practiced for years. "How about that breakfast. I promise you'll feel much better after some eggs."

Rya was happy to see Thane's color return after his meal, and she was equally happy to have proved to Gavin that she was right. The group gathered their possessions, and mounted the horses. As they rode out of the village Rya could see the brown stain of blood on the road from where the man had broken his nose, and the drag marks that had followed.

Avoiding Danek took some work as all the roads seemed to pull the group towards the middle of Trava, but Thane had done an excellent job of keeping them off Centrum Road and close to the coast. The journey had led them through a large orchard of orange trees, filling the air with the sweet citrus smell of the fruit. Strawberries overgrew their plot and the rogue ones had fallen onto the dirt path, leaving sticky pink spots behind as the horses trotted over them.

Each patch of land they passed was different than the last, and each one beautiful. The rows of crops lined up cross hatched patterns added depth to the low rolling hills. The colors were brighter than Rya had ever seen before. The yellow of the lemons almost glowed in the daylight. The rich greens of the watermelons complimented the vines growing around them. The territory was a quilt,

316

every plot unique as if it spoke to the variety of people that called Trava home. A part of Rya was sad to see it behind them, but with the border to the Imani Plains in front of them, they had no time to waste.

THIRTY-FIVE

The roads through Imani were all wide and smoothed over, thanks to the ranchers that drove herds of livestock from one end to the other. Tall grass covered most of the land except for the few flat-topped trees that offered the animals shade in midday heat. The cattle that roamed the open space were branded, each design representing one of the lord's houses in the area. As they rode near one of the villages, they could see smaller fenced off pastures that housed goats or sheep, obviously belonging to families of lower status.

"Do you think we'll make it by sundown?" Sora asked. He was fanning himself as the sunlight beat down on them. Imani enjoyed the warmth of the summer and fall longer than any other kingdom, and the weather was determined to hold off winter as long as possible.

"We should," Cam answered. "One more night in a real bed, then it's back to sleeping on the ground."

"Maybe we should splurge and get our own rooms this time," Gavin added from behind them. "I wouldn't mind having a moment's peace before marching into a battle."

"I don't know that we can afford that," Cam replied. "I think it's better to save the coin we have left and maybe buy some food for when we leave Imani. Being back in the wilderness is going to be rough, and I don't want to end up in the situation we had before."

"Cam's right," Thane nodded. "The last thing we need is to be going to war and empty stomachs."

"Fine," Gavin grumbled. "But this time you're sleeping on the floor. I can't handle another night of you kicking me in your sleep."

All over Imani groups of shingled buildings calling themselves villages popped up. Living close together gave the regular citizens a sense of comfort and safety. No one wanted to be out on their own trying to keep the lords from absorbing their small piece of land into their own. Cam had expected Saraba to mostly be the same, perhaps with a few more shabby homes on the outskirts. She was completely wrong.

All the money the king of Imani spent on his kingdom obviously went into maintaining the small city.

The buildings were still made of wood, but the grain was smooth and without splinters. Each home was painted a different color, and stood at least a story, if not two, higher than any others they'd seen along the way. The roads were made of cobblestone, lined with torches for the night, and cleaner than anyone would have expected. Shops were tucked in between houses, flower stalls sat on the corners, and the smell of a bakery filled the air.

The inn they were searching for sat on the end of a long drive, flanked by a bar on one side, and a small market on the other. The exterior was a sky blue and each of the four floors held large windows that tilted open to allow the fresh air to flow into the rooms. The inside was equally impressive, with a large dining area and kitchen to one side, and a parlor for games on the other.

"Here," Norell said, taking the bag of coin from Cam's hand. "I'll get the rooms, you ask what time dinner is served."

Cam had tracked down one of the cooks and gotten the information they needed when Norell returned to her with a key in hand, and led her away from the rest of the group.

"Take this." Norell shoved the brass at Cam. "Room 40, top floor. I'll be up soon. I just have to deal with something first."

The look on her cousin's face was tense, and Cam couldn't help but wonder what Thane had done this time to make her so annoyed.

She took the key and climbed the four flights of stairs, finally coming to the door with the 40 carved into the rich wood. She unlocked it and walked in, not ready for what she found. The space was bright and airy, thanks to the windows she'd seen outside. The bed was larger than any they'd slept in so far, and she collapsed on the plush bedding. The sheets smelled of fresh air and flowers, and she rolled over to take a big whiff. After breathing in the clean scent, she stood and looked out the window. The king of Imani's home was in the center of the scene, placed atop a small slope, the white walls glistened as the sun set behind the massive castle. It was impressive, as was the whole town of Saraba, but she grew sad for those living elsewhere in Imani. If you weren't here in the heart of it, you were lost and forgotten, left on your own to survive the brutal world of ranchers.

A light tap on the door broke her thoughts, and she huffed as she walked to the door.

"Sorry," she called out. "I thought I left it open for you."

When she pulled on the handle, she expected to see Norell waiting for her, but found a slightly confused Rya standing in the hall instead.

"I thought you were Norell," Cam explained. "She said she'd be up soon."

"She won't be," Rya replied. "She approached me downstairs, and told me that she's going to be staying in the room with Sora tonight. She said she's had enough of your company, and asked if I wouldn't mind staying in here with you."

"What? Really?"

"Yes," Rya smiled. "Also, she said it should be *very* clear to both of us that she will be tired of you for one night only, and that we shouldn't expect this ever again."

"Oh." Cam stood in the open doorway, trying desperately to ignore the bright shade of red she knew her face had turned.

"So—can I come in?"

"Of course," Cam stammered. "Sorry. I just was in shock, that's all."

The room seemed smaller with Rya in it, and the air had grown a few degrees warmer. The confidence Cam had the night at the lake was hiding somewhere deep inside her, pushed away by some awkward nerves that were controlling her now. She had never intended on things to go that far by the water, but now that they were alone in the bedroom, she was completely aware of what would happen.

"You can relax," Rya urged. She was sitting on the bed with her back against the wall, looking as calm as anyone could be. It made Cam feel even worse for being flustered. Rya patted the spot next to her. "Come sit with me."

Cam wanted to say something, but couldn't find words, so she simply nodded. *Did the bed get smaller?* She thought as she crawled up next to Rya. They were so close, legs on top of each other's, bodies pressed together. The heat that had lit up Cam's face was now spreading to over areas of her as well.

"Nothing has to happen," Rya whispered. She leaned over and kissed Cam on the forehead, soft and light. "I just want to spend time with you. We could lay like this all night, not moving at all, and I would be happier than I have ever been."

Rya's words drove out any of the anxiety Cam had been feeling, allowing the want she had before to take over. She leaned in closer to Rya and pressed her lips against hers. Her tongue started to slide between them to explore. Rya returned the kiss, pressing her body against Cam's. Their arms wrapped around each other, hands moving over the other's body. Skin touched skin as their clothing shifted, and the warmth cut through Cam like a knife. In a flash, she sat up and grabbed the bottom of her shirt, pulling it off over her head in one swift motion. The breeze

323

chilled her naked torso, but before it could take hold, Rya was on top of her, straddling her body. Her tongue danced with Cam's, while her hands moved across Cam's bare skin. The warm brush of her fingers on Cam's breast made her shudder, and she breathed a moan into the queen's mouth.

"Is this alright?" Rya asked. She looked more innocent than Cam had ever seen. Her eyes wanting to touch her more, but also full of care and concern. "Are you sure about this?"

"Yes," Cam nodded. "But if you're not, that's alright."

Rya's regular smirk reappeared. "I'm definitely sure."

Cam grabbed at Rya's shirt, and tried to pull it off, getting it stuck around Rya's neck. The queen laughed, then yanked it off herself and tossed it somewhere on the floor. Cam stopped for a moment, taking in the sight of her olive skin glowing in dimming light. Her fingers traced the edges of her body, while her lips continued moving against Rya's. The sounds were getting more difficult to control, and they broke free every time the queen's skin brushed her nipples so Cam could gasp for air.

Rya's hand moved lower now, unlacing the front of Cam's pants. The velvet touch of Rya's fingers on her soft flesh brought a different sound, one that Cam had never made before.

"Are you okay?" Rya asked once more. "Should I keep going?"

The burning desire inside Cam grew hungry. The brief moment that Rya had leaned away to ask her was like someone had yanked the world out from under her. She struggled to find her voice, finally able to answer.

"Yes," she breathed. "Please."

The heat of Rya's fingers met the heat between her legs, and she gasped again. Her body moved on its own against her, begging for more. Her fingers dug into Rya's back. Her breathing quickened, and she pressed her mouth against Rya's ear, moaning her pleasure into it. Fire surged throughout her entire body, her muscles tensing with each motion of her hips.

The night Nix had attacked them, when she touched Rya, she had felt everything the queen did. Their hearts had become one, and the rage and fear that filled her filled Cam as well. Now, as their bodies pressed together, and the pleasure grew to its peak, she was once again connected to Rya. They were two halves of the same heart. The flame exploded within Cam, and her body shook as the waves washed over her, leaving her exhausted and limp in their wake.

Rya leaned over her, and tenderly touched her lips to Cam's, soft and sweet.

"How was that?" she asked.

Cam pressed her forehead to Rya's, breathing slow and steady while her body calmed itself.

"Wonderful," Cam replied. After a few more breaths she sat up, grinning at the queen in the darkness. "Now, it's your turn."

THIRTY-SIX

Waking up in Cam's arms was the greatest gift Rya had ever received. She watched the rise and fall of the princess' chest as she slept, and she couldn't help but smile. It was the most peace she'd ever had. The rest of the world had melted away for one night, and they were the only two people left. She'd forgotten all about her past that haunted her, and she'd pushed away all thoughts of what was to come. She was able to focus on Cam and simply enjoy the feeling of being in love. Norell had given her that, and she knew she could never thank her.

The knock on the door shattered the perfect bubble she was hiding in, and she knew the time had come to return to the real world. She shook Cam's arm, laughing as she swatted away her hand to try and keep sleeping.

"You have to get up."

"Let's stay here," Cam mumbled. "This is our home now."

"Come on," Rya urged. She slipped out of the bed, knowing that as long as she was under the sheets with her, Cam would never move. The moment Cam felt her absence her eyes snapped open, and she sat upright.

"Did you sleep well?" Cam asked. Her voice was too innocent, and Rya knew she wanted to say more. "I did," Cam added. "I had a great night's sleep."

"Yes," Rya answered with a grin. "I slept very well, thank you."

"Good."

"When will you learn, if you have something on your mind just say it."

"It's just—" Cam hesitated. "—Sora said you had others brought to your room before. I'm not a child, I know what happened and I'm not jealous of that, I just want to know..."

Rya leaned in and kissed her mouth.

"Yes," Rya nodded. "You were the best."

"You don't have to say that if it's not true."

"Anyone I met before, they were just a way to satisfy a fleeting urge. What you and I have, and what happened between us last night, that was the most amazing experience I've ever had. I couldn't tell you a single thing about any previous lover, because one night with you has wiped them from my brain completely. They don't exist in my world any longer; there's only you."

Cam jumped from the bed, throwing her arms around Rya. Their kisses were softer than the deep passionate ones from the night before, but full of just as much emotion. They stood pressed together, still unclothed, holding on to each other for one last moment.

After breakfast was eaten and the supplies were purchased, Rya stood outside the inn with the others, waiting for Thane's direction.

"I just need to fetch the horses." He pointed at Gavin and Cam. "You two can help me with that. Once we're saddled it's only a days' ride to the Obsidian Isles' border. We will be outside your kingdom by nightfall."

Gavin smiled, excited at the idea of seeing his home again after years of hiding, but Rya couldn't muster a grin, even a fake one.

Sora kicked at the dirt nearby, bored as he waited for the others to return. His distracted mind left Rya practically alone with Norell.

"I want to thank you." Rya looked Norell in the eye, wanting to make sure her sincerity was known. "I know how much you hate me, and you giving us that night together must have been hard for you. She's lucky to have you as her family."

Norell shifted, uncomfortable with the kind words coming from Rya's mouth. They had been bickering so long, neither of them was sure how to navigate calm waters.

"I don't hate you," Norell finally replied. "You're a little annoying, but I don't hate you. You've been wonderful to Cam, better than I thought was possible from you."

"Thanks, I guess."

"Cam has spent her entire life worrying about what kind of queen she's going to be. She's trained harder and longer than anyone else, and studied more than anyone else, all with the goal of being as loved by the people as King Mikkel. I've always worried that she is so focused on being like him, that she's lost sight of who she wants to be, and what she really wants. The one time she focused on making herself happy, it backfired and she was left broken hearted. I only wanted to protect her from that pain, but in the end, it doesn't matter. Gavin is going to pass his judgment, and Cam will be devastated, but I can see that this short time you've had together is enough to make that pain worth it. She'll have a better memory of you than she would have if I stood in the way."

"I know she'll be alright," Rya smiled. "As long as she has you, Cam will always survive. They all will. You're the backbone that keeps them in line. Without you, Thane and Cam would be lost."

Norell held out her hand as a peace offering to Rya, but she couldn't accept it. With the Isles so close she couldn't end it like that. She reached out and grabbed Norell's arm, pulling her towards her and wrapping her arms around her stiff body. The girl froze, uncertain of what to do, but after a moment, Rya smiled as she hugged her back.

"That's enough," Norell growled, and Rya released her.

They each took a step back from the other as the sound of the horses on the stone road clicked louder. Thane stopped in front of Rya, handing her Eclipse's reins with a knowing stare.

"I know what happened last night," he whispered, and Rya's cheeks turned pink. "It will only make saying goodbye harder."

"I know but—"

"But I'm glad you had that," he interrupted. "She deserves to know how you feel."

Thane walked away and began mounting Rainy. Rya watched him help Norell up behind him, and she realized that she'd never actually told Cam what was in her heart. She'd hinted at it, she'd told other people, she'd even expressed it physically, but the words have never escaped her lips. To Rya, love was a joy she was unworthy of, and she knew that if she said those three words, Cam would repeat them. Rya still had a plan and Gavin stood in her way of the throne. She knew she could never accept Cam's love knowing what was still to come.

THIRTY-SEVEN

The Obsidian Isles were close enough to touch. The Bardo Mountains that lined the northwest of the region towered in front of them, and the sea crashed far to the east. The soft dirt of the plains had already begun merging with the rocky ground of the Isles. Bare areas with black soil stuck out among the grass, and the smell of the ocean wafted in on the evening's breeze. Each step brought them closer to home, and each step tore at Rya's heart.

The marker stood out like a giant in front of her, though in reality it barely reached the horses' shoulders. The wooden signpost signals the official start of the Isles' land. They stopped just past it, and Gavin jumped down off his horse, touching the earth of his home. His eyes flashed with pain and anger, but also joy at his return. It was a mixture of emotion that she too felt in that moment, though for completely different reasons.

"We should make camp near here," Gavin said, pushing himself back to his feet. "The further in we go, the harder the land becomes. You won't find a comfortable night's sleep on the volcanic rock."

They began unpacking their camp as they'd done a dozen times before. It seemed like ages had passed since their first night in a rickety cabin. They had come so far, and grown so close. It would be a million times harder to leave them now than it would have been in the Ashen Forest, but Rya couldn't imagine the journey without them. They had softened her heart, and made her believe in hope when she thought she never would.

If she hadn't of stopped to watch them work, she would have missed it—the sound rustling in the tall grass around them. She shouted, but the footsteps were already rushing towards them. The figures were almost hidden in the grass, with only their rounded backs visible. Thane had his sword in hand, standing back to back with Gavin who held a long blade he'd brought from the Cape. It was curved at the end, made for slicing fish and certain to do damage to any man who attacked.

Cam was on the other side of the circle, far from Rya's reach. She wanted to scream for her to run. She wanted to save them all from harm, but there wasn't time. Nix burst from the bushes, tackling Rya and driving them both to the ground. All around, the camp members of the

Kael emerged from hiding and started to slash at anyone near them.

Thane was locked in a sword fight against a young man with blond hair. If it weren't for the dark cloak and scars, she wouldn't have been able to tell them apart.

Norell was on the ground, clutching her left leg. Her hand was covered in blood as she tried to hold the wound closed, her other hand thrusting a dagger at the assailant. Sora crawled over and grabbed Norell's spear and, with a shout, jabbed it into the back of the man's calf. He fell to his knees with a howl, and Norell started slashing at him with the knife.

Gavin was on top of his attacker, wrestling the young Kael woman to the ground, ready to strike, but he hesitated. Her eyes sparked as she spotted his weakness and, in an instant, she had flipped him onto his back and knocked him unconscious with the hilt of the very knife he had at her throat.

She couldn't find Cam, and the panic set in. Nix was still on top of her. They'd been fighting for his dagger since he attacked, but her focus had shifted to Cam and he knew it. He yanked the weapon from her grip and lifted it in the air, ready to plunge it into her flesh. Her palms found his face before he could strike, and the charge of magic exploded from her. Screaming, he fell backwards, clutching the burning skin on his face. Each cheek raw in the shape of her hands.

Rya scrambled to her feet, ready for his next attack but he just stood in front of her, laughing. It was haunting and hollow, and his maniacal grin stretched the skin tight on his face, showing the outline of his skull underneath.

The queen's eyes darted between the killer and the scene around her, still searching for Cam's face. A wave of relief washed over her when Cam appeared at her side, her arrow at the ready.

"What are you waiting for?" One of the other assassins shouted. "Finish it."

The other members of the Kael had stopped their fighting, holding each of Rya's friend's captive as they waited for Nix to strike. Norell was still on the ground, her hands pressing against her leg while the young woman who had attacked Gavin held her by the hair. The man Sora had stabbed in the calf had grabbed him and held him against his chest. Sora's boots dangled a foot above the ground while the man held the tip of Norell's spear at the boy's throat. Thane had lost his battle as well, and was sprawled on his back in the dirt next to Gavin's motionless body, his victor standing over him with two swords pointed at his chest.

"Nice to see you again," Nix smiled, talking directly to Sora. "I'm disappointed to see the company you keep."

"Shut up," Sora snapped.

"Not so friendly," he laughed. "Too bad."

"I won't tell you again," the Kael woman shouted. She was glaring at Nix who was still chuckling to himself. "Kill her."

His smile faded.

Cam's eyes narrowed.

His hand squeezed the hilt of his dagger.

She pointed the shining tip of her arrow at the center of his chest.

He shouted.

She released.

The hit was hard and unexpected, and Cam gasped as she hit the ground, all the air leaving her lungs. Nix had dodged the shot, rolling under the arrow's path and exploding upwards into her body. It happened so fast that Rya had missed it. By the time she realized what happened, Cam was clutching her chest as she passed out. Her body lay still behind the assassin who was now the only thing standing between the queen and her love.

Rya's watched her hands move in slow motion, rising before her and burning white hot. She could have killed him from a hundred yards away, could have used her powers to strangle him without a touch, but that wasn't good enough. She wanted to feel the life draining from him. She wanted to feel the weight of his body in her hands. She needed to touch his cold dead flesh with her own fiery skin. She walked forward, one foot in front of the other and wrapped her fingers around his throat.

He didn't scream, not like before. This time he was ready for the scorching pain of her touch. His legs failed him, and he dropped to his knees, but still he didn't make a sound. His lips curled into a sneer, and his teeth gnashed together while he fought against her force.

"You'll never win," she hissed, tightening her hold. She summoned every ounce of power she had, joyous at the red glow of his skin under her grip.

"We—will—see," he gurgled. His face started to fade, the rich brown color dulling before her eyes. She squeezed harder, mixing the strength of her magic with her own muscles, driving him closer to death with each second passing.

She sensed the blade entering her flesh before its sting could register in her mind. The pain exploded from her thigh, and she staggered backwards a few steps before falling. She rested on her hands, trying to ignore the blood seeping from her leg, but the drops were coloring the dirt with her defeat. Nix knelt where she'd dropped him, holding the two-inch silver blade he'd had hidden in his boot. His color and smile had returned, and Rya screamed as she cursed.

Her fingers twitched, and her magic raged to an inferno. Her newly healed wrist cracked under the pressure of her magic, and her energy was being eaten with each second that passed. She had only one more chance, and she had to take it now.

Another pain erupted from her palm, and for a moment Rya thought her own power had finally consumed her body. The sight of the knife protruding from her hand told her she was wrong. Nix had thrown the dagger at her only weapon, sinking the blade into the center of her palm with such force that it came out the other side.

"Let's end this," Nix spat.

He grabbed one of the swords from his comrade, Thane's sword, and held it hovering inches from her the base of her neck. He was watching with wide eyes, breathing in her fear. This was it. This was how she would die, at the hand of a hired man, surrounded by those who gave everything to help her.

Rya would never forget the squish of the skin and the smell of the blood. Nix's eyes lost their glow, and his body slacked. Cam's hand was still wrapped around the shaft of the arrow she'd drove into his neck, her hands soaked in red. She let go as he dropped to his knees.

"You're a fool," he breathed, barely audible, clinging to the last moments of his life. "You'll never change her."

"That's the thing," Cam replied, "I never wanted to."

The assassin slumped to the ground. His blood spread across the dirt, staining the blades of grass that edged the area. Cam raised her arrow at the next assassin, surprised to find that he was helping Thane off the ground.

"We have no business here," the lady explained. She'd released Norell and was helping her limping partner walk away. "Nix was supposed to complete his job, and he did not. The Kael do not fail; therefore, he was not truly one of us."

The assassins disappeared into the same brush they'd come from, leaving the battered group alone to tend their wounds.

THIRTY-EIGHT

"It's nothing," Rya insisted. She was trying to keep a brave face, but the pain of removing the knife from her hand was too much to bare. She'd almost thrown up when Thane yanked it free, and had to keep her head turned while Norell bandaged it. The gash on her thigh wasn't as bad, but it did require sitting through some rough stitches. She tried to remind herself that they all had injuries, they all had new scars to add to their body.

Norell proved to be the biggest asset after the fight. The young woman didn't make a sound as she stitched up her own leg, wincing only once as she tested its strength after. Seconds later, she was dashing around, tending to everyone else and ignoring her own pain. Sora trailed behind her, handing over whatever she needed, and acting as her assistant. Rya knew the boy was worried, but as long as he kept busy, he wouldn't give in to it. He was no stranger to a beating, but the sight of Rya's blood upset him, and he needed a distraction.

Gavin cringed as his fingers traced the edges of his new stitches.

"You'll get used to it," Rya said, pointing to the pink scar above her brow. "You're lucky it's above your ear, once it heals you can grow your hair out over it. No one will ever see it."

"I won't do that," he replied. "I'm tired of hiding my scars. They are marks of where I've been, and they are nothing to be ashamed of." He reached out, brushing his thumb over the raised skin she'd pointed to. "If you hide the trials you've been through, how will anyone know how far you've come?"

As he walked away her insides twisted. She watched him talking to Sora, placing a comforting hand on the boy's shoulder. Thane stroked Norell's cheek, and he offered her his usual sweet smile. A few feet away, Nix's body rested where he'd fallen. He looked so young in the moonlight, like the child he was before the Kael stole his innocence. Cam was close by, reloading the last of their supplies onto the horses. The idea of sleeping on that patch of ground for the night was too much for any of them.

Rya crossed the space, looking once at Thane. In that split second, he knew, and he gave her a subtle nod as if to say "*I understand.*" She took Cam's hand, leading her a few

342

feet from the rest of them. She wanted to keep the others in sight, she knew Cam would need them after it was over.

"We're almost ready to go," Cam said, confused. "We'll be tired, but I'll feel better being far from this place."

"Cam," she whispered. Her courage was shaky, but she forced it to hold. "Cam, you can't come with me."

"What," she laughed. "You're joking, right?"

"I'm sorry, but you need to return to the Ashen Forest. I can't have you come to the Isles."

Her smile dropped, her eyes searching for any sign that it wasn't true. "No," Cam argued. "I won't let you go."

The tears began streaming down Rya's face. Cam reached up and tried to wipe them away as she started to cry as well.

"You're under my protection," the princess replied. "I swore I'd keep you safe, remember? You can't leave me now. You need me."

She pressed her forehead against Cam's and closed her eyes. The words would come now, and she couldn't look at Cam's face as she said them.

"I had a plan," she explained. She knew the others could hear her, but she didn't care. "When I made the deal with Gavin back at the cape, I knew the only way out of it would be to kill him, but I can't do that now. I don't know what Gavin's choice will be, or if the people will have the justice they're calling for, but I can tell you I'm not afraid.

All my courage and strength come from your love. I've spent my entire life in a cage, beaten and twisted into what someone else envisioned. They all wanted me to be what they created, but you only wanted me to be myself. While the rest of the world wanted to keep me locked up, you set me free. I never thought I would love anyone, or be worthy of love, until you showed me it was possible. You saved me, Cam. No matter what happens after this, remember that you saved me."

"You can't—can't give in like that," the princess cried.

"I'm not giving in," Rya replied. She forced herself to look into Cam's eyes. Her heart pounded against her ribs, and with each second that passed more of her soul shattered like glass. The sharp edges tore through her organs, cutting deep grooves throughout her body. "I *am* fighting, it's just a different battle than you want it to be. I can't live my life in hiding, and I'm tired of running. I need to make things right for Gavin, and for Sora. It's my fault that they've been through so much, and this is my chance to fix that. I need to prove that the love you have for me is justified, and that I deserve it. When the time comes, I'll stand before the people of the Isles and take whatever punishment Gavin chooses to give, knowing that I've done everything I could have done to redeem myself."

"Let me come with you."

"No," Rya argued. "You have a life to return to. People need you. Norell and Thane need you to get them back to the forest. Your father needs you, and Eirik needs you. Don't forget they are waiting for your return. You mean so much to them. Besides, we both know you will never stand by and watch me be punished, and I won't risk you getting in trouble trying to save me. I don't want you to see that. You found something in me that no one else bothered to look for. You've unlocked a part of my soul I thought was long dead, and I want you to remember me as I am now when we're together, and not as I will be alone in my final moments."

Cam hiccupped. "No—this can't be it."

"You have to let me go. I'm ready to be my true self. I'm ready to be free." Rya wept. "I love you, Cam. I love you with everything I have. Thank you for showing me who I truly am inside."

Rya leaned in and, through the wetness of their tears, kissed her one last time. She turned her back just as Cam collapsed sobbing on the ground, but she couldn't comfort her. Norell was already moving towards the princess, ready to do what she always did. She placed a gentle touch on Rya's shoulder as they passed, a simple gesture that said everything Norell couldn't.

"Here, take Eclipse." Thane was handing her the reins. His smile was still present, but his tears kept it from reaching his cheeks. "We can't send you into the Isles on foot."

"Thank you," she whispered. Her voice was as broken as her heart.

"I'll make sure he gets back to you," Gavin added. His face was the only one not tear stained in that moment, but Rya finally recognized the young man in him she'd known before. His look was tender, full of kindness, and she knew she'd made the right choice.

She hoisted herself into the saddle, keeping her head down while Sora situated himself behind her. His thin arms wrapped around her waist, trying to ease her pain though he knew it was hopeless. She clicked her tongue, and Eclipse started to walk.

In that last moment the only sound that reached her ears was Cam's voice, calling to her with the only words she ever needed.

"I love you, Rya! I always will."

WALLS DOWN

They'd been riding non-stop for hours, and it had been years since Gavin had been forced to do that. He was used to working on a boat in the middle of the Nestian Ocean, which required a different type of balance, and he wasn't used to the pain in his legs the saddle was providing. It didn't help that his head was still foggy from the night before. Thankfully they'd found a stream flowing along the path, and an old stump near the water's edge that he claimed it before anyone else could.

Trava was known for its crops, but that also meant it lacked a lot of shade and the sun was starting to wear on him. He wiped the sweat from his neck, while the others led their horses to quench their thirst.

"It's a lot different than being up north, isn't it?" Thane had appeared next to him, gathering his hair back into a bun. "It's usually starting to frost in the Ashen Forest. I miss that right now."

Gavin nodded, but Thane didn't see it. He was too busy watching the stream. Cam had a hold of Rya's arm, and was desperately trying to drag her into the flowing water. Rya struggled against the princess, laughing too hard to really fight back. Their feet dipped into the cold and Cam screamed. Norell came out from behind the horses, hands on her hips, glaring at the pair of them.

"Do you really have to act so childish?" She asked in a huff.

Gavin caught the look between the two before Norell had a chance. They rushed towards her, each grabbing one of the arms and pulled her with them into the flowing brook.

"Sora," she cried out, "help me."

But the boy sat on the edge of the path and laughed while they continued to drag her into the water.

"You'll be sorry," Norell shrieked. Her toes were already wet, but they were still pulling and laughing. Even Norell was giggling between her threats and arguments.

Everything happened so fast it was hard to say who was at fault. One minute they were standing upright, the next they were falling. Before anyone could blink the trio of girls had landed face first in the stream. Thane was cringing next to him, which wasn't a good sign.

Norell stood up, soaking wet from head to toe and still standing in six inches of water. Cam and Rya were still sitting in the stream, afraid to move. Norell flipped the wet locks from her face and shook her head.

"You both need a babysitter." Laughter burst from Norell's mouth, and a second later the rest of them had joined in with their own.

She helped the other two up from the stream and they walked to the road to ring out their clothing as best as they could.

"Good news is they'll dry quickly in this warmth," Thane smiled. "They won't have a damp piece of clothing by the time we reach the plains." He looked down at Gavin's thoughtful face and paused. "Something on your mind?

"I don't understand," Gavin said, shaking his head. "I've never seen her so relaxed."

"Who, Rya?"

"Yes. When we were back in the Isles I remember her being calm and collected, but I can't say I ever heard her laugh before—even when she seemed happy. With the stories they tell I can't imagine she's done much laughing since I've left either."

"I don't know that she's had much reason to," Thane replied. "I don't know all her past, but I've heard bits of it from her, and from Cam. If I were Rya, I would find it hard to muster a smile some days, let alone allow myself to enjoy anything."

"You all really care about her, don't you?"

"Yes, we do. Not just because Cam likes her, and not because she's a queen, but because she's a joy to be around when she's not worrying about her impending death."

"You're a good man, Thane," Gavin nodded. "You all must be amazing people to be able to see past her actions, and care about the person underneath."

"Thanks," Thane replied. He walked back towards the horses, but Gavin stayed seated on his stump.

"A good man," he repeated to himself. "Or an extremely foolish one."

THIRTY-NINE

Night had almost passed them by but still they rode. It wasn't the eager pace of the day before, but a slow walk that's only purpose was to put space between Rya and the piece of her heart she'd left behind.

"The sun's coming up," Gavin pointed out. "Maybe we should rest for a bit."

"Sure," she nodded. Nix had taken her energy, and Cam her emotion. There was no fight left in her, and that wasn't how she wanted to meet Kasen.

They stopped the horses and started setting up a small campsite. Sora moved like a rabbit, quickly jumping from one task to the next. He'd learned everything they'd needed from watching the others, and now that they were gone, he took on all their duties himself.

Rya sat on her blankets staring over the sea in the distance. The sun was coming up over the water, dulled by the low fog that hung over the Isles' mornings. Her new wounds ached, but it was nothing compared to the pain pounding in her heart.

"I can't find wood for a fire," Sora said, kicking the ground.

"Come here." She waved him towards her with a forced smile. "You can lay with me."

He climbed under her blanket, and curled up next to her. She laid her arm over him, using her body like armor to protect him, but she couldn't shield him for herself. The reveal of her plan, and the decision to let Gavin live was a blow to him. He followed her now, knowing that he too would lose her. She squeezed him tighter.

Sleep came easy, it was the dreams that were hard. Flashes of Nix and his daggers. The image of Cam's face. Thane's easy smile. Norell's eye roll. They were all torture. Every time Rya's eyes flew open it was a little brighter outside, contrasting the dark ghosts that haunted her sleep.

"Are you alright?" Gavin was sitting around a small smoking pile of grass and bits of wood.

"Yes, I'm fine," she lied.

"I think we need to take a day here. You were just stabbed in the leg, and my head is killing. We aren't in any condition to charge in there, swords waving."

Rya nodded. Sora was still asleep at her side, and she slide out careful not to disturb him.

"You got the fire going," she mentioned, motioning to the sad pile of burning debris.

"As much as I could. I remembered the shore usually has driftwood. I wanted to get more, but I didn't want you to wake and think I'd run off."

"It wouldn't surprise me if you did. I admitted I'd planned on killing you and usually enough to send someone running the other way."

"I always knew that was a risk I was taking," he joked. "Did you mean what you said?" He asked in a more serious tone. "You're going to abide by whatever decision I make?"

"Yes, as long as you promise me one thing—Sora will be kept safe. If I have your word that he'll be alright, I won't fight you. I understand the position you'll be in. I know you'll want to listen to your subjects, especially after being gone for so long."

"No thanks to you," he added. "But I can promise you I'll take care of Sora. He's a good kid with a big heart, and he's quite the little fighter."

"Thank you." A small weight lifted from her shoulders. It didn't matter what her future held, her family would be safe.

Gavin stroked the fire with a thin stick. "I'm sorry. I know leaving them wasn't easy for you, I can see now how much they mean to you, and I'm sorry that I doubted it before."

She felt the urge to cry again but the tears wouldn't come, they were all dried up.

"We were supposed to be married," he continued. "I imagine that would be torture for you."

"Why's that?"

"If you love Cam like that, how could you have been happy about marrying me."

"Why not?" She shrugged. "I've never been particular about men versus women. I see the beauty in both."

"Do you think you would have loved me? If I hadn't left, do you think you would have felt for me what you feel for her?"

"I'm not sure. You were a sweet boy, with a kind heart. You were always soft-spoken and calm, and your voice reassured me that everything would be alright, but you wanted to be everything everyone wanted from you. That was your downfall. I found your innocence and gentle nature endearing, but as you know your father disagreed. He tried to beat it out of you, and had you remained in the Isles, he may have succeeded. You may have bent to his will, and if that had happened I would have hated you."

"I would never be like him."

"You can say that now because you were ripped free from his hold. I know you think your years in the Ivory

354

Cape was a punishment, but I think it was a blessing. You were able to grow into the man you should be. You were given Clint, and you were able to live without the pressures of Gerrod's expectations. The only reason you're going to make a great king now is *because* you left."

"You're not trying to soften me, are you?" His smirk was the one he held as a child.

"No," she chuckled. "I'm just being honest. It's about time I try it out, don't you think?"

"It suits you."

And with those words another piece of her burden was lifted. She crawled back into the blankets next to Sora, and closed her eyes. She still dreamed of Cam's face, but it was different. They were together, standing on one of the Ashen Forest's hills, overlooking the distant shore. The princess was smiling and laughing. Their hands held each other, warm with their love. They were happy, and that was all Rya could hope for.

FORTY

Journeying through the Obsidian Isles was far easier than it should have been. Kasen knew they were coming, and they'd expected to be met with guards at every settlement they saw, but they came across no one. The roads were deserted except for them, and not a single soul passed them by from their first camp to the next. The second day they skirted a village seeing only a handful of people milling around the narrow streets, all of them women and children. In fact, they hadn't seen a single man during the three-day journey.

"This is insane," Gavin complained. They were lying on their stomachs, crawling to the cliff edge to get a better look. The sea crashed below them, spraying a mist into the air, making the entire area smell of salt. "Why are we hiding like a snake in the grass? Why can't we just stroll up there and tell them who I am?"

"That's why," Rya said, pointing down the hill to the castle's outer wall. The perimeter of the keep was guarded on all sides by a vast army. It was larger than she'd left it, and for a moment she her hope deflated.

"I thought the army was fighting in the Ashen Forest."

"They were," she confirmed. "But Kasen called them all back when he realized we were heading north to find you."

They were silent as they watched the men below. A few sat sharpening swords, or cleaning armor, but most were huddled around the fire pits, looking tired and sad.

"Look closer." She nudged him. "It's all the men from the villages."

Gavin's eyes scanned the group. "You're right. He's pulled them all to help guard the castle. These aren't fighters, they are fishermen. He's got children armed and standing guard, and old men who have no place in battle."

"It should make for an easy fight. Half of them don't know what they're doing."

"No," Gavin argued. "You won't charge through the crowd attacking anyone who moves. Those are innocent villagers. I doubt Father Kasen gave them a choice in whether they fight or not."

"What do you propose we do, then?" Rya asked, annoyed. "They have every entrance to the castle surrounded. Even if we ignore the innocent victims, he still has real guards down there, with real swords."

"We do the only thing we can do. We walk in peacefully and try to talk to them."

"You're not serious, are you?"

"It's the best option we have. They have to know Kasen is using them. Why else would he force them to live outside the walls while he stays hidden inside? We just need to convince them it's better for them and their families to turn on him. By the time we reach the gates we'll have the full force of his army standing behind us."

"You're insane," she scoffed. "We can try it your way, but the second it goes wrong I'm blasting someone."

"Deal."

She followed Gavin down the road that led to from the cliff side to the shore, both of them preferring his face be the first the people saw. Sora was behind her. He'd refused to stay at the top like she knew he would. She could have made him by trapping him with magic, but with their time together coming to a close, she couldn't steal any of it from him.

When he'd insisted on coming with them, she'd armed him with the set of daggers Nix had abandoned in death. The weight of the blades in his hands gave him pause, and he shook his head.

"I don't want them. Nix used them to hurt you, I can't take them."

"They were made for killing," she explained. "But in your hands, they will only harm those who try to harm you. They won't be used for evil any longer."

"I don't know," he winced. His hands tightened around the hilts.

Rya smiled. "If anything, my blood has strengthened them."

The slope of the ground evened out, and the trio marched towards the horde of men. From up high the camp looked shabby and the men unhappy, but now that they were closer Rya could see how horrible the conditions actually were. The tents were patched together and placed nearly on top of each other. The tight spaces didn't allow the air to flow between them and the scent of sea water, sweat, and bodily fluids hung like a fog over the entire area. Rya held her nose as they zigzagged their way through the first few rows.

"Someone's here," a voice shouted.

"Is it Father Kasen?" another asked.

All around them chatter bounced from tent to tent, and the men started to come out from their shelters. They converged on the small group, circling them with questioning eyes. Some had swords at the ready, but most were worn and weak, unwilling or unable to start a fight.

Gavin pushed forward, searching for an open space in the cluster of mess. Rya grabbed Sora by the sleeve and followed. The last thing she wanted was to get lost in a sea of dirty men. Gavin stopped in a small cleared circle. Remnants of a fire pit sat in the center, but the embers were long dead.

The group was growing more confused and restless with their arrival, and Rya was getting nervous. Gavin kicked over a crate and stepped up onto it with his arms stretched out.

"People of the Obsidian Isles," he shouted. "I ask you to come forward and hear my words."

Others added to the mob, and the circle started to close in on them. Someone pushed Rya from behind, and instinctively she summoned a ball of fire from her hand. It hovered above her flesh, poised for defense.

"It's the Black Queen," one of the men yelled, and suddenly everyone was backing away, giving her a wide berth.

"I am Queen Rya," she replied, speaking as loudly as she could. "I know Father Kasen has been feeding you lies. I did not murder King Gerrod, and while I know many of you won't believe me, I've brought someone you may listen to." She gestured to the young man standing on the crate in front of her. "I give to you Prince Gavin, son of Gerrod, and rightful heir to the Obsidian Isles."

A collective gasp filled the air, and all the faces scanned Gavin with curiosity and mistrust. He'd been gone for years, growing into a man, and it had only just occurred to her that they may not recognize him. Her heart pounded in her chest as she waited for their reaction.

"The prince is dead," someone called out. "He was killed after he was kidnapped."

"That's what Kasen wanted you to think," Gavin answered. "He told many lies to many people, including myself. He is the one who stole me from my castle in the dead of night. He made me believe that my life was in danger here. He sent me to the Ivory Cape to hide until it was safe. After I was out of reach, he convinced my father I'd been kidnapped, and eventually that I'd been murdered. These are only a few of the lies we know about. Who knows how many other deceitful schemes he's been a part of. What about you all? What has he told you about the reason you're out stationed outside these walls?"

A murmur carried through the crowd.

"There's a great threat against our kingdom," a man shouted in reply. "The Father told us that he needs our help to keep the Isles safe. He's promised to pay us each in gold once the task is complete."

"Let me ask you this," Gavin continued. "If a war is coming to the Isles, how will Kasen pay you after you've given your life to protect him? Has he promised to send money to your families once you're dead? If he cared about you at all, why would he have you camped out in your own filth and feces? Why would he have you getting sick out here in the cold while he's inside feasting next to a fire?"

The noise from the group grew louder, and Gavin kept going.

"What about his challenge to the Ashen Forest? He sent the men to fight our neighbors when there's been no cause to bring violence against them. A true leader would be fighting alongside you. Instead he's hiding behind you all, waiting for everyone else to win his battles for him."

The mutterings had turned into a roar. Rya shrank into the background, allowing Gavin the spotlight. They were looking at him with glowing faces, their eyes sparkling with the desire to stand by his side. This was his army, his people, and they would fight for him.

"I say," Gavin shouted, "we put an end to Kasen's lies. Allow me to enter the castle to confront him. Follow me into the outer ward, and I'll stand him before you to answer for his cowardice. Let's take back the Isles!"

Cheers erupted all around them, and men started to run off in every direction. They spread the word throughout the entire camp that the prince had returned.

FORTY-ONE

Tents were knocked aside, kicked out of the way by those joining Gavin's fight. He marched towards the castle gates with a fire in his eyes. Swords, pitchforks, and spears all raised behind him, bouncing with the chants of his followers.

"That was easy," Rya said in a hushed voice, walking next to him.

"Everyone wants to keep hope. Kasen has treated them poorly, and because of that they were eager to believe in something better."

"Not all of them."

A wall of men was forming in front of them, blocking the main gates and pointing their weapons towards the oncoming mass. The crowd had been split, some wanting to follow their lost prince, others not trusting his words. The faces in front of Rya were confused and frustrated, searching for some direction but none came. Anyone who would shout orders had hidden themselves inside the walls, leaving the rest to fend off the oncoming crowd.

Gavin held up his hand, stopping his army a few yards in front of the line.

"Let us in," he shouted. "Our fight is not with you."

The patter of feet on stone was faint, but she could hear it. Archers had taken their place along the top of the turrets.

"We defend the king of the Isles," one of the soldiers yelled.

"You serve a false king," Gavin replied. "He has no right to wear the crown, not when your queen stands at my side, very much alive. I'm your prince, Gavin Hemply of the Obsidian Isles. If you won't fight for Queen Rya, then at least fight for me."

The wall of men did not move.

Gavin turned his back to them, facing the men who were willing to give their life for his. "If a battle is what they want, then that's what we will give them. If any man yields, do not take his life. If any of them renounces loyalty to Kasen, he will be allowed to live. We only fight those who attack us in the name of the traitor."

The hours spent with Cam in the forest had tuned Rya's ears, and she picked up on the thunk of the bowstrings even at a distance. The split second it took for the arrows to reach Gavin's back was enough for her. A wall of ice appeared between them, and the arrows struck the cold barrier instead of his skin. He turned to find the tips protruding out of the ice, still reaching for his body.

The world erupted around them. Men rushed forward, charging at the ones guarding the gate. A blast of sparks shot from the clashing of metal on metal. Gavin had disappeared, but Sora stayed at Rya's side, waving his daggers at anyone who dared to come close. She spun around with her hand out, forming a circle of flame around the two of them for protection as her still healing bones splintered. She could smell the blood as swords found their marks. The arrows landed in the crowd, the archers clearly not caring who they wounded. The shaft of one stuck out from the ground at her feet, and she grabbed Sora by the arm, pulling him with her as jumped over the fire and ran towards the gates.

On both sides of the blocked opening men were scaling the walls, trying to make their way over before they were struck down from above. Her eyes found Gavin thrusting his sword into the belly of a solider. She pushed her way to his side, grabbing him by the arm. He turned with his blade raised, ready to strike, but stopped when he recognized her face.

"I can open the gates," she exclaimed. "If you can keep the men off me, I can use my power to turn the cranks."

"But your hand—" he argued. He pointed at the arm she cradled against her body.

"I don't need both, I promise I can do it."

The prince nodded, and him and Sora took their place at her back, placing themselves between herself and the fighting. She could see the cranks through a slit in the wall. All she needed was the time to concentrate, and she could move them. She'd spent years cutting herself off from everything around her, but now that she'd opened her heart it seemed her other senses opened with it, and the screams of the dying was louder than she'd expected. She focused her energy on the metal of the handle. She imagined it in her hand, and could feel the cold touch of it in her palm. Slowly it turned, clicking once and then again. Click after click the rope curled around itself, and the bars began to rise.

The men didn't wait for the gate to completely open. They crawled under the rising bars in the second the opening was big enough. Many of the men loyal to Kasen dropped their weapons at the sight of the entry. A single tip of the scales and they were no longer quite willing to die for their Father.

Gavin's men flooded the outer ward. Each building was taken by the crowd; those claiming loyalty to Kasen were restrained, and the rest ran outside to join the cheering mob as they moved on to the next building. In no time at all, townsfolk had claimed the ward in the name of Prince Gavin, but that wasn't the end.

The inner ward came next. Anyone living within the castle walls had heard the commotion and tried barricading themselves indoors. It wasn't enough to stop the persistence of the villagers. Doors were broken down and they flooded into each home. Once more, anyone on Gavin's side was allowed to walk free, everyone else was bound and gagged. With both the inner and outer ward under his command, Gavin stopped his still growing army at the gate to the castle courtyard.

A stone path cut through the center and ended at a staircase that led to the castle's front doors. Poised at the top of its steps stood Father Kasen.

He wore the deep purple cloak reserved for royal celebrations, and had placed the crown on top of his religious cap, combining the two as his symbol of ultimate power. He looked the part of a fearless leader, but Rya could see his hands trembling in the sleeves of those ceremonial robes.

Gavin put a hand on Rya's shoulder. Her blood boiled at the sight of Kasen standing where she should be, but she knew they had to do this Gavin's way. She nodded to the prince and he walked into the courtyard with herself only a few steps behind him. The mass of people who had followed them stayed at the entrance, including Sora.

"Arrest these intruders," Kasen shouted. "Rya has murdered your king and she must pay for her crime."

"Lies," Gavin replied. He spoke loud enough to bridge the distance, but kept his tone calm. "You've told nothing but lies to these people. Like when you told them I had died. As you can see, I'm alive, and here to take back my kingdom."

Two guards ran down the steps, but as they got closer to the prince they hesitated, unsure of who they should be following. Most of the soldiers had already fled, and the few that remained stood in the shadows, waiting to see how the argument played out. The only one still by Kasen's side was Normand, the head of the Obsidian army. Gavin, however, had an entire village at his back, ready to fight if he commanded it.

Hundreds of pairs of lungs held their breath, waiting to see who made the first move.

FORTY-TWO

Tension filled the air, thicker than the stink of the men Kasen had left outside the castle walls. He narrowed his eyes, smirking at Rya from the top of the staircase.

"This man is an impostor," he shouted. "He's convinced you that he's the prince, but I know that to be false. Prince Gavin is dead, and whoever this young man is he's nothing more than a pawn in Rya's game, sent here to confuse you."

The crowd shifted, restless and uncertain.

"You've allowed yourself to be fooled," he continued. "If he truly is the son of Gerrod, why doesn't he prove it?"

Rya's biggest fear had come true. She had crossed Kelda to find Gavin and bring him home, but there was no way for her to prove he was the prince they'd lost. She'd searched her brain from the beginning, trying to find a way to validate his lineage, but came up short every time. Kasen was a smart man and he knew she would have no way to provide proof of Gavin's claim. The air had left her lungs, but the prince simply smiled.

"Normand," he called out. "I see you standing by your rulers' side. I applaud you for staying true to your word as a soldier of the Obsidian army. You're a good man who has fought for his king, including my father. You were in the room during many of my lessons with him. I'm sure you remember them as well as I do."

Rya paused while Gavin walked across the stone pathway, stopping at the bottom of the castle's steps. He held up his hand, showing the back of it to the old guard.

"This scar is from when I was five. I was whining about the dinner we were having, and my father grew angry and threw his knife at me. I cried and bled all over the table, but he never batted an eye. You helped me clean the wound after he'd left. Surely you remember that."

He took a few steps up the stairs.

"That's not proof," Kasen stammered. "He could have learned that story from anyone in the room at the time."

"How about when I was seven and I climbed onto the roof of the aviary with paper wings I'd made myself. I had watched my mother launch herself off the tallest tower in the castle, and I thought if I tried hard enough, I could fly like her, and follow her wherever she'd gone. You grabbed me at the last second, pulling me from the edge. You scolded me, but you never told my father because you knew his punishment would be worse than what I had attempted."

Gavin climbed a few more steps. Normand's sword inched down to his side, and Kasen's face turned beat red.

"He's lying!" Kasen screamed. He knew he was losing. "He's not the prince. I swear it."

"Or we can talk about my tenth birthday. Father had given me a sword, but not the light ones the other boys trained with. This was a full-length broadsword, and it was as thick as I'd ever seen. He made me lift it, even though it took both hands and hurt my arms. When I complained he forced me to stand in my room, holding my arms in front of me for hours on end. If they fell even a little you were supposed to whip me, but you looked away a few times, allowing me a brief moment of relief."

It was over. Kasen had no defense left. Gavin was at the top of the steps, inches away from the Father's face and no one fought to stop him.

"Seize this man," Gavin ordered.

Rya rushed up the steps, stopping at Gavin's side. The guards had stepped forward once more, their swords all pointed in Kasen's direction. Norman grabbed his arms, yanking them behind him.

"Let me go!" he shrieked. His eyes darted back and forth between her and Gavin, resting on the prince. "This is her doing," he whimpered. "She's tricked you. She killed your father."

She shook her head. "No, Gerrod was killed by you. It was part of your plan all along. Admit it."

"I admit nothing," he spat. "I'm a man of the church, you can't do this to me."

"The church won't erase your crimes," Gavin replied. "Nothing can do that."

He struggled against Normand's grip while he screamed. "I did what I had to. You know all about that don't you, Rya? Gerrod was going to ruin this kingdom, he had to be stopped. Then you came along, with all your ideas of ruling and control, taking away all I'd worked for. It wasn't fair. I put in decades here—it's mine. The Obsidian Isles are mine!"

"Take him to the dungeon," Gavin commanded. "He can wait in the dark while I decide what to do with him. However long that takes."

"And what about her?" One of the guards asked, pointing to Rya. "What do we do about the Black Queen?"

Gavin looked around at the hundreds of eyes on him and swallowed. "Take her to her tower, and lock her inside. Her judgment will come later."

The soldier stepped in front of her, watching as she put her hands out in front of her. He had expected her magic, he had never thought he'd offer her wrists to him to be chained.

FORTY-THREE

The throne room had always been a cold place, stripped of all warmth and comfort, and chilling to those who stood before the queen. Rya had spent years on the platform, looking over the subjects who summoned enough bravery to ask her for a favor. Now it was her turn to look up at the throne, and it was her turn to wait with a pounding heart to hear her fate.

Fourteen days had passed since they'd taken back the castle. Fourteen nights had tormented her with unsettling sleep, her dreams taunting her with the faces of those she loved. It was already punishment to be unaware of their outcome. She had no idea if Cam and the others had reached the Ashen Forest. No one would tell her what Sora was doing, where he was, or if Gavin had stood by his word to keep the boy safe. She had been locked away in the room she was so desperate to return to, only to be dying to escape the Isles' once more.

The men that guarded her door had talked of Kasen's death sentence. He'd been charged with the Gerrod's murder after suggesting the late king was poisoned. It was also punishment for attacking the Ashen Forest. In Gavin's opinion, it was a horrible act to wage a war against a neighboring kingdom unprovoked. Kasen had lived three days in his cell before he was hanged. His body was thrown into the sea without the ceremony and celebration given to the rest of the Isles' people. She was about to find out if her end would be the same, or if Gavin would leave her to waste away in the dungeons.

The doors to the throne room swung open, and the faces all turned her direction. People were packed inside, filling any empty space they could, from the center aisle to all four walls. She stood in the open doorway, the toes of her shoes brushing the black carpet that created the path to the throne. They craned their necks to see her, to look upon her sullen face with joy and happiness. She would not give them what they wanted, she refused to show any emotion, but kept her eyes on the new king sitting before her, and walked down the aisle.

Words were spoken as she passed, some too fowl to ever repeat in good company. Others hissed at her. They would never know the truth behind her reign. They would never learn how many children she had saved from the slaver, or how she'd freed a once beaten wife to live on her own without fear. They could never understand the horror she had suffered of being used and abused her whole life, and how she vowed to save others from that same fate. They knew her as evil, as the Black Queen who did everything for her own gain, who loved no one and who no one loved in return. That didn't matter now because she knew they were wrong. She knew she had a heart, that she did some good in this world, and that somehow she'd managed to find the love she'd always dreamed of.

Gavin rose from the chair that once was her seat, and stood before her and all his people. He held up a hand, silencing the last of the hushed curses and quieting the room. The air churned with energy as each person awaited his verdict.

"Queen Rya, you stand before me charged with many injustices against the people of the Obsidian Isles. You have claimed before that everything you've done was within your right as ruler, and that you've committed no crimes. While that is technically true, I would agree that the actions you've taken against the people you reigned over were harsh and unnecessary, and therefore it is my right as the new king to decide a punishment for those actions.

"I have listened to many stories, from most of the different villages within the Isles borders, all telling me of the horrible Black Queen. I would be a fool to ignore these tales, and to do so would be unfair to those who lived them. However, I myself have seen your true nature. I have watched you care for the ones close to you, and I've seen the good that lies deep within. It's true that your heart was once wicked and poisoned, but with each day that passes it's healing itself a little more. Because of this, I would be equally foolish to sentence you to death, as I did for Father Kasen. I refuse to throw away someone who stands a chance at being saved."

Rya's heart stopped in her chest, and she couldn't breathe. This couldn't be true. He couldn't be pardoning her. Gasps and chatter broke out among the crowd, and King Gavin held up his hand again, silencing the people.

He continued, "Your sentence will not be death, but you will not leave here unpunished. I am stripping you of your title as queen and all the honors that come with it. From today on you are no greater than a commoner, with nothing to your name. I understand the danger your magic poses to the people around you, and that without being able to control it, I can never guarantee their safety. Because of that, you are hereby banished from the Obsidian Isles forever. You will be led from this castle to the kingdom's border, and if you're ever seen within our boundaries again you will be killed on sight. For your sake, I hope you can find some kingdom that will be kind enough to take you in."

He winked at her with last of his words. Her mouth hung open, and her stomach turned. A man grabbed her by the arm and led her back down the aisle. She could never to thank him for what he'd just done, she would be forced out of the Isles and they would part ways forever. She could only hope he realized the enormity of his decision.

The man kept hold of her until they reached the front doors of the castle. He pushed them open and nodded to the next solider, a small framed young man in a plain uniform.

"Sora," she gasped, nearly crying.

"Come," he smiled, offering his arm to her. "It's time to go."

Rya held him as they walked down the stairs and to the edge of the courtyard. It was the same spot where, only days before, they had faced Kasen and exposed his lies. The scene had been witnessed by hundreds, but now it was only her, Sora, and one more surprise.

Two horses stood on the other side of the archway, one smaller and spotted, and one she'd grown to know all too well.

"Eclipse" she smiled. She ran her hands over his coat before resting her cheek against him. "He really is a good horse."

"He's *your* good horse," Sora replied. He climbed onto the other, grinning down at her. "King Gavin has given me the task of taking you to the border, from there I'm to return Eclipse to the Ashen Forest as he promised."

"I can't believe he made you an official guard." He beamed at him in the crisp, clean uniform. He'd come from so little, and now he would always have a status among the people.

"Well, almost." He ran a hand over his slicked back hair. "The king also said that if I didn't return from this assignment, he would not come looking for me as I haven't been officially sworn into his service. I would just be another young man who disappeared to live his life somewhere else."

Rya was crying now, unable to fathom how Gavin had given her so much. He had broken the last remaining bars of her cage, and freed her to live the life she'd always dreamed of. She wasn't the Black Queen any longer, she was just Rya.

"Where to?" Sora asked, already knowing the answer.

Rya laughed. "I heard the Ashen Forest takes in people like us."

FORTY-FOUR

Cam sat on the edge of the ditch, her legs dangling over the lip. The first snowfall had left the ground wet and icy, chilling her through her pants, but she didn't care. This is where it all started, where she'd saved Rya the first time. She knew Thane and Norell were close by, resting on a fallen tree a few feet behind her, watching her carefully. They were always within arm's reach these days, not wanting to leave her alone. The first nights after Rya left were broken apart by Cam's screams in the night. She couldn't sleep more than an hour without a terrifying nightmare jarring her awake. It wasn't long before Norell took to sleeping next to her. Even after they'd returned to the castle, Norell would crawl into Cam's bed after dark, making sure she was never alone when the terrors came.

"Does my father know we're out here?" She asked, staring into the dirt below.

"Yes," Norell nodded. "He said he's certain any threat from the Isles or the Kael is over. You're free to do whatever you wish, just like before."

Norell's words echoed in Cam's head. *Like before.* She could go hunting whenever she'd like. *Like before.* She could roam the entire kingdom without worry. *Like before.* It didn't matter what she did, nothing would ever be as it was before.

Her mind drifted away, replacing the cold words with an even colder face. It was Gavin in front of her. His mouth was angry and twisted like the first day they'd met. He was furious Rya had left him in the Ivory Cape. He would never forgive her. The image made her stomach sick.

"Do you—think she's still alive?" Cam asked, interrupting whatever Thane had been rambling about. "Do you think he went easy on her, giving her a sentence in the cells instead of—the other option? I can't imagine her down there in a dark hole. What if he decided to do worse? What if he's torturing her? I just wish someone would send us word of what's happened."

Norell was at her side now, her arm around Cam's shoulder, her eyes shifting to Thane.

"No one is sending us a hawk," Thane answered. "They're never going to tell us what happened."

"Why not?" Cam asked, her neck snapping around to glare at him.

"Because I asked Gavin and Sora not to."

Cam could hear the blood pumping in her ears, she could feel it in her temple. Her eyes swelled with tears, and she could do nothing to stop them.

Norell kissed the side of her head. "I know you're angry with Thane, but he did what was right." Her tone was too soft, the same voice she'd used when Cam's mother had died, and it broke Cam even more. Norell continued, "you can't allow yourself to be consumed with what's happened to her. You should be focusing on the time you spent together. Forget the Black Queen, and focus on Rya, the girl you knew and loved. Remember the way you two laughed together, the way her sass and sarcasm kept Guthry on his toes, and the gentle nature she had with the children here. Don't think about the Isles; think about the love you two shared, and how her heart was forever changed by you, and yours by her. Allow that to be the Rya you keep in your memories."

Cam wiped the tears from her cheek with the sleeve of her coat. Her lower half was numb now, and soon it would be dark. It was time to go home, time to leave this place, and Rya behind. She stood on wobbly legs, holding onto Norell's arm for support.

They had turned their backs on the edging, ignoring the rustle of the autumn's last few leaves. When the sound of feet crunching the frozen forest floor reached her, Cam turned and saw the most beautiful sight she could have imagined. Rya was running at them up through the trees, smiling from ear to ear.

"It's you," Cam gasped. She rushed forward, and the girls collided like two stars in the sky, exploding in a hail of light and sparks. Rya kissed her, her hand on the back of Cam's head, fingers in her hair. The heat from her magic warmed her scalp, and melted Cam's insides. Cam's arms wrapped around Rya's waist, determined to never let go. It seemed like an eternity that they stood entangled, but when Rya pulled back it was still too soon.

"What are you doing here?" Cam asked, laughing through the stream of tears that flowed down her face.

"Well," Rya smirked. "I've been banished from my homeland, and I've come to the Ashen Forest seeking safety."

"In that case," Cam replied, unable to contain her happiness. "You have my word as the Ashen princess, I will always protect you."

ACKNOWLEDGMENTS

The Poison Within wasn't my first book, but it took more out of me than anything I've done previously. There's no way I could have reached my dream of publishing this story without the help of the people around me.

First, I need to thank Bonnie, my love and my life. If I didn't have your support, I would have never become the writer I am. Thank you for dealing with the late-night typing sessions, the hours I spend erasing and rewriting a single sentence, and the tons of money we spend on Diet Coke to keep me powered. Your love and enthusiasm for my writing gives me the courage to keep coming up with stories.

A whole-hearted, massive thank you goes to Cece Ewing. You're the best friend I could have asked for, and my number one person to bounce ideas off of. You've never let me down, and I won't trust anyone else to take my words into their hands from now on. When I sat down to write Rya's story it was always with you in mind. Her redemption was yours from the beginning, and I'm so glad you came to love her as much as I did.

Thank you to my parents and my family for their ongoing support. I know the fantasy genre isn't your thing, but you've always had my back and I love you.

I need to thank my mix-matched team that helped me along the way. Jen Lew, Mike Ries, and Erin Ford who read parts for me along the way. Kristine Slipson, and Ashleigh Davis, who were always there to answer my horse questions. To Vanessa Martinez, thanks for being my archery expert.

A special thanks goes to YouTube and hundreds of channels that provide someone like me with the skills to do Photoshop and create the covers and maps I'm able to design. The people who post tutorials and free photos, the ones who create and share their artwork with the world, they are the reason I'm able to do what I do. Without you I'd be lost.

Last but not least thank you to anyone reading this. Whether you're a fan of my work from the beginning (Chantal and Jessica I'm talking about you) or you've just recently picked it up, I'm grateful to you for taking the time to read my writing.

Manufactured by Amazon.ca
Bolton, ON

15805148R00231